# Ghosts of Bliss Bayou

## Jack Massa

 Triskelion Books

Published by
Triskelion Books
www.triskelionbooks.com

This is a work of fiction. All of the characters, organizations, and events portrayed in this novel are either products of the author's imagination or are used fictitiously.

ISBN: 978-0-9976461-2-2

Print Edition published November 2016

Cover design by Ida Jansson, http://amygdaladesign.net/

## 1. That awkward feeling when you wake up and the nightmare is with you in the room

My eyes fly open, and I stare at the clock: 5:13 a.m.

Something is on top of me. It presses down on my shoulder and hip. Cool, slimy breath brushes my ear. I hear my own breathing, loud and frantic, and over it, a whisper: "Abigail Renshaw...we have found you."

My terror changes to blind panic.

"Get off me!" I mean it for a scream, but it comes out a pathetic whimper. I try to push and struggle, but the bed hardly moves. I feel the thing's breath on my cheek, a wet, decaying smell like a stagnant pool in a swamp.

*The same smell as in the nightmare.* I remember it now. Running through dark, muddy woods. Something chasing me. I tripped over a fallen branch, and the something picked me up, carried me, flung me into the water. Then I was sinking into a freezing blackness, my arms and legs paralyzed so I couldn't struggle.

Paralyzed like now.

"This cannot be happening!" My voice sounds grim, sharpened by outrage. I suck in a deep breath, get both hands under me, and push with all my strength.

I spring up in the bed and turn to look.

The thing is still there.

I see it now, a floating deep, deep blackness with strands of gray mist. It streams across the room to the corner. There it swirls and thickens.

Now a shape hovers in the corner: a blond middle-aged woman. She's tall and stiff, in a long black dress, a necklace of white pearls. She has thin lips and proud, glaring eyes. She stares at me with...recognition. Not hate, but a kind of contempt, like I'm some insect she's found in her kitchen.

"No," I whisper. "You can't be here. You are not real."

For several moments we just stare at each other, Abby Renshaw and the woman in pearls. The room is freezing, and I get angrier and angrier. I pull off the covers and climb out of bed, my eyes never leaving her eyes.

"You are not real. Go away!"

I take a step toward her, then another. The woman's expression never changes. I force myself to go closer and closer, afraid, but also furious. This is *my* room, the only place in the universe that belongs to me, where I can be myself without pretending or trying to please everyone else. No crazy hallucination is going to take that away.

I reach toward it, thinking that if I can just touch it, it will disappear.

I touch it, and it disappears.

Now I'm blinking like an idiot, waving my hands in the dark corner. Nothing. The room's no longer cold, but *now* I shiver.

I crawl back to the bed and pull up the covers.

The clock shows 5:20 a.m.

♒

I lie with the covers up to my chin, checking every few moments through half-opened eyes in case it comes back. This is the third time in the last week I've had the nightmare about the swamp and drowning. And I've dreamed of that woman before, somewhere in the mix.

But this is the first time she leaked out of the dream world into my room. *My* room. And that thing on top of me, with the slimy breath and creepy voice? Was that her or something else altogether?

This is getting seriously scary.

I've had hallucinations before. Heard voices in my head, saw people and creatures that couldn't possibly be there.

But that was years ago. That was twelve-year-old Abby Renshaw, the geeky, lonely girl with no friends and too much imagination. Too much fear.

I'm supposed to be the new, improved Abby now. I get good grades, I run on the track team, I go to parties. I've kissed a few boys. Okay, I'm a little slow in the boyfriend department, I admit. I'm still shy and weird. But like Franklin, my friend in the drama club, says: where's the line between weird and interesting anyway?

I like to tell myself I'm not weird, just interesting—that I'm not so different from everyone else.

But then why am I so afraid?

The future. It's the first of May, and I turn seventeen in August. One more year at Hudson Heights High, and then...what? College applications. Where should I apply? What should I major in? What am I going to do with the rest of my life? I need to think about my future, Mom keeps telling me. As if I can think of anything else. I feel like I'm running, running, running toward the edge of a cliff, and then...

What?

Running makes me feel better though.

When it's light outside, I climb out of bed and put on my workout clothes. Weekdays I train after school with the team, but weekends I usually go for a run in the morning by myself. The dawns are still chilly here in New Jersey, so I wear leggings under my shorts—bright orange leggings—and my royal blue track team sweatshirt with the Hudson Fighting Eagles logo. Extra thick white socks, and my neon blue and orange Nikes. Nothing's more reassuring than a good pair of running shoes.

I have lingering shakes from the nightmare, so I'm very careful to make no noise as I tiptoe past Mom's room. I still think of it as Mom's, although she's shared it with my stepfather, Jim, since they got married last December. Jim's all right. He tries to be friendly while still respecting my space. No attempts to be "Dad," which is good.

Downstairs I grab a bottle of Dasani from the pantry, then go out the back door. I sip the water as I do my warm-ups in the driveway. The sky's pearly gray, and a cool breeze is shaking the new leaves on the oaks and sycamores. Perfect weather.

I jog down the driveway, then hit my stride at the street. I'll head downtown, then over the highway to the nature preserve on the Palisades. With the route set, my brain flips into autopilot, and I can think about other stuff.

Like my hallucinations.

I've always been the sensitive, imaginative type. Hyperaware of other people's feelings. Sometimes I can tell what they're going to say before they say it. And I've always been prone to anxiety. But when I started to go through puberty, things got really bad. I was afraid all the time, and then I started to hear voices in my head. Scary voices, telling me I might as well just die, that I had no future, that I was cursed.

Just like my dad.

Then I started seeing things, nightmare things while I was awake: faceless people in black robes, goblins from video games, reptiles that walked upright on short, bowed legs. At first they were just shapes at the edges of my vision, and they skittered away as soon as I looked. Then they stayed longer.

It all got pretty horrible.

I tried to ignore it, to hide it from Mom, to pretend it would go away. But a few months after I turned thirteen, I had a breakdown. I was too scared even to get out of bed. Mom took me to a shrink, who put me on meds and recommended a therapist.

The therapist, Dr. Mark, was actually a good guy. He assured us that hallucinations in a kid my age were not all that unusual. He helped me work through my fears about the future and my feelings about losing my dad when I was seven and Mom moving us up from Florida to New Jersey.

Between the anti-anxiety meds and the sessions with Dr. Mark, the hallucinations faded away.

*If they were hallucinations.*

Of course they were. Now I'm being stupid.

I've reached downtown, and I'm running along Englewood Boulevard, almost to the one-mile point. There's already some traffic, so I have to wait for the light before crossing Clinton Avenue. It's uphill from here for a half mile, and I concentrate on my stride, trying not to think of anything. At the top of the road is a small park. An asphalt path takes me past the baseball field, and I cross pedestrian bridges over Route 9 and then the Palisades Parkway. I enter the nature preserve, where it's all quiet and peaceful. I usually love running here, but this morning I'm wary. I check every tree, expecting something to jump out.

Nothing does.

When I reach the end of the path, I stop for a breather. No one's around. I'm alone in the world, gazing down over the eighty-foot cliffs to the Hudson River. Downstream I can see the Washington Bridge, and beyond it the impossible megalopolis of Manhattan. The view is breathtaking, enormous, terrifying.

*That's the real world, Abby.*

Sometimes I think it's a dying world, that with overpopulation and the threat of environmental collapse, it can't possibly survive another fifty years. Other times I think it will last forever, and it's just me who can't survive, that I'll never find my place in the world.

Mom has. Mom and Jim drive into Manhattan every day. Mom's made a great success of her life, coming up here after Dad died, tugging a lost seven-year-old daughter along. She started in a branch bank and worked her way up. Now's she's a financial analyst and makes a really good living.

I'm proud of my mom. She's smart, and she's a fighter.

And I'm a fighter too. I've shown it in the past, dealing with my "issues." I show it on the track. I'm not going to give in to the fear and run off the edge of the cliff.

Even though the cliff is right here in front of me. Literally.

I think about that for a second. Then I turn and start for home.

〰

When I reach the house, Mom and Jim are in the kitchen, having toast and coffee. They're dressed in golf clothes, with their bags of clubs leaning nearby. Since early April they've gone golfing at the country club every Saturday morning. They're not the type to sleep in on the weekends.

"How was your run?" Jim says as I open the fridge and grab a yogurt.

"Fine, thanks."

"Abby," Mom says, "we're having dinner tomorrow at Trudi's. You need to be ready to leave at one."

Trudi is Jim's sister. She has an apartment on Park Avenue and two daughters around my age—Julie a year older and Kristen a year younger. They go to an exclusive prep school on the West Side, and they are both beautiful and oh-so-polished. I feel like a nerdy ugly dumpling by comparison. Of course, *they* already know where they want to go to college—Yale and Smith, thank you very much.

I really don't like visiting them. And it must be showing on my face.

"It's important that you come with us," Mom says. "Trudi and the girls are being nice enough to put you up for three weeks. The least you can do is try to be friendly."

The three weeks are in June, right after school ends. Mom and Jim will be touring Europe on their long-delayed honeymoon, and I'll be sleeping on a futon in Trudi's den. This was the last-resort arrangement for little Abby. Mom wanted me to go to a camp in the Catskills for a combination of intensive track training and college prep classes. I just wanted to stay home by myself and chill. No way, not at your age, Mom said. We argued over it until the deadline passed for applying to the camp.

Mom's parents might have been another option, but they live in an over-55 community and really don't have the room. So I'm stuck with the futon. I thought I was resigned to it, though now the thought of being trapped in Manhattan for three weeks makes me panicky. What if the hallucinations continue? What if I really start to lose it?

As I'm lifting a spoonful of yogurt to my mouth, something catches my eye. I glance into the dining room and see Julie and Kristen and Trudi, all standing there plain as can be, smiling at me. Behind them is a floating image—the black cloud-thing from my nightmare.

I squinch my eyes tight and look again. Still there.

"Abby, are you okay?"

"Yes. Yes, I'm fine, Mom." I toss the yogurt in the trash and rush out the other door to the hallway. As I run up the stairs I yell back, "I'll be ready tomorrow at one. I promise."

Upstairs, I lock the bathroom door and lean my back against it. Eventually the fear rush passes, and my breathing slows down. I turn on the shower and strip off my clothes. I step under the hot water and close my eyes.

This. Cannot. Happen.

I wish there were someone I could talk to about it. But Dr. Mark moved out of state sometime after I stopped seeing him, and I certainly don't want to look for another therapist. I don't want to put Mom through that. I don't want her to know I'm in trouble again.

As for my friends at school...no way. They only know smart-student, track-team Abby. The girl who's pretty much like everyone else. Show them crazy psycho Abby? Uh-uh. I can imagine it all over school and the internet: *Abby Renshaw, freak of nature. Her eyesight's so good, she sees things that aren't there.*

No. I've *got* to figure this out by myself.

The hot water feels really good, relaxing. I pour out shampoo and rub it hard into my hair and scalp.

I go back to the techniques Dr. Mark taught me. He saw the hallucinations as messengers from my subconscious, clues to feelings I was repressing. Figure out the clues, confront the feelings, and the creepies will go away.

It worked before, pretty much...

So what do Trudi and her daughters represent to me? They've got their lives together, and I don't. That's simple. Compared with Julie and Kristen, I feel inadequate, and it scares me. But I know this already. These feelings aren't new, although they have grown worse lately.

What about Ghost Woman? There I draw a blank. I don't know who she is. As for the feelings she brings up...just strangeness. I'm not really afraid of her. She's just some dark, impenetrable mystery.

I'm not getting very far, Dr. Mark.

What about the dream of the swamp? That's something. It reminds me of the woods around my Grandma's house in Florida, where I used to visit when I was little. It's a place in the boonies: unpaved, sandy roads and weedy lawns and huge trees hung with Spanish moss. And there are springs nearby with fast-flowing crystal-blue water. Except Grandma lives on a kind of backwater: Bliss Bayou. I couldn't play near the water because there were snakes and sometimes alligators. Besides, the edges of the banks changed all the time, depending on how much rain there'd been. They were always slick and muddy, with shallow pools.

Just like in my nightmare.

I'm feeling nervous again, but it's a good nervous, like I'm onto something. I finish rinsing off and step out of the shower. I put on my terry robe and toss my running clothes in the hamper. I don't bother with the blow dryer, just wrap up my hair in a towel.

Back in my room, I close and lock the door—although Mom and Jim have probably left by now. I flop on the bed and think about my Grandma.

In my first memory of her, I'm only two or three and I'm sitting on her lap, feeling warm and safe and...loved. When I got a little older, I would often spend whole days at her house. I would follow her around and watch everything she did—gardening, baking cookies, embroidery. She was always so calm and patient, explaining everything to me. Sometimes we'd sit on her porch swing in the afternoon, rocking back and forth and telling each other stories.

Her house was like a hundred years old, Victorian. Tall, arched windows to let in the Florida light, and creaky floors with dark wooden slats. As I picture those floors, another dream fragment sparks in my brain...

I'm standing in a room with high ceilings, like in Grandma's house. It's dark, lit only by candles. The floor is painted with a white circle and weird symbols or hieroglyphs. People in white robes are standing around the circle, murmuring and chanting. The air is very cold, and there's this powerful sense of an invisible presence.

I sit up on my bed and shudder.

Well, Dr. Mark. It seems pretty clear the dreams are pointing to my Grandma's house in Florida. And not just the house, but the woods around it, and the water.

The town is called Harmony Springs. My dad grew up there, in the big house on the bayou. He met Mom at the University of

Florida, where he was studying for an MBA and Mom was an undergrad. After they got married, they moved into a housing development near downtown. Dad became a real estate broker, and Mom helped him in the business. She worked a lot of the time, even after I came along, which is why I spent so many days with Grandma.

From early on, I knew there was trouble between Mom and Dad. Lying in bed at night, I would hear them fighting. More and more as I got older, Dad would come home smelling weird and stumbling. Mom told me he was sick, but it didn't take me long to understand that "sick" meant drinking. He was never violent, just morbid and dull. Sometimes he would moan and burst into tears. One night he told Mom that she should just leave him and take the child, that he was cursed. I was old enough to have an idea of what that meant, and it's always stuck with me. So, in a horrible kind of way, it made sense, the way Dad died. Late one night he drove the wrong way on the interstate and smashed his SUV into an oncoming truck.

Remembering all this is getting me depressed, but not any closer to solving my problems.

I stand up and shake it off. I put on some clothes: underwear and yoga pants, T-shirt, thick white socks. I dry my hair with the towel and then brush out the tangles. My legs are aching, and I remember I didn't stretch out after running. Stupid. I do long, gentle stretches, breathing deeply and keeping my eyes closed. I don't want to see any more "visitors."

While I'm relaxing with my eyes shut, a thought occurs to me. After I finish stretching, I open the drawer in my bedside table, reach all the way to the back, and pull out my cards.

The first time I saw Tarot cards was at a party when I was fourteen. One of the girls had a deck, and she showed them to us. We sat around giggling as she told our fortunes.

I was fascinated. Every card had a picture, and every picture seemed like a window into a strange world where everything was sharp and clear in a way the real world never is. The following week I bought my own cards and started studying them. I found all kinds of information online: the history of the Tarot, different decks, multiple ways to lay out the cards and read them. And whole schools of occult philosophy, attributing meanings to the cards way beyond telling fortunes. Most of it goes deeper than I understand. For me, it's mainly about the pictures. I can look at the cards in a spread, and it's like they speak to me, explaining the unseen forces that surround whatever I'm reading about.

I did say I was a little weird, right? The Tarot is part of that, part of the secret Abby, the girl with too much imagination.

I mostly keep her under control. When I started seeing Dr. Mark, I gave up online gaming. I figured it was contributing to my hallucination problems. And this year I've been so involved with school and the track team and making some new friends around the drama club, that I've hardly even touched the Tarot.

But now I'm having black clouds and creepy women in pearls leaking out of my dreams, so I think maybe I'm repressing too much. I decide to give the cards another try.

I shuffle the pack and ask the unseen forces for help. *Why am I having these hallucinations? What can I do about it?*

I lay down a Celtic Cross spread. There are lots of wands and swords, contending forces, pain and sorrow. In the position of my hopes and fears is the Tower Struck by Lightning, utter destruction. But my eyes are drawn to the crown position—the High Priestess. I've read that she's actually a goddess, seated on her throne at the place of balance between the positive and negative polarities of the Universe. I stare at her serene face and her robes. In the picture, the robes turn into a waterfall and then a blue stream that flows away. It flows down through all the other cards that have pictures of water— the Stream of Life that gives birth to everything.

In the outcome position is the Empress. She is another version of the same goddess. She's seated on a bench in a beautiful garden, beside the same blue stream. Looking at her face reminds me of Grandma.

*The Empress is Grandma, and the stream is Bliss Bayou.*

That thought comes into my mind with a thud. And suddenly I know what I have to do.

I haven't seen Grandma since we moved nine years ago. At first we would talk on the phone every few weeks, but as I grew older we seemed to have less and less to say to each other. The past few years it's been limited to birthday and Christmas cards. We haven't spoken in three or four years.

*But I have to go see her.* The cards are definitely telling me so. And rationally, it makes sense. If the nightmares are caused by subconscious stuff from my childhood, going back to where I lived then might be the way to deal with it.

And I think I can. Those three weeks when Mom and Jim are in Europe—instead of being trapped in New York, I could fly down to Florida. I have some money in the bank from working last summer, so I could pay for the trip. Although Mom will probably pay for it, assuming I can convince her.

Assuming I can convince Grandma.

I don't know if she'll want me barging in and disrupting her life for three weeks. I flash back to the last time I saw her, just before we moved. I stood on her porch, hugging her, crying and crying. I was seven, but I was acting like a two-year-old. And I could feel Grandma sobbing too, although she tried to hide it. She had lost her only son, and now she was losing her granddaughter. Mom promised we would come back and visit often. But that never happened.

Will Grandma be mad at me for not calling her more, for losing touch? Will she even want to see me? I don't know, but I've got to find out.

I'm nervous and scared and excited all at the same time. I go scrambling though my desk, looking for her phone number. When I find the old address book, my hands are shaking. I pick up my phone and try to compose myself, to think of what I'll say. But I can't think at all. I just keep seeing the picture of the Empress, kind and reassuring.

I tap in the number and touch the call button. I hold the phone to my ear and listen to the beeps and then the ringing sounds.

No answer. After five rings, a machine kicks in, and I hear Grandma's voice. I open my mouth to leave a message, but then I freeze and hang up.

It's ten o'clock on a Saturday morning. I remember that Grandma owns an antique shop now. She bought it a few years after we moved. She's probably at the shop, but I don't know the number there, or even the name.

Damn. I'll just have to keep trying.

〰〰

I call again at noon and one thirty and two thirty. Still no answer. In between I fix myself a huge breakfast of scrambled eggs and toast and jam but end up throwing most of it away, my stomach too nervous for food. I prowl around downstairs, checking the dining room in particular for any sign of Trudi and her daughters. Just in case.

When Jim and Mom come home, I retreat to my room. I boot up my tablet and get online, visiting some Tarot sites and reading the forums. Then I get on Google Earth and look at Harmony Springs. The area around the town has changed some. There are more housing developments and a new shopping plaza mixed in with the cattle ranches and patches of wetland. But the historic downtown looks exactly the same, and it's amazing—a few blocks of old shops and commercial buildings, the streets lined with huge, twisted oak trees draped in moss. And Victorian houses with wraparound porches and pointed turrets. The street-level pictures make me all warm and nostalgic. I feel this ridiculous yearning to be there.

At a quarter after four I call Grandma again, and she picks up. When she says, "Hello," my heart jumps into my throat.

"Hello, Grandma? This is Abby...your granddaughter."

After what seems a painfully long pause: "Abby? Well, it's been a long time."

"I know, Grandma. How are you?"

"Oh, I'm fine. Getting older, you know. How are you?"

"I'm fine. Well, I've been missing you, and...um...here's the thing. School ends on June 12th, and I was wondering if I might come visit you."

"Oh..."

I rush ahead. "See, Mom's going to Europe for three weeks, and, well, I know it's a lot to ask, but I can pay for my own food and stuff."

"Oh, it's not that, Abby. I'm just surprised."

"I know. I haven't been good about keeping in touch with you, Grandma. I'm sorry." My voice sounds all wimpy and desperate. *Grimace.*

"Abby. Are you sure you're all right?"

"Oh, yeah. So, what do you think?"

"I'd love to have you visit. I'd be thrilled."

I try to keep wimpy and desperate relief out of my voice. "Thanks, Grandma. That's great."

"But I want to be sure you know what you're getting into. It's pretty quiet here. The town hasn't changed much."

"That's fine. Really."

"And I don't have internet at the house. Or cable. But they do have Wi-Fi in the library and the coffee shop downtown, and that's only a bike ride away. You can borrow my old bike anytime you want."

She's still my loving Grandma, explaining everything in her calm, patient way.

"It sounds wonderful. Thank you so much."

We talk a little longer. I tell her I still need to square it with Mom. Or rather, spring it on her. Mom will certainly want to call her to make sure it's all cool. She asks how Mom is doing, and if I'm getting along okay with the new husband, what's-his-name. I tell her that's all good, and that Mom and I will be talking with her soon.

After I hang up I take three long breaths, set my shoulders, and go to find Mom.

≈

Downstairs, Jim's flopped out in the den, watching golf on TV. Mom's at her desk in the home office, working on her laptop. I might hesitate to interrupt her, except she's always busy with something. Besides, the more distracted she is, the easier it might be to get this past her.

I knock on the glass-paneled door, then go in and close it behind me. She gives me her vague multitasking look.

"Sorry to bother you, Mom. Can we talk for a second?"

"Sure, hon. What's up?"

I stand at the edge of her desk. Her eyes have roamed back to the screen. "Here's the thing: I've got a new plan for what to do while you're in Europe."

"Not that again. It's already been settled."

"No, only by default, remember? Now I've got a better idea. I'm going to visit Grandma Renshaw in Florida."

After a second this sinks in, and Mom's eyebrows pop up. Multitasking look switches instantly to laser-burning look. "You can't be serious."

"Yes, I am. I just got off the phone with her. She said she'd be thrilled to have me."

"But Abby, you haven't been there since you were a child. You've forgotten what it's like. It's a stuffy little town in the middle of nowhere. You'll be bored out of your mind."

I'm ready for that one. "No, I won't. I can run, I can go kayaking, I can help Grandma in her shop, and I'll have the summer reading list for next year's honors classes. Besides, it's only three weeks."

Mom glances unhappily at her screen. She doesn't have time for this. But that doesn't mean she's ready to surrender. "What would we tell Trudi?"

"That Grandma just invited me, which is the truth. Trudi won't mind; she'll be relieved. She was only doing it to be nice."

Mom can't argue with that. She considers for a second, then frowns at me. "Abby, I'm not sure I'm comfortable with this. I know she's your grandmother, but it's been so long—"

"Yes, she's my grandmother. And I love her. And when we moved away, you said we'd go back to visit. But we never have."

Now Mom looks hurt, and I realize I've punched a guilt button.

"Abby, I never meant to separate you from Kathryn. I know you love her."

"I know, Mom. We couldn't afford trips to Florida those first few years. But now it's different, and I have the chance. And it means a lot to me."

*I can't tell you how much.*

Mom thinks it over. Then she gets up, and I follow her into the den. She tells Jim my plan and asks what he thinks. Jim gives me an appraising stare, but I can tell he's thinking how this will get his sister off the hook. He shrugs. As long as my grandmother's on board with it, he doesn't see a problem.

I love Jim. What a great guy.

Mom suddenly hugs me very tight. "I want you to call me every week. And text me every day so I know you're all right."

"I will, Mom. I promise."

~~~

I float upstairs, my stomach full of butterflies. And moths. And maybe one or two hornets. My brain is racing with all kinds of thoughts: plane reservations, what to pack, Grandma, Dr. Mark, the ghostly woman in the black dress, the High Priestess in her waterfall clothes.

It's almost five o'clock, and I'm supposed to go to the movies tonight with Franklin and a few other kids from the drama club. The idea makes me queasy—I imagine hallucinations jumping off the screen into the dark theater. This is not a good plan. I text Franklin my apologies.

I'm still queasy, and then I realize I'm ravenous. I've hardly eaten all day.

I go downstairs and offer to fix dinner. I find salmon in the freezer, and I bake it and fix fried rice with veggies and Chinese tea. It's been a while since I cooked for them, and Mom and Jim both appreciate it. Jim jokes that the trip to Florida seems to agree with me.

I just smile.

After dinner, Mom calls Grandma Renshaw, and we both talk to her. Mom stays on the line a long time. She's strained at first, but they talk a lot about me, and Mom slowly relaxes. When she hangs up, she actually looks satisfied.

〰

In the middle of the night, I gasp and sit up in bed. I'm terrified, and I don't know why.

Then I see it: the black cloud seething with strings of gray mist. It hovers near the foot of my bed. The room is icy cold, and I smell swampy decay.

I jump up on the bed. I've had self-defense classes, and I take an attack pose: facing it sideways, my feet spread wide, hands raised and curled into fists. I don't know if you can punch a hallucination, but if it comes near, I intend to find out.

It seems to read my thoughts and hesitates. Then it starts to roll in on itself and grow smaller. Just before it blinks out of sight, I hear the creepy, slithering voice:

"We will meet you at the springs."

Instantly the room is warm and normal seeming.

"All right, then," I answer, "you slimy creep."

But I feel okay. Because the dark, scary energy is gone. Really gone.

For now.

I take a deep breath, drop down on my bed, and go back to sleep.

## 2. I'm not the only one with an apparition problem

"Once more unto the breach, dear friends!" Timothy jerks the steering wheel and the van screeches off the highway, heading for a gap in the trees that might or might not be a road.

I'm in the front seat, and the violent turn almost throws me into Timothy's lap. When I regain my balance, I see we've plunged through the low-hanging fronds and are now swerving down a bumpy, unpaved road. The track is lined with ferns and towering trees draped in Spanish moss. It looks like an enchanted forest and brings up memories of the road to Grandma's house.

"I think this might finally be the place, Timothy."

"For Abby, England, and St. George," Timothy mutters.

Timothy, my shuttle driver, is a heavyset fortyish guy with curly black hair and a thick mustache. He's told me all about himself in the more than two-hours since we left the Orlando airport. He grew up in Belarus, where he learned English watching the BBC on television. He studied Shakespeare at university and seems to have memorized lots of the speeches. He emigrated to the US in the 1990s, then drove a taxi in New York for ten years before concluding he was not going to make it as an actor and that he could drive for a living just as well in Florida. He speaks with an odd blend of accents: Russian, British, and Brooklyn.

I moved to the front seat after Timothy dropped off the last of his other passengers in Lakeland. From there we drove for miles and miles on two-lane rural roads. I got more and more nervous as we neared Harmony Springs, then all gushy-excited as we drove through the historic downtown. But after we passed the cemetery and the last blocks of old wood-frame houses, things started getting weird.

The GPS kept telling Timothy to turn where there were no turns, then to make U-turns. Timothy checked the address with me and found out he had punched it in wrong: Blissful Street instead of Bliss Road. He reset the GPS, and it took us in another direction, back through town and up a county road.

But soon the directions got loopy again. I tried using the map on my phone but couldn't get a reliable signal. (So much for my clever plan of using the phone as a hotspot at Grandma's house.) Finally Timothy switched off the GPS in disgust.

So that's how we ended up speeding back and forth on County Road 245, turning into every gap in the trees that looked like it might be a driveway or street. Which is how we found this enchanted forest trail we're on now, which I really hope will lead us to Grandma's.

The trail merges onto another, wider road of packed sand, and I start to lose hope again. This looks not at all familiar.

Up ahead a big house appears, steep roofs and gables looming over a line of hedges. Timothy slows down as we round the bend and stops next to the mailbox. Vans and pickup trucks are parked in the front yard. Two shirtless guys are carrying a plank from one of the trucks toward the house, and they give us a "what are you doing here?" look.

"I don't suppose this is the place." Timothy sighs.

But I'm staring up at the tall, broken-down house—Victorian-style, almost a mansion, with boarded-up windows and sagging roofs. Then I look to the right, where a muddy path leads down to a dock on dark, sluggish water.

I feel a tarantula crawling inside my chest. I've seen this place in my nightmares.

"Abby! Are you all right?"

I'm gripping the armrest, knuckles white. "Yes. I'm all right. And no, this isn't the place."

"Well, never fear." Timothy unbuckles his seat belt and pops open the door. "I will go and inquire of yonder swains."

Since that night I threatened to punch out the creepy black cloud, I've not seen any more hallucinations. Even the nightmares went away for a while. But in the last two weeks, as my trip to Florida got closer, they started up again, vivid and weird as ever. I started to remember more details: people in robes doing strange rituals in painted circles; the blond woman in the black dress and pearls walking around, looking lost and lonely; two girls in long white dresses, standing beside the rushing blue water of the springs. But the dreams always end the same way—me being grabbed from behind and flung into black water to drown. Looking again at the boat dock, I'm sure that's where it happens.

"Good news. I think we have the answer." Timothy climbs back into the van. "This very street is Bliss Road. We follow it back the other way, and we should find your destination."

I sit quiet as he backs up the van and sets off the way we came. I suppose it's possible I saw this house and the dock as a young child and incorporated them into the scary dreams. But that idea's not very satisfying, since I have no conscious memory of seeing this place, except in the nightmares.

"Ay, now am I in Arden; the more fool I," Timothy mutters under his breath. "But travelers must be content."

I don't answer. The joy and excitement I've been feeling about seeing Grandma is all deflated. Now I'm worried, reminded of the reason I had to come here. As we bump along the road, I scan the deep green and gray shadows, watching for hallucinations.

Ten minutes later we've looped around in a half circle, past two more old houses, and then I see the one I know is Grandma's. It's in better shape than the nightmare mansion on the other side of the bayou, but still it looks rickety and run-down, and smaller than I remember.

A lot of the houses around here date to the 1890s, when well-to-do Northerners founded a kind of colony around the springs. One of those founders was Thomas Renshaw, my great-great-grandfather, and this house has been in the family ever since. Now it looks sad, overgrown with weeds and vines and in need of a paint job.

We climb out of the van, and Timothy starts to unload my suitcases. Contrary to my arrival fantasy, Grandma has not flung open the front door and rushed across the porch to welcome me. Air conditioners are groaning away at two of the windows, so she probably didn't even hear the van pull up.

Timothy plops my luggage on the soft ground and stands there, wearing an expectant smile under his Orlando Magic baseball cap. I realize I need to tip him. I open my backpack and fish out my wallet.

Sometimes I sense people's feelings and even imagine I can hear their thoughts. In this case, I sense how Timothy is hot and tired and feeling pressured to get back to Orlando and pick up his next round of fares. Because this trip took so long, he's thinking he'll probably have to work late and might even get bawled out by his boss.

Despite all this, he's been nothing but kind and cheerful.

Thinking that Mom would not approve such generosity, I hand him a twenty. "I'm sorry to have been so difficult."

Timothy grins and holds up the bill. "If these spirits have offended, I'll think of this, and all is mended!"

I know that one: the ending of *A Midsummer Night's Dream*. We read it in tenth grade. It somehow seems appropriate.

≈

I watch Timothy drive away, and then I'm standing alone in the enchanted forest. The sky is a silvery overcast, as it has been all day, and the air is humid and shimmering hot. I hear insects chirping and a breeze rustling in the towering trees. So here I am, returned to the place of my childhood, trying to put myself back together so I can turn into a grown-up.

And I have no idea if I can.

The front door swings open, and Grandma calls my name. She doesn't move so effortlessly as in my fantasy, but still she hurries across the porch. I break into a run, meet her at the bottom of the steps, and hug her.

It's strange finding that she's shorter than me. Should have been prepared for that. I'm five seven, so I guess Grandma's about five foot five. And she feels smaller in other ways, diminished, almost frail, and that's kind of scary. But as she hugs me back, I feel that my strong, caring Grandma is still in there, and I touch some of the love and security I've missed so much.

She holds me at arm's length. "Let me look at you. What a glorious young woman you've become! I thought you'd never get here. I expected you earlier."

"I'm sorry. The driver had a really hard time finding this place."

She nods. "We *are* out in the sticks. I did warn you."

"I don't care. I'm just so glad to see you, Grandma."

Together we wrangle my luggage up the steps and into the house. We set it in the hallway at the foot of the stairs. Grandma leads me into the living room, where it's cooler and one of the window AC units is chugging away.

The ceilings and windows are high, and the room full of the silvery forest light. But I have the same impression I had outside, that the house is sad, forlorn. The furniture and rugs are dingy, and there's a faint moldy smell.

Grandma picks up on my thoughts. "It's not much, but I do my best to keep it up. Down here a house requires a lot of maintenance."

The last thing I want is for her to feel defensive. "It's just strange being here after so long."

"Disappointed?"

"No! Really."

"Hungry?"

I haven't eaten since breakfast, and it must be three or four. "Starving."

She brightens. "Come into the kitchen, and we'll see what we can do."

The kitchen's immaculate, with the clean, bakery-like smell I remember. Grandma and I spent many, many hours in here when I was a little girl. I sit at the table sipping iced tea while she fixes me a sandwich.

We chat about school, the track team, her shop. She took the afternoon off from the shop so she could be here when I arrived. She didn't have to close it, since it adjoins an old bookstore, and the guy who runs that is watching it for her.

"We've got three businesses sharing an old warehouse space," she explains. "We help each other out, almost like a co-op. Anyway, this is the quiet time of year, so there won't be much activity...Why are you grinning?"

"Things are so laid back here. *So* unlike New Jersey. I think this is just what I need."

"Well, I'm glad to hear it."

She sets a plate in front of me: tuna on wheat bread, with carrot sticks and chips. I dive in, and everything is delicious.

As she watches me, a fond smile appears. Between mouthfuls I smile back. "God, I missed you, Grandma."

This makes her eyes sparkle, like she could almost cry. "I missed you too, Abby. More than I wanted to admit. I'd pretty much given up on having any part in your life."

That makes *me* want to cry. And that emotion drags up a whole lot more—all I've been through since Dad died, the grief of losing him, the pain of separating from Grandma and my home, the nightmares and hallucinations when I got older, my insecurities about the future, my fears of losing my mind.

Before I know it, I'm swallowing hard to keep back the tears.

"I'm sorry," Grandma says. "I didn't mean to make you sad."

"That's okay. I'm fine."

But she's staring at me hard. "You were such a sensitive little girl. And I get the feeling you still are. Do you want to talk about it?"

Wow. Where to begin? I take a sip of tea. I wasn't planning to tell her about the nightmares. She doesn't even know about my hallucination episodes when I was twelve—unless Mom told her, which I'm sure not.

As I'm trying to think what to say, I realize I'm hearing the faint wail of a siren—an ambulance or police car. For a second I even think it might be a hallucination, but then I see that Grandma hears it too. As it gets louder, we stare at each other with growing alarm.

"That's not usual around here," she says.

The siren is getting closer and closer. I follow Grandma out the back door, where the wraparound porch overlooks the yard and the bayou. Grandma looks off to the left, in the direction of the sound. When it seems the siren is almost on top of us, I see spinning blue lights through the trees. Police car.

"That's the Parkers' house," Grandma says. "What in god's name is going on?"

She's not going to wait to find out. She marches down the steps and around the corner of the house. I have to walk pretty fast to keep up.

By the time we reach the stand of trees that separates the two properties, the siren has stopped, but I still see the blue lights flashing through the undergrowth. I follow Grandma down a narrow footpath through the ferns and bushes. The path ends near the spot where the police car is parked, at the side of the house. The car doors stand open, and I read "Harmony Springs Police" painted on one of them. Two officers are trotting across the backyard to where an old man is kneeling, propped up on one hand as if trying to catch his breath. Near the house, a white-haired woman in a flower-print dress stands by the back porch. Grandma hurries over to her, and I follow.

"Emily," Grandma says. "What in the world?"

"Oh, Kathryn! I saw the devil!" She grabs hold of Grandma's shoulders. "I know it sounds crazy, but I swear to god. Satan himself. He was standing right there at the edge of our yard, dripping wet, like he'd gone for swim in the bayou."

"It's all right," Grandma says. "The police are here now. Everything's going to be all right."

Across the lawn, the police officers are bending down beside the elderly man, helping him to his feet.

"I've never been so scared in my life." Mrs. Parker is breathless, nearly hysterical. "John saw it too, not just me. He said it was just some clown trying to scare us. He told me to call the police, then he went out with his shotgun. But Satan didn't move, just stood there watching our house. Then I heard his voice inside my head. He said, 'Leave this place.' And then I saw my husband collapse."

She breaks down sobbing, and Grandma holds her.

I'm wondering what the frick is going on here. And then I'm wondering if it could possibly have something to do with *my* hallucinations.

One of the officers is walking down to the edge of the yard, where Satan was sighted. The other is supporting John Parker as they walk slowly toward us.

"He's all right, Mrs. Parker," the officer says. "We think it was just a dizzy spell. Of course, we'll get an ambulance out here if you want."

"No ambulance!" Mr. Parker growls at him. "I'm not getting stuck with no co-pay!"

"Don't worry about that, sir. We'll drive you to the hospital if you want to get checked out. No charge for that, I promise. Why don't you rest here a few minutes and think it over."

The police officer helps Mr. Parker sit down on the porch steps.

Only now I'm not sure he is an officer. He's young, not much older than me. Tall and lanky, more like a high school basketball player than a full-grown man. And although he wears the same blue shirt, black trousers, and sky-blue cap as his partner, he doesn't have a badge or gun.

He nods politely. "Miss Emily. Miss Kathryn." He glances at me, and for an instant I think I see that look a boy gives you when he kind of likes what he sees.

He clears his throat. "Miss Emily, can you tell me exactly what you saw?"

Mrs. Parker has sat down next to her husband. It takes a moment before she replies in a hoarse whisper. "I think I saw Satan."

"No, you didn't!" Mr. Parker snaps. "What we saw was some jackass playing a prank or trying to scare us. Probably the same jackass who showed up at the Hilton place last week dressed as the skunk ape."

"You mean this has happened before?" They all turn to me, and I realize that was my outside voice. *Oops.*

Grandma inserts introductions: "Emily, John, Ray-Ray, this is my granddaughter, Abigail. She's down visiting me from New Jersey. These are my neighbors, John and Emily Parker, and this is Ray-Ray Quick, son of our chief of police."

Ray-Ray Quick? What kind of name is that? (Luckily, this was *not* my outside voice.)

Now here comes the other officer, the full-grown one with the gun. "I didn't see any tracks or breaks in the grass." He sets down Mr. Parker's shotgun, which he's retrieved from the lawn, and beside it the cartridges, which he has wisely unloaded.

"I understand you saw this intruder also, Mrs. Parker?"

Emily nods, lips pressed thin.

"Do you think you can come over and show me exactly where you saw him?"

She goes white. "I don't think I want to."

"She doesn't have to," Mr. Parker says. "I told you exactly where he was. Standing right next to that cypress. And dripping wet, like he just stepped out of the bayou."

The officer twists his mouth, looking stymied. "Ray-Ray, you want to take another look over there? Maybe I missed something."

"Sure, Dan."

Ray-Ray walks off across the yard. Dan suggests we go inside, where it's cooler, and the Parkers can tell him everything from the beginning. Grandma tags along to give Mrs. Parker support. As they're climbing the steps, I hesitate, then decide to follow Ray-Ray.

Sometimes I'm impulsive, and this is one of those times.

When I approach, he is scouting the back of the yard, where the mowed grass gives way to deeper grass and sedges. The ground is soggy under my running shoes, sloping down toward the dark, still waters of Bliss Bayou.

Ray-Ray glances at me, then goes back to his investigation.

"Excuse me, officer. But did I understand correctly? Something like this happened once before?"

He answers without looking up. "Yes. And I'm not an officer, just a summer intern."

Summer intern, son of the police chief. That explains the uniform and the not-carrying-a-gun. "So what exactly happened at the Hilton place? And what is a, uh...skunk ape?"

He flicks me a smile. I'm glad to see he has a sense of humor.

"The skunk ape is the Florida version of Bigfoot. Just a legend that some people claim to have seen and that a few people have made up hoaxes around."

"So you think that's what's happening here? Someone dressing up to spoof people? Or frighten them?"

Ray-Ray shakes his head. "I don't know what to think. But I sure don't see any sign that anyone's walked through here recently. Do you?"

He and Dan have been careful to stay on the edge of the yard and not disturb the deep grass near the cypress. I scan the area and look closely at the spot where the devil was supposed to have appeared.

"No. I don't." *At least no one with a physical body.*

Ray-Ray touches his cap and walks off. "Ma'am."

*Ma'am?*

I tag after him, hustling to keep up with his long strides. "So, officially the police have no explanation for this or for what happened at the Hilton place?"

He stops and looks down at me. "*Officially?* What are you, with CNN? You ought to meet my sister."

"What do you mean?"

"Never mind." He stalks away again.

"Wait." I hurry after him. "Listen. I didn't mean to sound pushy. But I just got here today, and I'm curious. You have to admit this is some weird shit."

He laughs at that and stops again. "Okay. I'm only an intern. Officially, I can't speak for the Harmony Springs police force...except that, as I'm sure my dad would tell you, the investigation is ongoing."

~~~

Later Grandma fills me in on the Parkers' interview with Officer Dan. We've had dinner and washed up, and now we sit together on the back porch swing, just like years ago. The air is cooling off, and crickets are buzzing like crazy in the June twilight.

Mr. and Mrs. Parker both agreed that the figure was black, mucky, and shiny wet, as if it had walked out of the bayou. Mrs. Parker said she saw devil horns, but Mr. Parker saw nothing like that. Mr. Parker said the figure never spoke, and Mrs. Parker did not repeat her statement that she heard a voice in her head saying, "Leave this place."

Dan took down all the information and verified that Mr. Parker was feeling okay. He and Ray-Ray left after making the Parkers promise that if they were bothered by any more intruders, they would call the police and not try to handle it themselves.

"I don't know if John will keep that promise," Grandma says. "As you saw, he's a feisty old bird."

"What do you know about the other incident, Grandma? The one with the skunk ape?"

"Oh, at Laura Hilton's. Her place is on the other side of the springs. That was also supposed to be a dark figure, but Laura claimed it was seven feet tall. Of course, she saw it in the twilight. It might have been the same person."

"So you think it's someone dressing up in costume to frighten people?"

"Not necessarily dressing up. Probably just some vagrant hanging around. We're in the backwoods here, and we get some weird characters coming through from time to time."

I mull that over for a bit. "But the police didn't find any tracks at the Parkers'. The grass was undisturbed."

"Well, they can miss things. Or the Parkers might have been mistaken about exactly where they saw the guy."

She doesn't sound entirely convinced, and I get a prickling sense she's not telling me everything.

"I don't want you worrying about this, Abby. We're safe here."

"Oh, I'm not scared. More curious." I guess I've been hoping people might actually be seeing something supernatural. Or else some kind of mass hallucination. Because that would make me feel less crazy. Less alone.

"Did the figure at Laura Hilton's say anything to her?"

"Well…" Grandma laughs. "Now that you mention it, she claimed to have heard it tell her to 'leave this place.' That's probably where Emily got the idea. I don't believe I've ever heard of a skunk ape talking before."

"Hmm." This is getting weirder and weirder. "Suppose it was a vagrant, like you say. Why would a vagrant say something like that?"

"You are the curious one!" Grandma sighs. "Okay, one of the rumors that came up last week—and I think it's a crackpot rumor—is that the skunk ape incident has to do with the development."

"What development?"

"There's a real estate company from Texas that's trying to buy up land around the springs to build luxury houses and a golf course."

"Yuck!" I find that thought almost as scary as my nightmares. I want this place to stay the way it is forever. It's my childhood. It's sacred.

"I know," Grandma says. "In Florida, there's always conflicts over development. Out here we're isolated enough that we've mostly been spared. But this time there's real pressure, and it's creating a rift in the community. Some of the owners want to sell out, poor folks who need the money, a few speculators who bought properties and now see their chance to cash in. The rest of us are against it. We're afraid that once developers get a foothold and put up a few mansions, it will ruin the springs. Then others will want to sell, and it will be like dominoes falling. It's happened before in other places."

"Wow. So someone might be trying to frighten more homeowners into selling?"

"That's the theory. I think it's pretty far-fetched. Don't you?"

"You're not thinking of selling, are you, Grandma?"

She peers off across the darkening backyard, toward the bayou. "No. I've lived in this house since I moved in with your grandfather. Over forty years. I'll hang on if I possibly can. I always wanted to pass the place down to you."

"To me?"

"Who else? You're my only heir. Of course, once I'm gone, you can do whatever you want with it."

My brain is whirling. Abby Renshaw, slightly insane girl from New Jersey and backwoods Florida heiress.

I put my hand on her forearm. "I hope you live a long, long time, Grandma. And that you never sell this place."

〰〰

Upstairs I have a big, airy bedroom in a corner of the house. Windows face the backyard and the woods to the side. Grandma's had one of her downstairs air conditioners brought up so the room will be cool enough for sleeping. It rattles and chugs away as I unpack.

Tired as I am from the trip and the long day, I am way too wired to sleep. Long after Grandma has said goodnight, I am up rearranging my clothes in the drawers and closets, checking for a phone signal (without success), and trying to get into one of the honors reading assignment books on my tablet (with very little success).

Finally I dig out my Tarot deck. I ask the cards about the dark figures seen by the Parkers and Laura Hilton. Are they men or hallucinations? Or something else?

The reading is hard to decipher. Swords, wands, pentacles, cups: all the suits are here and seem to tell different stories. In the position of the environment is the Knight of Cups, and he reminds me of Ray-Ray Quick. I stare at him for a while and notice that I'm smiling.

I focus on the crown position, the High Priestess again, the goddess at the point of balance, the source of the waters...the source of the springs. She stares back at me—kind, serene, powerful.

*What are you trying to tell me?*

Now I feel a presence in the room, a cool, mysterious power, like a breeze lifting me up in a dream. I stand and walk to the window that faces the woods.

On the ground below, at the edge of the trees, a woman is staring up at me. Not the stern blond woman in black I've seen before. This one is young and slender and seems very alive. She wears a long white skirt, a white blouse, and a straw bonnet, like a sun hat. She reminds me of the girls in white dresses I dreamed about, the ones standing beside the springs.

I literally pinch my arm to be sure I'm not dreaming.

I have no fear, like with the other hallucinations. Only this deep sense of wonder. I feel I know her, and that she means me well.

Slowly she raises her right hand in greeting.

I wave back. Then I squeeze my eyes shut and look again. She's gone. I see only a wall of trees under the black sky.

### 3. Have you ever heard of a curse on the Renshaws?

Next morning, we're having a late breakfast in the kitchen when I hear knocking on the front door.

"Now what?" Grandma sounds flustered. She's had more excitement in the past twenty-four hours than she's used to, for sure.

I go and open the door.

A girl grins at me. Short, curly orange hair and a face full of freckles. She's about my age and height, but curvier.

"Hi, you must be Abigail. I'm Molly Quick. My brother said I should meet you."

"Oh...Ray-Ray?"

"Yeah. Mind if I come in?"

"No...sure." I step back, and she brushes past me.

"Is your grandmother here?"

"Yeah. We're having breakfast. Come on in."

She follows me down the hall.

"Oh, it's you, Molly," Grandma says. "Can I get you some breakfast?"

"No, thank you, Miss Kathryn. Well, maybe just coffee, if you can pour it over ice. It's going to be another hot day."

I volunteer to get it so Grandma doesn't have to get up. Molly sits down at the table.

"So what brings you out here on a Sunday morning?" Grandma asks.

"Research," Molly replies. "I heard about the devil showing up next door."

Grandma laughs. "I hope you're not going to write *that* in the *Quick Report*." She explains to me: "Molly is a budding newswoman. She writes a blog about Harmony Springs. Pretty good stuff, too."

"Thank you!" Molly sounds pleased. "But I'm actually starting a new blog. With more of an investigative slant. All these weird events, they're looking less and less like coincidence."

"Now, Molly—"

"Seriously, Miss Kathryn. First Pete Hastings is bitten by a cottonmouth, then Laura Hilton is visited by the skunk ape, and now the Parkers see Satan in their backyard."

I set the iced coffee down in front of Molly. "What's this about a cottonmouth?"

"That was three weeks ago," Grandma says. "Pete was clearing out some weeds and surprised a snake. It happens around here. Molly, there's no reason to believe that's related to these other things."

"No reason to conclude it's not," Molly says, "without investigating. That's why I rode out this morning, to talk to the Parkers. Unfortunately, they were not very talkative. They seemed pretty upset. They told me everything they have to say is in the police report, which of course I've already read."

She's added milk and sugar, and now she gulps down half the glass of coffee. "This is delicious, thanks. So, I understand you two went over to the Parkers' when you heard the siren..."

Grandma confirms that we hurried over there, and no, she didn't see any intruders—natural or supernatural.

"How about you, Abigail? Or is it Abby?"

"Abby. It's just like Grandma said. We arrived after the fact and didn't really see anything."

"Ray-Ray told me you went with him to look at the spot where the figure appeared."

"Well...not *with him*, exactly."

Molly gives us her grin. "He wouldn't admit it, of course, but from the way he described you, I'd say he thinks you're cute."

*Really?* That's nice. I guess he's not so bad either...

Now both of them are grinning at me. I hope I'm not blushing. I think I am.

"So, what do you think?" Molly asks. "I mean, about these strange reports of intruders?"

"Oh, I don't know. I'm new around here."

"Yeah. I understand you lived here as a little girl? How does it feel to be back? What are your impressions of the town so far?"

Not sure how many impressions I want to share. Particularly with someone who's going to post them online. "Well, I just got in yesterday."

"I can show you around if you like. It's a quiet little town—apart from these possibly paranormal events, of course. My favorite hangouts are the library and Springs of Coffee. That's this little coffee shop and bakery on Main Street. They have Wi-Fi."

"That's good to know." I touch the phone in the back pocket of my shorts. "We don't have a signal out here. And I need to text my mom today."

"You can ride in with me now if you want. They open at eleven on Sundays."

"No, thanks. I'm going with Grandma to help in her shop today."

"Oh, you can meet me there if you want," Grandma says. "I won't open up 'til noon or twelve thirty."

Well...I don't want to seem unfriendly. And despite all the nosey questions, I like Molly. Her enthusiasm's kind of charming.

〜〜〜

So ten minutes later, with my tablet in my backpack and the backpack slung over my shoulder, I'm climbing onto Molly Quick's electric bike. The bike seems patched together, with an old, rusty frame and motor but a seat and deep-tread tires that look like new additions.

"Are you sure this is safe for two people?"

"Absolutely! Would the daughter of the chief of police suggest an unsafe ride?"

"I don't know you well enough to answer that."

"Ha! Then you'll just have to hold on and trust me."

Molly walks the bike in a half circle so it's pointing away from the house. She instructs me to wrap my arms around her waist. She turns the key, and the motor hums to life. We start off with a jolt. Molly twists the handles to accelerate, and we go streaming down the tree-lined road with the wind in our faces.

I've never ridden on any kind of motorbike before. "Hey! This is really fun."

"I know!" Molly says. "I love the electric motor. Eco-friendly. And quiet, so I can sneak up on people."

"Do you sneak up on people a lot?"

"Oh, I never have. But as an investigative journalist, who knows when I might need to start?"

We ride down Bliss Road in the direction opposite the way I arrived yesterday. The trail curves past three more old houses set back in the trees, then merges onto a narrow blacktop. A short time later, we're on the outskirts of town.

We turn onto Main Street and cruise past houses and shops under the huge oak trees hung with Spanish moss. There's almost no traffic, except in the parking lot of the Presbyterian church.

Molly pulls into the side yard of Springs of Coffee and leaves the bike leaning against the brick wall. Inside, she introduces me to the gay couple who own the place. Benjamin is the baker and Lewis is the barista and "business genius." They seem really nice, and they treat Molly like family. Benjamin insists we sample some pieces of blueberry muffin.

Molly orders a caramel macchiato and I ask for an iced chai. We sit down at a little table in the corner and fire up our computers. While mine is booting, I check my phone: two texts from Mom. The first, from yesterday, tells me they've landed in Paris and are having a grand time, and asks how I'm doing. The second, from this morning, says, "Where R U? U promised to text everyday!"

I thumb in a reply: "I am great. no signal at Grandma's. messages may be irregular. stop worrying bout me and enjoy ur vacation!"

After we pick up our drinks, we both get involved with our screens. I've been so charged up with settling in at Grandma's and the excitement at the Parkers' house that I've hardly noticed not having internet. Now it hits me hard, and I get a burst of anxiety about catching up. I look at the latest posts from my teammates and add comments and emojis. I check in on Franklin and some of our friends from the drama club.

Franklin is maybe my best friend. I met him three years ago, when we were both patients of Dr. Mark. Like me, he has anxiety disorder and suffers from too much imagination. But since we got to high school, he's done really well. He's extremely smart, and he's acing all his classes. And getting involved with the drama club has really helped him bloom socially. We talk a lot about books and plays. He's tried to get me to join the club, but it's just not my thing. I do love hanging around with them and watching them all perform. I make a good audience.

So I send Franklin a text to let him know I've arrived safely and that my phone access is limited. Then I think I ought to post something of my own, so I snap a picture of the coffee shop and post that I'm at Springs of Coffee in Harmony Springs. I think of taking one of Molly and adding "with my new friend Molly," but I guess that would be false. I mean, she's not really my friend, is she?

After considering this, I look up to find Molly staring at me with a thoughtful expression.

"About the Parkers," she says. "Dan's report stated there was no sign of disturbance in the grass where they claimed to have seen the intruder. Did you see anything?"

"No."

"But the Parkers were pretty definite about the spot, right?"

"Yes."

"So wouldn't you say that's evidence that this could be an actual paranormal event?"

She would obviously like to think so. I have to admit, so would I. But I fall back on "I really don't know what to say. I can't explain about the grass."

Molly nods. "It's not as far-fetched as it might sound. The history of Harmony Springs is full of paranormal stories."

A wriggle of fear starts in my stomach. "You mean like apparitions and ghosts?"

"Sure. The families who founded the town were spiritualists. The Greenes, the Hollingsworths, the Aldens"—she gestures at me with an open hand—"the Renshaws."

The wriggle turns into a cringe. "I didn't know that."

"Oh yeah. I've read a lot about it. Old newspapers and diaries over at the library. Alden was a rich guy from Boston and Greene was a minister in Indiana, but they were both into the occult. The story is that on the same night in 1882, they were visited in a dream by a spirit named Lebab. Lebab told them both to come to the springs and build a community. There was no town here then, just a little backwoods settlement."

Molly pauses to sip her coffee.

"Go on." I'm staring at her, enthralled. Why have I never heard this before?

"Well, it gets more interesting. The spiritualist community grew and seems to have split into different factions. Some of them practiced magic, I mean, rituals where they conjured spirits and raised powers to do things for them. Others said that this was dangerous and called it sorcery."

Her eyes focus in on mine. "Did you ever hear anything about a *curse* on the Renshaws?"

I lean back, hunch my shoulders, put my hands under the table and curl them into fists. I know I'm overreacting big-time, but it feels like she's just punched me between the eyes.

"Abby?"

My voice is choked. "I...that's sort of a painful subject. My dad said he was cursed. He died in a car wreck."

Molly looks horrified, then guilty. "Oh, I'm sorry. My big mouth! I ought to just shut up."

"No, please! Tell me what you know about it."

She goes on reluctantly. "Well, I don't know a lot. It's not the kind of thing that got written up in the newspapers. But I've heard a few older folks mention it. And it's in one old diary I found. There was a young woman named Annie Renshaw in the second generation. She was the daughter of the Renshaw family who moved here from the north. Supposedly, she and some of her friends were very skilled in magic. When they were still teenagers, they got in contact with some powerful spirit or entity, but it turned out to be evil. Eventually Annie Renshaw went insane and drowned herself in Bliss Spring."

"Bliss Spring? Is that the bayou?"

"Yeah, now it's the bayou, but it used to be a spring. See, originally there were five springs: Bliss and the other four upstream. But sometime after Annie Renshaw drowned, the source of Bliss Spring closed up, and it became a backwater."

"But...who put the curse on us?"

Molly shrugs. "The story is that Annie did, just before she drowned. She was possessed by all this evil, and since she was never going to have any children, she put a curse on her brothers and sister and all their descendants."

"Wow...wow." This does *not* feel like some quaint horror story from the last century. This feels like the hidden truth of my own past—the cause of my nightmares, the source of *my* mental instability.

"Really, Abby. I'm sorry. I know I talk too much. But it's just that I'm so curious and interested in things. People around here understand that they can just tell me to back off when I go too far. Please don't hate me."

I'm finding it a little hard to breathe. "I don't hate you...Really, I appreciate your telling me. I'm curious about this myself."

"Thanks." Molly looks relieved. "But please, if I ever get too nosey, just tell me to shut up."

## 4. Drowning six or seven times an hour

A little past noon, I say good-bye to Molly and walk the few blocks to Grandma's shop. While yesterday was overcast and humid, today is hot and dry. Sunlight filters through the oak leaves and casts wavy shadows on the ancient, broken sidewalks. The buildings and overgrown yards all look like they haven't changed in a hundred years—not since the time of Annie Renshaw. But the modern world is also right in my face: cars and pickup trucks driving by, advertisements in the shop windows for the theme parks in Orlando, a road sign about the development issue:

> Save Harmony Springs
> Community Meeting June 24

Grandma's shop is one of three businesses in a brick building. The sidewalk is raised a couple of steps above street level and bordered with an iron rail. The lettering on the front window says "Glenda's Antiques." Grandma told me that Glenda was actually three owners ago, but no one's ever seen a good reason to change the name.

Grandma is busy with a customer, so I look around. The small space is packed with china, picture frames, glassware and silverware, crystal, even some antique clothes. Not much furniture— just a few small tables and stools, nothing Grandma couldn't move herself. Some of it smells a little musty, but there's not a speck of dust. I think how much work it must be for Grandma to keep it all tidy.

I'm spacing out, staring into a case of old costume jewelry, when Grandma's voice startles me. "So, what do you think of the place?"

"Oh...pretty sweet. I can't believe you manage all this by yourself."

"Well, it keeps me busy." I can feel she's very proud of it. "How was your visit with Molly?"

I try to keep the stress out of my voice. "Fine...She's an interesting girl."

Grandma smiles. "She comes on a little strong sometimes, but I like her."

I want to ask what she knows about Annie Renshaw. But then I think how hard it hit me to hear the story from Molly. Any talk of a Renshaw curse is bound to be painful for Grandma too, so I leave it alone.

I spend the afternoon learning about the shop. In between customers, Grandma shows me the stock and how to use the cash register and credit card device. The side walls have big openings that lead to other shops, and Grandma takes me to meet her neighbors.

On one side is Palmer's Books, a space much bigger than Grandma's, and crammed with all kinds of books—floor to ceiling, in narrow aisles. The owner, Kevin Palmer, is a Black man around Grandma's age. He's a retired anthropology professor from the University of Florida, and he asks me about my honors reading list. On the other side is the Harmony Gallery, which sells original arts and crafts—pottery, jewelry, paintings, and stained glass. It's run by a fortyish woman named Jenny Nesheim. She looks Swedish or Norwegian, with short blond hair and very pale skin. She likes to knit, and in the air conditioning she wears a handmade shawl.

Processing all this new information keeps my mind off my anxieties. By the time we've closed the shop and are driving home in Grandma's old Honda Odyssey, I'm wondering why the talk with Molly freaked me out so much.

Seriously, the fact that some people a hundred years ago might have been into the occult and that one of them might have come to a bad end has nothing to do me. As for the skunk ape and the devil, they were probably just intruders—vagrants, as Grandma said, or somebody dressing up as a hoax.

All this paranormal talk is making my imagination run wild.

That's what the rational part of me says. That's what Dr. Mark would tell me.

And yet, as we near Grandma's house and I glimpse the dull water through the trees, fear gnaws at the pit of my stomach.

I haven't run in over two days. No question my body and brain are missing the calming influence. It's about six, and the weather is cooling off. Since it's June, there will still be at least a couple more hours of daylight. So when we pull up into the front yard, I tell Grandma not to wait dinner for me, that I'm going for a run. She says okay, but warns me to keep to the roads and not venture into the underbrush.

I change into workout clothes and put on one of the three pairs of running shoes I brought on the trip. Outside, I stretch and take in deep breaths to center myself. I start up Bliss Road in the direction away from town. The hard-packed sand has ruts and potholes, so I have to watch my step. Just as well—concentrating on that keeps my mind off other things.

The road loops around the top end of the bayou and then down toward the houses on the other side. This is the way Timothy drove me yesterday. I come to the fork and run all the way out to the county road. After I double back, I figure I've run about two miles. So I continue down Bliss Road toward the house where Timothy stopped, the house I recognized from the nightmares.

The thought of seeing it again scares me, but also makes me determined. I'm feeling like Abby the athlete, strong and tough, and my rational mind tells me to confront the place. The fear rises as I get closer, but it's nothing I can't handle.

I stop in front of the house and look it over. No workmen are around, and the place is deserted. No sounds but a faint hissing of insects.

The fear is growing.

*Face it, Abby. Face it down.*

I jog toward the water, where the path twists down the slope, turns onto a little boardwalk, then reaches the old dock. That is where I dreamed of drowning. I wonder if it's where Annie drowned. Somehow, I'm certain it is.

*Face it and make it go away.*

I walk down the path, setting one foot in front of the other. On my right, something slithers away through the weeds. I sidestep a puddle and keep going.

I place one foot on the boards, then the other.

The world explodes around me, freezing cold and wet.

*I've fallen into the water.*

It's not possible. I was like thirty feet from the dock.

I'm struggling, thrashing my arms. I know how to swim, but it doesn't matter. Something is dragging me down. I open my mouth to scream, and the water rushes in, down my throat, into my lungs. In terrible pain I look up. The gray light is far overhead, and I'm sinking...

Then I'm coughing and retching, agony in my chest. I'm on my hands and knees on the rough boards.

*A hallucination—but so real.*

I straighten my back, clutching my chest with both hands. I can hardly believe my skin and clothes are dry. I raise my head. And then I see him.

He stands on the boardwalk, black and dripping wet, framed against the water in the dim light. When I saw him before, he was just a floating cloud. Now he has the form of an ape or slouching man—long arms, bulky shoulders, oval head, no eyes or mouth, no face at all, just a flat, inky blackness. Like some hideous cartoon, a slimy living shadow.

As he reaches for me, I hear his slithery voice. "Little Renshaw, I can save you."

I twist around, jump up, and run.

My legs feel heavy, the muscles almost paralyzed. After a few steps I slip and fall face down into the puddle. Gasping, I swallow a mouthful of filthy water. I lift my head, coughing.

Anger rushes in, wiping out some of the fear. *I will not drown in a mud puddle!*

I get back on my feet and splash through the water.

I've almost reached the road when the earth disappears under me, and I plunge back into the bayou. This time I know it's an illusion. But that doesn't stop my thrashing and sinking, or the suffocating pain in my lungs.

When I come back to myself, I'm bent over, coughing.

And he's there again, standing right in front of me, reaching with long, wet fingers. "You cannot escape this. Not unless you come to me."

I scream and roll away from him.

I stagger to my feet and run.

≈

By the time I get back to Grandma's house, it's night. An owl is hooting somewhere in the woods.

I drowned twice more along the way. In one of the falls I bruised my knee, and I'm limping. My mouth is swollen from landing on a root, and I've spit out some blood.

I struggle up the porch steps and find the front door locked. I don't want Grandma to see me like this, all scared and beaten up. I hope I can make it to my room without being seen, so I limp around to the back door.

But Grandma's sitting in the kitchen with a cup of tea. "There you are. I was—" She jumps up. "Abby! What happened to you?"

I raise my hands to keep her away. "I'm all right. I had a fall."

"You weren't attacked?"

"No! No, I'm all right."

She grabs hold of my arms. "Child, you're not all right. Let me see!"

Panicking, I look into her eyes. And then I lose it. I slump against her, and all my fear bursts out in a loud, wailing cry.

"Abby!"

For just a moment I feel her shoulder against my cheek. Then the floor opens, and I fall into the black water...

〰

When I come back to reality, we're both on the kitchen floor. Grandma is holding me, rocking me like a baby.

"It's all right. It's all right." But she looks terrified.

"Oh, Grandma. I'm sorry. I'm so sorry to dump this on you."

"Abby, please tell me. What is the matter?"

Over her shoulder I see the slimy shadow guy slouching in the doorway. "I'm losing my mind."

"What do you mean? Do you want me to call your mother?"

"No! Please. Please don't call her!"

"All right. All right. But you need to calm down. You're not taking drugs, are you?"

"No. I used to be on anxiety meds, but...it's not that."

"Then what?"

Panting, sobbing, I try to explain. The nightmares, the real reason I came here...and what happened tonight.

"I had hallucinations before. When I was twelve. They put me on meds. But this is the worst it's ever been. I keep drowning over and over. I'm so afraid."

"Abby, this is serious. I think I should take you to the hospital."

"No! Please, Grandma. I've always been able to get hold of myself before. Please give me more time." I'm afraid that if I'm checked into a psychiatric hospital now, I'll never come out.

"All right," Grandma says. "No one will hurt you. I promise."

She helps me into the living room, and I sit down on the couch. She brings a wet cloth to wash off some of the mud, and ice for my knee and swollen face. When I've calmed down a little, she asks me to describe the hallucinations. I tell her about the goblins and creatures I used to see and the creepy black cloud in my bedroom in New Jersey. I've started to tell her how tonight he's manifested as a shadow man, when the room disappears and I drown again.

When it ends, I'm shaking uncontrollably. "Oh, Grandma. I just want to die! I'm cursed. Just like my dad."

She grips me hard by the arms. "Don't say that, Abby! Don't *ever* say that!"

I break down sobbing, and she hugs me and strokes my head. When I've settled down some, she asks me about the nightmares—to keep me talking, to keep me *here*.

I tell her everything I can remember: being chased through the woods, the blond woman in black, the girls in white dresses, the circle of people in hooded robes. As Grandma listens, her expression changes, like it's all starting to make some sense.

"And the figure that looks like a shadow. Is he in the nightmares too?"

He's followed us into the living room, and I look over at him standing in the corner. "I don't think so. Not that I remember."

"Do you mean he's here now? You see him now?"

I nod.

Grandma clutches my hand. She stares at the corner, like she's trying to see him too. "Tell me exactly what you see."

I describe the bulky, glistening shape, the long arms, the empty blackness where there should be a face. "He's like the figure the

Parkers described, but without the devil horns. Maybe he's the skunk ape too."

Grandma's eyes are wide. "Abby, if this keeps up, I'll have to take you to the hospital. There may be no other choice. But there is one thing I can try—if you'll trust me."

"Anything, Grandma. I trust you."

"Then wait right here. And don't be afraid."

She crosses the room to the hallway, and I hear her climb the stairs. I sit with my knees tucked, hugging myself, not looking at Shadow Man.

In a little while, Grandma comes down. She's wearing a robe of blue velvet with brocaded silver birds, and a silver chain for a belt. She's carrying a knife.

"Is the spirit still here?" she asks.

I break out of my shock enough to answer. "Yes."

"Show me exactly where."

I point to the spot. He seems to be watching Grandma now, tense like a cat.

Grandma comes over and stands between me and Shadow Man. She points the knife at the ceiling. She takes a deep breath and holds it for a second, and then a tone comes from deep in her chest: "Ooooohhhhhhhhh."

I'm stunned and frightened, but I also sense protection rising around us.

Grandma repeats the tone twice more. Then she extends the knife in front of her and slowly walks around the couch. Staring at the knife, I see faint blue light coming from the tip. She draws a circle with this light, with her and me inside the circle and Shadow Man outside it.

Then she steps over in front of Shadow Man and points the knife directly at him. She traces a five-pointed star in the air, and when she speaks, her voice is deep and strong.

"I am an initiate of the Circle of Harmony. I have tasted the waters of the Five Springs. In the name of the founders of our order, in the name of the spirit Lebab, in the name of the Great Goddess Who Shapes All Things, I banish you from my presence and from this place and time. *Go now*, and leave us in peace!"

With these last words, she thrusts the knife and the shadow flickers out—like the dark in a room when a light is switched on.

"Is he gone, Abby?"

Bewildered and amazed, I can only nod.

Grandma sinks into a chair, exhausted.

When I'm finally able to speak, I say, "Grandma, what just happened? What did you do?"

"Abby, that was magic."

## 5. Magic is not what you think

"I haven't tried anything like that in a long, long time," Grandma says. "I'd forgotten how much energy it takes."

I just stare at her, speechless.

"I know, Abby. You must be wondering about all this." She gestures at her robe, the knife still in her hand. "Maybe now you think I'm the one who's crazy. But the important thing is, it seems to have worked. At least for the moment."

"I saw blue light coming out of your knife."

"You saw that? That's remarkable. I visualized the light when I drew the circle. But the fact you could actually see it—well, not many people are that gifted. Is the light still there?"

"Yes, but dimmer. It seems to be fading." I'm straining to fit all this into my head. "So, does this mean it's all real? My hallucinations are real?"

"I don't know." Grandma sighs. "I'm not an expert...There's someone I can call. She might be able to help us." She pushes herself out of the chair.

"Where are you going?"

"Just to the other room, sweetie. Don't worry. You can come with me if you want."

I follow her, feeling like a weepy three-year-old who's gotten hurt and needs to cling to her mother. We go into the little sunroom, which Grandma has furnished as a study. She searches through an old phone book and picks up her landline phone.

"Who are you calling, Grandma?" I ask as she presses the buttons.

"An old friend. She's going to be surprised to hear from me."

After a moment she speaks into the phone. "Hello, Violet? This is Kat Renshaw...Yes, I know it's been a while. I hope it's not too late to call you?... Fine. Listen, Vi, I need your help—badly. A spiritual matter... Yeah, that's right. It's my granddaughter, Abigail. She's having visions, horrible, uncontrollable. I think, well, she may be under psychic attack...I don't know 'by what.' She assumed they were hallucinations. She's had them a long time, but tonight it got really scary. She said it was the worst ever. When I couldn't calm her down, I tried a banishing, and that seems to have driven it away...Yes...I'm not sure. I don't know what to do next. That's why I'm calling you...Yes, we can come right over. Thank you, Vi. I really appreciate this."

Grandma sets down the phone. "We're going to go see Violet, honey. I think she can help us."

"All right." I remember that I'm sweaty and filthy. "Can I take a shower first?"

Grandma laughs and glances at her sleeves. "Of course. I'll need to change out of this too."

〰〰

We're driving down Bliss Road in the direction of town. The car windows are open, and the night air is damp and cool. I hear an owl again, hooting over a chorus of frogs.

I glance at myself in the visor mirror—red eyes over dark circles, and the right side of my mouth has a beautiful bruise. I look like some poor, abused waif.

But at least my emotions have quieted—enough that I'm able to think. And ask questions. I look over at Grandma. "Tell me about Violet."

"Well, she's an old friend. When I first met your grandfather, he and I studied with her."

"Studied?"

"Yes, magic. You see, Abby, magic is not what you think. It's not like what you see in the movies. It's a discipline for...growing yourself mentally and spiritually. Although some of it does involve working with forces outside yourself, and it can give you power over those forces. But the main point is to give you self-knowledge and self-control. People have been practicing that kind of magic since the early days of Harmony Springs. And Violet probably knows more about it than anyone."

I'm quiet for a while, taking this in. We've turned onto the paved road, and up ahead I see a few lights through the trees, the first houses on the outskirts of town.

"So you told her that my hallucinations were visions. And that you thought I was under psychic attack."

"Yeah, I'm not sure about that... I suppose there are two ways to look at what happened tonight. One, some spirit or force was attacking you, and the banishing ritual drove it away. Or two, it *was* a hallucination, all in your head, but the fact that I did something that seemed reassuring and powerful was enough to bring you out of that psychological state. One thing I learned from studying magic is that there is always more than one way to explain things."

We drive through a neighborhood of old houses built in what they call cracker style—wood-frame cabins with porches on big, wooded lots. Grandma pulls into one of these and parks in the driveway. In front of us is a Toyota RAV, and I notice a Palmer's Books sign painted on the door.

"Oh, I forgot to mention," Grandma says. "Kevin will be here. You met Kevin at the bookshop today. He and Violet are...domestic partners."

When Grandma knocks, it's Kevin who opens the door. He's wearing striped pajamas, slippers, and a blue silk robe. "Come on in. Hope you don't mind that I didn't dress."

"Of course not," Grandma answers. "We appreciate your letting us barge in on short notice."

We walk into a tiny parlor cluttered with furniture and stacks of books. No air conditioner, just a ceiling fan whirling overhead. The night air flows in through open windows.

"Hello! Welcome!" Violet comes in from the kitchen. She and I lock eyes, and I sway back—like the force of her presence knocked me off balance.

She's a plump, moon-faced woman, a little taller than me. She looks about ten years older than Grandma or Kevin, but she's beaming and full of life. Her shoulder-length hair is dyed red with purple streaks, and she wears dangling silver earrings.

After hugging Grandma, she turns to me. "Abigail, so nice to meet you." She squeezes both my hands. "Come into the kitchen. Will you take some tea?"

"Thanks," Grandma says. "That would be lovely."

Violet puts on the kettle, and we all sit down at the kitchen table.

"Let me see your hands," Violet says.

She holds both my hands and examines the palms. "Oh, very good." She traces an index finger over some of the lines. "All the talent and sensitivity of the Renshaws—and then some. But you're also very strong, and tough."

I feel anything but strong and tough at the moment. I haven't eaten since lunch, and I'm actually kind of woozy.

Violet can apparently read my mind. She pushes a shiny brown loaf in front of me. "Have some apple bread. Kevie, would you get her a plate?"

Kevin brings a plate and butter knife, and Violet cuts a thick slice for me.

I bite into the apple bread and talk with my mouth full. "Oh, this is so good. Thank you!"

"Poor thing didn't get any dinner," Grandma says.

"Do you read Tarot cards?" Violet asks me.

Whoa. Violet can *definitely* read my mind. "How did you know that?"

She grins. "I didn't. Just a question."

"You read Tarot cards?" Grandma asks.

So it occurs to me: I'm sitting in the kitchen of an old wood cabin late at night in the middle of Florida, with my grandmother (who, by the way, does magic) and a sixty-something Black man (who's a retired anthropology professor) and a seventy-something Caucasian woman with red and purple hair (who can maybe read my mind), eating sweet, doughy apple bread and about to discuss the Tarot.

I wonder how my friends on the track team are spending *their* summer vacations.

I explain how I got started with the cards, and a little of what I've read online.

"So you've studied some occult philosophy," Violet says.

I tell her I have, but that I don't really understand most of it.

"What about Astrology? Palmistry? Numerology?"

I shake my head.

"Tell me about when you first started seeing the visions."

The kettle whistles, and Kevin fixes the tea. Violet cuts me a second slice of apple bread. I describe what happened when I was twelve—the voices in my head, the goblins and reptile people. And how I had my breakdown and ended up on meds, and my therapy with Dr. Mark. Then I tell them what's happened the past two months—first the nightmares, then the hallucinations (or visions), the slithering cloud-thing and the woman in black with the pearls. And tonight, Shadow Man and the drowning over and over.

Strangely, I'm not at all ashamed to confess this stuff in front of Violet, Kevin, and Grandma. Pouring it all out just brings me a sense of relief. I guess the apple bread and herbal tea are helping too. When I'm done, I feel calmer and safer than I have all evening.

"I think I'll do a reading," Violet says.

She goes into another room and returns with her Tarot cards. She brushes away crumbs, spreads a silk handkerchief on the table, and lays out the cards so I can see them. It's a different deck than I'm used to, and I'm not even sure I've seen it online. Most of the suit cards don't have pictures, just symbols and numbers. The pictures there are look like old-style paintings, Renaissance or medieval. When she hands me the deck to shuffle, the cards seem to tingle with energy.

She lays down a spread, and we all stare at the cards in silence. I can't read much meaning, except that it all feels very serious.

Finally Violet looks into my eyes. "I think you are very psychic, like all the Renshaws. Kevie, my anthropologist friend here, would say you have the gifts of a natural shaman—that is, to see visions, to walk in other worlds, to communicate with spirits. When your father died, it wounded you badly, and then you moved away to a strange place and felt frightened and alone. When your body started changing with puberty, you fell victim to obsessions—which, because you are a natural visionary, manifested as malevolent beings."

"So are you saying they were *real* creatures—spirits? Not hallucinations, like everyone told me?"

Violet takes a deep breath. "This is difficult to understand, Abby. Hallucinations are projections from your unconscious mind. Spirits—and everything else we see and know—are projections from the Great Mind that is the Universe. Ultimately, both of those minds are the same." She leans closer. "So ultimately, visions and hallucinations are just different forms of the same thing."

Wow. I need time to wrap my head around that one. Like a hundred years. And yet inside me, it seems to make a weird kind of sense. "Go on."

"Well, they treated you with psychiatric drugs, which desensitized you. And therapy, which gave your rational mind tools to close down the doorways through which your visions were appearing. So eventually the visions went away."

"What about now?"

Violet clenches her lips. "Now...something else is going on. I'm not sure what. But it definitely has to do with Harmony Springs, and it definitely means you no good. That's obvious from what you went through tonight. And yet..." She points to the Temperance card, a gray angel standing with one foot on land and one in the water. "There is also a protective spirit watching over you."

We're all silent again for some moments. Then Grandma says, "So what should we do?"

"Well..." Violet moves to collect the cards. "I like the fact that she responded so well to the banishing rite. I think we three should cast a sphere of protection around her. How does that sound to you, Abby?"

"I'm not sure what it means. But it sounds great."

"Good," Violet says. "Do you trust us?"

That makes me anxious again. I think about my mom and what she would say. And all the "normal" kids back in New Jersey—how crazy all of this would sound to them. It seems my mental instability has taken a sharp left turn, bringing me to a place that feels all kind and supportive but might really be insane. It's like the secret Abby who reads Tarot cards and studies occult stuff on the internet is taking over—and that might not be a good thing.

But then I glance at Grandma, and she gives me a slight nod. I know that, as much as anyone in the world, she loves me and wants what's best for me.

"Yes...I trust you."

Violet smiles. "I like that you thought it over. We'll cast a protective sphere before you leave. That should help for a while. But like I said, Abby, you are extremely sensitive, extremely *open*. Your openness is both a strength and a weakness. The best thing I can do for you is teach you to protect yourself."

I nod immediately. "I'm all for that."

Violet turns to Grandma. "You know, Kat, the way to do that is to initiate her."

Grandma's mouth tenses, like she thought this might be coming but feels uncertain. She looks at me. "It's up to her, of course."

Violet takes that as permission to go on. "Abby, we're talking about initiating you into our magical path, the Circle of Harmony. This path was created by the people who founded the town, including your ancestor, Thomas Renshaw. It consists of beautiful rituals and a large body of occult knowledge. Its purpose is to grow the human mind and soul, to make us *true magicians*—that is, men and women of power."

*Whoa.* "What would I have to do?"

"First, you should know that the fortunes of the Circle have fluctuated over the years. It almost died out in the middle of the last century. I was initiated when I was a little older than you by some of the last practicing members at the time. Later I initiated a few others, including your grandmother and grandfather. Most of them have passed on. Your grandmother left the Circle some years ago, although circumstances may now be bringing her back. But that's for her to decide and to tell you about. Right now, only Kevin and I still actively practice.

"And that means we don't have the resources to stage the rituals the way they did in the past. But I think with the three of us we can muster the energy for a Rite of Initiation."

Kevin nods, and then Grandma does too.

"But you have to understand, Abby. As an initiate, you would take on certain obligations. You must promise to follow the path faithfully and to the best of your ability. Most importantly, you must swear that you will use any occult powers you gain only to bring good and harmony into the world. That's the center of our teaching. It may sound easy, but believe me, it's not. As power grows, it's more and more tempting to use it for self-gratification, and easier and easier to be seduced by evil forces. You need to think about all this carefully before you decide."

Her tone communicates to me how serious this is. It's a lifelong obligation—the kind of thing only an adult can choose. I don't know if I'm grown-up enough to decide. It feels really scary.

But then, not as scary as drowning over and over.

"I understand...I'll need to think about it." I want my voice to sound firm, but it cracks a little.

"Sure." Violet stretches. "I'll give you some stuff to read. Then you can talk it over with me or Kevin or your grandmother when you're ready."

〰〰

Afterward I help Kevin do the dishes while Grandma and Violet talk in the parlor. When we join them, the ceiling fan is off and the windows closed. Five candles burn at different points in the room, each set next to a white porcelain cup filled with water.

We stand in the center of the parlor. Violet traces a circle in the air, using a wooden wand as long as her forearm, with a crystal fastened on the end. Then she, Kevin, and Grandma circle around me and join hands.

They chant—long, deep notes like Grandma did earlier. With their three voices, the sound grows so strong that the house seems to vibrate. Violet speaks their intention: to form a sphere of pure, protective light around me, to make it strong and enduring, to repel all evil forces and allow only good to enter in.

Then they just stand, breathing quietly. I sense the sphere of protection forming around me, created by their thoughts, their will. After a while I can see it shining—the pale, crystal-blue color of the springs.

〰〰

On the way home, Grandma and I are both quiet. In my lap I hold a small stack of typewritten pages that Violet gave me to read. Grandma focuses hard on the road, and I can feel she is really tired. I think of all she's been through in the last day and a half, so it's no wonder. I keep my mouth shut and let her concentrate on driving.

As soon as we enter the house, she turns to me in the hallway and asks if I'm okay.

"Yes." I'm actually more than okay—I'm amazed. Like I've climbed a big rock and am looking out over this vast, misty country I didn't know was there. "I've got a lot to think about."

"I know, sweetie. We both need a good night's sleep. But if anything happens during the night, you come and wake me up, okay?"

I hug her. "I will, Grandma. Thank you for everything."

♒

Up in my room, after I've changed clothes and brushed my teeth, I sit on the bed and read the papers Violet gave me. The first is titled "The Circle of Harmony," and it says:

> Lo, this is the manifesto of the Circle of Harmony, which is a Path of Initiation into True Magic, as revealed by the spirit LEBAB. That which is written here is secret and must not be taken lightly.

> LEBAB came to certain persons in a dream and showed them a vision of light. And in the light they saw Five Springs of the purest blue water. And LEBAB named the Springs: Love, Endurance, Balance, Amity, and Bliss. And he showed them where these Springs flowed on the Earthly plane, and had done from time immemorial, in the land of Florida.

> But these Springs are not merely waters of the Earth, but manifestations of the One Spiritual Source. And each Spring is a Fountain, and each Fountain a waymarker on the Path of True Magic. These things are secret and must not be taken lightly.

> And the names of the Springs have these meanings, and each is a Principle of the Path:

1. Love - Love of the truth, which first inspires the quest of the Magician.

2. Endurance - The strength and persistence required to follow the Path.

3. Balance - In all things, body, mind, and soul, required for worthy attainment.

4. Amity - The will to harmonious relations with all Beings in all Worlds.

5. Bliss - The prize of Union with All That Is, which is the ultimate goal of the quest.

And it was shown how the first letters of the Five Names of the Springs spell the name LEBAB, who is the True Spirit of the Springs. And it was further shown how the letters reversed spell BABEL, for the evil and confusion that inevitably comes to those who seek Occult knowledge without pure intent and strict adherence to the Principles. These things are secret and must not be taken lightly.

After reading this three times, I turn to the other paper. This one is called "Admonitions to the Candidate." It seems to be what they gave people to prepare them for initiation. It says that anyone who aspires to the path of true magic must leave behind selfishness and lust for power. Only those who pledge themselves heart and soul to the Five Principles may enter the Circle of Harmony.

I glance at the next several pages. By now my eyelids are so heavy, I can barely keep awake. I look around the room, checking for Shadow Man or any other non-hallucinations.

Nothing. I feel totally safe and at peace. I put the pages away, lie down on my side, and pull the sheet up to my chin.

〰〰

When I wake up, it's morning, with silvery light shining through the windows. I remember a dream. I was with the two girls in the old-fashioned dresses. The three of us were walking beside the springs, talking like three friends. One of the girls was tall and willowy, with beautiful black hair in ringlets. I think she was Annie

Renshaw. The other one was blond, tall, but with a stronger build. Something about her made me uneasy.

Now I'm lying on my back, staring at the high ceiling. I hear something, and at first I think it's a bird or animal in the woods. But it goes on and on and begins to sound like crying.

I get out of bed. Barefoot, in boxers and a tee, I open the door and listen. The sound is coming from Grandma's room. I step over there quietly. The door is partway open, and I peek inside. Grandma is lying in bed, sobbing.

"Grandma, are you all right?"

"Oh, Abby!...Are *you* all right?"

"Yes. I'm fine."

I walk over to her bed as she sits up and wipes her eyes. I realize then that she was crying so quietly that I couldn't possibly have heard it from the other room. Yet somehow, I did.

"Can I do anything?"

"No, sweetie. It's all right." She takes her eyeglasses from the bedside table and slips them on. "When you get old...sometimes you think about the past and...grieve over what you've lost. But I didn't mean for you to catch me feeling sorry for myself."

"Oh, Grandma. Please don't apologize. I put you through so much awful stuff yesterday. You'll probably think twice before inviting me here again."

Grandma squeezes my wrist. "Don't even think that, Abby. I am so happy you are here. I feel you are a brave and beautiful young woman with an amazing future. And there is nothing I'd rather do than help you get there."

This chokes me up, so I don't answer for a moment. My mind wanders back to last night, to the terror of drowning, and the magic that rescued me. And the papers Violet gave me to read.

"Do you think I should be initiated into the Circle?"

"I think that is entirely up to you."

"But...there's so much about it I don't understand. You were part of it. Can you tell me what it was like, and..."

"And why I left? Yes, of course. You have a right to know all that. But how about some coffee first?"

Downstairs, I fix the coffee while Grandma mixes dough for biscuits. After she puts them in the oven, we take our coffee mugs out to the back porch. We sit on the swing, our old favorite place for talking together. We're still in our night clothes, and the air feels warm and soft. I think again how much I love the laid-back life here—except, of course, for the scary visions and psychic attacks.

"So, I started reading Tarot cards when I was a teenager," Grandma tells me. "Just like you. When I met your grandfather, I would sometimes do readings for him. He found that very interesting and got into studying books on metaphysics. George was a great reader, you know. This was in the 1960s, and like lots of young people, we were interested in New Age ideas. Around the time George inherited this house and we moved in together, we found out about Violet and her Circle. Violet did a reading for us, and we both liked what she was about. When she invited us, we decided to initiate."

"What was that like?"

"Oh, it was pretty magical. Like being in a play, everyone dressed up in robes and flowers, and with parts to speak. But on another level it felt really powerful, like—like rearranging your internal furniture in a major way.

"After the initiation, well, there was lots of study and meditation, spiritual exercises. We would meet as a group and practice together...breathing in unison, visualizing, all of it designed to open you up spiritually and build your mental powers. And there were more rituals as you progressed through the stages, one for each of the Five Springs, you know? That's probably mentioned in what Violet gave you to read."

I nod. "So, was it worthwhile? Did you feel like it made you a better person? Gave you self-control?"

Grandma's eyes are far away. "Yes, I would say so. I was always more of a follower. Your grandfather was really good at it—the talent of the Renshaws, you know? But I'd say it had a lot of meaning for me too."

"So why did you stop?"

While I'm waiting for her answer, the buzzer on the oven goes off. Grandma goes to take out the biscuits.

When she comes back, she's moving slowly, and her face is sad. "I was telling you about...after your grandfather died. I felt so lost and hurt. I thought we would have our whole lives together, and it turned out to be only a few years. Your daddy was just a toddler, so I had to keep it together for his sake. I just wasn't as interested in the Circle anymore. It hurt too much to work on that stuff without George beside me."

"I'm so sorry, Grandma. I didn't mean to—"

"There's more. You should hear it all, Abby. I did stay in touch with Violet and the others, and I did sometimes go to their rituals. I never let your father know about it when he was a child. But as he got older and started having problems...in high school, you know, he started drinking and got into drugs for a time. He grew up without a father, you see. I did my best. I did everything I could think of to help him grow up right. That included working with Violet, doing magic to help him. She said there was a limit to what she could do without his consent, and he didn't want anything to do with it, thought it was all crazy. Still, Violet and I did some concentrated work to protect him. And it seemed to help. For a few years he straightened out. He got through college, used some of the money we'd inherited from his father to open the real estate business. But he was always so sensitive and high-strung. Every little setback threw him off-kilter. The drinking got worse again. Somewhere he'd heard this idea about the curse of the Renshaws, and it became like an obsession. I tried everything to help him, including magic. But this time it did no good. He was too far gone, closed off from any help...you pretty much know the rest."

"I guess so."

"Well, after he died, I put away all my magical stuff. I couldn't bear to take it up again. I felt that if it couldn't save my husband or my son, what good was it? So that's why I stopped working with Violet and her Circle."

Wow. Grandma's never talked to me about any of this. I guess no adult has ever talked to me about their deep wounds this way. I don't know what to say to her. I just stare off at the woods, not thinking about magic or my problems at all, just *feeling* the reflection of all Grandma's pain. And imagining what it must have been like to carry it all those years.

"Well, now you know the story." Grandma leans forward and pushes herself to her feet. "Let's get some breakfast."

∼∼∼

After breakfast we get dressed and drive into town to open the shop. I bring my tablet, planning to spend part of the day on my summer reading assignments. But after swapping texts with Mom and checking a few things online, I pick up the pages Violet gave me.

I reread the Circle of Harmony manifesto and then read "Admonitions to the Candidate" a couple of times. It's not as complicated as I remember from last night. It mainly talks about purity of intention and examining your own thoughts and ideas, questioning where they come from. Except for the Victorian writing style, it's actually similar to the things Dr. Mark taught me.

But that doesn't bring me any closer to deciding about Initiation.

Here in the bright daylight, with people coming and going in the shop and cars driving by outside, it all seems so unreal. I start wondering again if it *is* unreal, if I've simply fallen off the sanity table. Maybe I need psychiatric intervention.

That makes me think of Franklin. The shop is quiet, so I send him a text, asking if he has time to talk. He sends me back a smiley face and then calls.

"Abigail Adams!"

"Benjamin Franklin! Thanks for calling me." This riff started when we saw *1776* together. Franklin is fond of musicals.

"Have you started *An American Tragedy* yet? It really sucks." He has the same honors reading list as me.

"Sorry to hear that. I was just about to read it."

"Sure you were. How 'bout this: you read the second half, and I'll read the first. Then we can fill each other in."

"Sounds very efficient. It's a deal."

I ask him how his summer is going so far. He's working in his uncle's clothing store and finds it really boring. But he is going into New York on Tuesday to see a play.

"And how are things in *rural* Florida?" he asks me.

"Well, I can't say boring." I hesitate. I wouldn't risk bringing this up with anyone else, but I've done Tarot readings for Franklin, and he has some idea of my secret side. "There are some people down here who are really into metaphysics and stuff."

"Yessss?"

"It's pretty interesting. I mean, they believe that spirits are real. And that magic is sort of real too."

"Abby. Do we need to up your meds?"

"I'm not on meds anymore."

"Do we need to *put* you back on meds?"

"Don't be snotty. What about 'There are more things in heaven and earth than are dreamed about in your philosophy, Horatio'?"

"Don't call me Horatio. And seriously, you need to be careful with that stuff. There's enough trouble with things that *are* dreamed about in our philosophy. Don't you think?"

"Yeah, I guess you're right." Maybe I just needed to hear him say that.

But I don't know...

"You need to keep things on track, Abigail. I mean, with your husband, John Adams, spending so much time goofing off at the Continental Congress..."

"I'll hold down the farm, Mr. Franklin. Don't worry."

〰

A little later a customer comes in, and I help Grandma wait on her. Then I spend some time dusting in the front of the shop. After that, things are quiet, so I pick up my tablet again and try to dive into *An American Tragedy*. Starting at the halfway point leaves me utterly lost, so I guess I'll have to rethink my deal with Franklin.

I put it down and wander next door to Palmer's Books. Kevin is waiting on a customer, so I browse the metaphysics section. Astrology, Numerology, Kabbalah...can all of it just be made-up junk? I wonder...

Kevin comes over to say hello. "How's our distance runner this morning?"

That makes me smile. "Fine. How's my favorite anthropology professor?"

He grins. "For a washed-up academic, I'm doing all right." He touches the side of his mouth, indicating the spot where my face is bruised. "No more ill effects from last night?"

"No. Whatever you guys did for me seems to have...driven the bad spirits away. Actually, I was hoping I could talk with you about that."

"Sure. Step into my office."

We go over behind the glass counter. Kevin sits on a tall metal stool next to the cash register and points me to an old office chair.

"So, I read the pages Violet gave me, and...well, some of it makes sense, but some of it just sounds so *weird*."

"Interesting choice of words," Kevin says. "Do you know the origin of the word *weird*? It comes from an Old English word meaning 'fate' or 'destiny.' Literally, 'that which comes.' So you could say the weird is that which comes to us that's beyond our ken. Beyond our understanding or control, but real nonetheless."

"Okay..."

"Sorry. I guess I'm not helping." Kevin sets his fingertips together, almost like he's praying. "You can look at it this way: the Universe is vast and incomprehensible. To try to understand it, the human mind creates maps. Science is one big set of maps. Magic is just another set. Both kinds of maps are valid in different ways. But the Universe will always be bigger and stranger than any map. Does that help?"

"I think so. Except that science is *real*, but magic—"

"Is equally real, just in a different way. Our culture, and I mean the mainstream culture, focuses exclusively on science. Science has brought us tremendous benefits and power. But I've studied other cultures—so-called primitive cultures—and I can tell you that their magic is also valid. And magic brings those people powers and benefits too, ones that we've lost."

"Like, for example?"

"Well, take you, for example. Around age twelve you started to manifest the talent of a shaman. In our culture, this is seen as a sickness, and it was treated with drugs and therapy to suppress your talent. In another culture, your gift would have been recognized. You would have been trained to cultivate your talent and use it for the good of the community. That would likely have proved a benefit to you and to others."

I think about that and have to admit it makes sense. I think about the Tarot cards and how I use them as a kind of map for seeing things in a different way. I was drawn to the Tarot, almost by instinct. Maybe I do have a special talent for these things.

A customer has come in, and Kevin chats with her for a while. After she wanders off, I ask him, "So, professor, do you know anything about curses?"

"Ah. The curse of the Renshaws. Yeah, I've heard of it. Well, from studying magical cultures, I do believe curses are real. And they *can* be passed down through generations. But I also know that curses are mainly effective on those who believe in them. Your grandfather, for example. He knew all about the curse, but he refused to believe in it."

"But he still died young."

Kevin's mouth turns down. "Yeah. Leukemia. But even after he got sick and was diagnosed, he never felt sorry for himself and never once talked about it as a curse. He said it was just a bad trip he had to go on."

"Sounds like you knew him pretty well."

"Oh, I did. We were friends all the way back to high school. And in those days, for a Black guy and a white guy to be friends was pretty rare. But George was a hell of a good guy, Abby. I think if he had lived, your father would have turned out differently. Your dad was not a bad person, but he was weak. I think he came to believe in the curse, and maybe that's part of what destroyed him."

Yeah. That hurts to think about. And where does it leave me? "I guess I need to be careful what I decide to believe in."

"Exactly," Kevin says. "You might say that's the whole theory of magic. What you believe—believe in your inner being—and think about all the time, that's what you tend to manifest in your life. So the path of the magician is to gain control of that so you can manifest positive things for yourself and for others."

Well...Kevin's take on all this certainly sounds reasonable. It's making me feel that maybe the whole magic thing *is* real. And that maybe I should go ahead with the Initiation. I tell Kevin this.

"It's not as scary or mysterious as it seems," he says. "Just think of it as a set of tools for working with your mind. Just a different set of maps."

## 6. Your mother and I were best friends

Around noon, as I'm mulling over whether believing in magic is actually realistic (Kevin's view) or a symptom of insanity (Franklin's), my phone does its incoming text chirp.

The message is from Mom: "Got an email from an old friend who heard you are in town. Going to look you up. Her name is Fiona."

As I'm staring stupidly at the phone, I hear "Whoa! What happened to you?"

Molly Quick is standing in front of the counter with a startled expression. I'm puzzled, then realize she's referring to my bruise.

"Oh...I tripped in the woods and hit a root." Naturally, I've prepared an edited version of the story, suitable for the public.

"Gawd! How did you manage that?"

"Running. In the dark."

Her mouth drops open. "What were you running from?"

"No, no. *Running*—like for fitness." Like I said, the edited version.

"Oh!" Molly shakes her head. "I always say too much exercise is more dangerous than not enough."

I laugh at that. "So what's with you? Any more possibly paranormal events?" I mean, of course, not counting the ones that happened to me, which I'm not going to tell her about.

"Nah. That story's dead. No clues, and nobody wants to talk about it. I'm putting *Quick Investigations* on hold and going back to the *Quick Report*. I'm writing about the development controversy.

*Everybody* wants to talk about that. Anyway, I stopped by to see if you might like to grab some lunch."

That actually sounds like a lot more fun than trying to read *An American Tragedy*. I check with Grandma, and she tells me to go on, and to bring her back a sandwich.

So Molly and I walk the three blocks to Springs of Coffee and order lunch. I get a big salad with cold cuts and a croissant. I've missed some meals lately and need to keep my calories up—even though with the bruised knee it will be a couple of days before I can run again. Molly gets a chicken salad sandwich and a blended iced coffee. I think the girl is a caffeine fiend.

Molly asks me what I know about the development issue, and I repeat the little bit Grandma told me. Molly, of course, knows a lot more. The Texas-Brighton Land Company started approaching property owners near the springs a couple of months ago, first by letter, then with phone calls. They were winding down a large development in south Texas and looking for a new project. They became interested in acquiring the land around the springs— preferably all of it—and let it be known that they were prepared to pay well above market value, as an incentive to sell. Some of the owners were interested and started talking it up with their neighbors. Others were dead against it, saying it would mean more roads, more crowding, and worst of all, ruining the character of the springs by tearing down a lot of the woods.

"That's how Grandma and I feel about it. But aren't the springs a National Historic Site?" I've seen the markers on Main Street.

"Only the downtown district," Molly says. "Not the properties up at the springs. Besides, just being on the National Register doesn't protect a place from being torn down. No, this is shaping up as a fight that could end up in court. The people who are against it are organizing. They're worried the developers will pour a lot of money in, buy some properties, and start bulldozing. Once that begins, it's hard to stop. Happens all the time in Florida. You and your grandmother might want to come to the meeting next week."

"Yeah. I've seen the signs."

"The committee's being led by a woman who owns a local real estate company along with her husband. She's actually a descendant of one of the town founders. Fiona Alden-Gathers."

The name sounds faintly familiar. Then I remember the text from Mom about her friend. I mention it to Molly.

"Is she the same Fiona?"

"I don't know her last name, but it could be. My mom worked in real estate."

"Great. I bet it is. If you meet her, could you put in a word? I'm trying to interview her for my blog, and her office hasn't returned my calls."

"Sure. Why not?"

"Thanks! You can tell her I'm sympathetic to the cause."

Molly seems to really appreciate this, and I sense it makes her more relaxed. For a while we talk about girl stuff—school, guys, plans for the future. Even though Molly is a year younger than me and just out of tenth grade, she already knows that she wants to apply to the School of Communication at FSU.

I, of course, am much vaguer about my plans.

But Molly says she can tell I'm really smart, and she's sure I'll figure it out. I'm beginning to see that under Molly's rapid-fire reporter facade, she's actually lonely and a little insecure. She goes to a county high school which is a twelve-mile bus ride away, so in the summer she doesn't get to see much of her school friends. The few kids who live around here are okay, she says, just not intellectual or interesting. "Unlike you, Abby."

Well. It's nice to be told you're both intellectual *and* interesting.

When we're done with lunch, Molly invites me to go kayaking with her later in the week. Grandma's told me over and over that she doesn't need me to stay at the shop all the time, so I accept.

~~~

At four thirty that afternoon, my phone rings.

"Hello. This is Fiona Alden-Gathers. Is this Abigail?"

"Yes."

"Hi. Your mother sent me your number. I heard you were in town visiting, and I wanted to give you a call. Your mother and I were best friends back in the day."

"Yes, hi. Mom texted me that you might call. It's nice of you."

"It's my pleasure. I remember you as a baby. How are you enjoying our quiet little town?"

"Oh, fine. I'm having a great time." *And it's been anything but quiet so far.*

"Not too boring after New York?"

"Well, I live in New Jersey. I don't go into the city that much."

"I see. Listen, Abigail, I've got some free time tomorrow afternoon. I thought I might take you out to lunch. I'd love to hear all about how your mother's doing. And you too, of course."

"Uh, that's really nice of you. Hold on a second. I'll check with my Grandma."

Grandma tells me it's fine to go ahead. She remembers her from the old days, when my dad and mom and Fiona all worked together. "Great," Fiona says. "I can pick you up at twelve thirty. Where will I find you?"

"At Grandma's shop, Glenda's Antiques, on Main Street."

"See you then."

After she beeps off, I ask Grandma what she knows about Fiona.

"I don't know her well. She left town a year or two before you and your mother did. Got married and moved to Atlanta. I understand she and her husband worked in real estate up there. A couple of years ago they opened an office in Florida, up near Ocala somewhere. I think they both still work in Atlanta too. She inherited the old Alden house across the bayou from us. They're putting a lot of money into fixing it up."

"Oh...the house with the construction going on? The one with the boat dock?"

"That's the one."

~~~

So the next day, waiting for Fiona to pick me up, I'm pretty apprehensive. Just thinking about the big house with the dock is enough to start nasty fears crawling in my stomach. I keep telling myself this is stupid. Just because she owns the house where I had my bad scare doesn't mean I should worry about meeting her. Besides, I haven't seen a hint of anything paranormal or hallucinatory since Grandma and her friends did their magic.

When Fiona arrives, I immediately feel at ease. She's brisk and pleasant, dressed in a tailored pantsuit. She chats a few minutes with Grandma, and I can tell she's really bright and good with people. She reminds me a lot of Mom in her professional mode.

I hope I'm dressed okay. I worried about what to wear and finally settled on a sundress and sandals. I put a barrette in my hair and even applied a little makeup to cover my fading bruise. I'm relieved when Fiona tells me how nice I look.

We go outside and get in her car, a Lexus hybrid SUV. She backs out of the parking space, makes a quick U-turn, and accelerates smoothly. Really nice car.

"I thought we'd drive out to I-75," Fiona says. "There are some good restaurants at the mall. Or if you'd rather, we could lunch at the country club."

"Either one sounds great. Thanks."

"Do you play golf?"

"No. I haven't taken that up yet. Mom and Jim play. Jim's her husband. I run on the track team."

"You look very fit. How about tennis?"

"Some. I'm not very good."

Fiona smiles. "I think you're probably too modest." She drives as fast as the traffic allows, keeping just three fingers on the wheel. "Tell me about school. What do you like to study?"

I tell her I like language arts and psychology, but I'm pretty good at math too. Fiona is so polished and accomplished that I feel pressure to say things she'll approve of. So when she asks about college plans, I tell her I'm undecided and toss out a few impressive names, schools where I think I'll apply. I'm also not sure yet what I'll major in, but I mention subjects I know Mom would like to hear—marketing, maybe finance.

That gives me a chance to turn it around and ask Fiona what she likes her work. I've noticed most adults like talking about themselves more than about me, and Fiona is no exception. I find out she loves the real estate business and has a great "synergistic" partnership with her husband, Adam. He's great at finances and planning, and she feels really confident "on the sales and people side."

"We've done very well up in Atlanta. But I'm really happier in Florida. It's where I grew up, you know? It's home. Eventually I'd like us to live here year-round."

We've taken County Road 245 north of town and then turned onto a state highway. There's little traffic, and Fiona flies past cattle ranches and patches of wetlands and woods. Then we start to pass developments with big tile-roofed houses behind concrete walls. Signs on the gates announce names like Paradise Prairies and River Ranch. Fiona tells me she has a house near here on a lake. A little later, she points out the country club.

After forty minutes we come to the mall, which is built next to the interstate. We go inside and walk past shops and salons and a high artificial waterfall. It feels a lot like New Jersey.

*This is the real world, Abby.* Harmony Springs, the enchanted forest, the nightmares and hallucinations—all seem a zillion miles away.

We have lunch at a continental café with white tablecloths, on a big terrace overlooking the mall. We eat crepes with crabmeat and drink Perrier from a bottle that the server keeps chilled in a silver ice bucket.

Fiona asks about Mom and Jim. I know enough about their work that I can answer semi-intelligently. I tell her how Mom tracks financial sectors and writes analysis reports and that Jim flies to London and Zurich several times a year. That seems to impress her.

"But this time they're in Europe for vacation. No work for three weeks. At least that's what Mom promised."

Fiona nods, smiling. "Your mom is very ambitious. I always admired her for that."

〜〜〜

On the way back, I remember my promise to Molly, so I ask Fiona about Save Harmony Springs. I can see immediately that I've touched a nerve.

"Those guys from Texas are the type who give developers a bad name. They come in and throw money around, knowing nothing about the people or the heritage of a place. Then they build acres of ugliness, leave the environment and the infrastructure a mess, and take their profits and run. When I heard about their plans, I just had to get involved."

"I'm really glad you feel that way. I guess someone like you can help a lot."

"I hope so. There are a number of strategies we can pursue to stop them. Denying permits, easements, environmental impact assessments. But it all gets into politics, and in the end depends on the community wanting to preserve its heritage. I hope you and your grandmother will come to the meeting next week."

I say that we plan to, then mention Molly. When she hears that Molly is on our side and wants to help spread the word, she says she'd be glad to do an interview. I take out my phone and text Molly, giving her Fiona's mobile number.

Fiona answered some phone calls and texts while we were at the mall. Now she says, "Speaking of the springs, I need to stop off at my house on the way back into town. I hope you don't mind."

"Oh, right. Your house on Bliss Bayou..."

"Just for a few minutes. I need to talk with the foreman about the new windows."

"Sure, that's fine." The skin prickles on the back of my neck. I've been terrified both times I went near that house. I met Shadow Man there less than two days ago. I search frantically for some excuse so I can ask her to drop me on Main Street first. But I can't think of anything that doesn't sound crazy.

I'll just have to tough it out and hope for the best.

So I'm pretty nervous when we turn off the county road and head for Bliss Bayou. I try to concentrate on holding up my side of the conversation. Fiona's explaining how she inherited the property from an aunt who died several years ago. The house hasn't been lived in since the 1990s.

"Parts of the structure needed to be rebuilt from the ground," she says. "It's cost us a ton of money, but Adam's been very understanding. It's important to me to restore the house to its original grandeur."

"I think that's really great. I love Grandma's house, and I know it's a struggle for her to keep it in good shape."

We pull up to the house. Pickup trucks are parked in the front yard, and the place is noisy with hammering and power saws. I'm anxious but feel none of the inexplicable terror I experienced the last two times I came here. I glance down at the bayou and see only the old dock and the quiet water gleaming in the sunlight.

Fiona asks if I'd like to come inside. I can't think of a good reason to refuse, so I put on a smile and say, "Sure."

Inside, the place is cluttered with scaffolds, ladders, and drop cloths. Workers are clattering around, and the air smells of sawdust and paint. But I can already see the house is going to be gorgeous—polished wood columns, arched doorways with stained glass, big, airy rooms with high ceilings. I can feel how proud Fiona is, and I make what I hope are appropriate comments of appreciation.

After she has her conference with the foreman, we head back to the car. I take a last look around as we drive away. Somehow, seeing the house this time—in the daylight, with Fiona, and going inside it—has reassured me.

Maybe the nightmares are over.

Maybe the magic work Grandma and Violet and Kevin did for me has solved the problem. Or maybe it just gave me some reassurance, and the fears lurking in my subconscious have been brought to light and vanquished, the way Dr. Mark used to explain.

Maybe I can just be plain-old, sane-old Abby Renshaw from now on.

That would be so nice.

## 7. I've never seen anyone as scared as I just saw you

Two days later, having experienced no relapse of my Abby-insanity, I keep my kayaking date with Molly. She meets me at the antique shop, and we ride her bike over to Founders Park.

The park stretches along the shore of Harmony River, about a mile and a half downstream from the headwaters of the springs. We cruise past tennis and basketball courts, a sandy baseball field, and picnic tables spread out in the shade of oaks and slash pines. There's also a swimming hole formed by an inlet of the river, and down from there is a place to rent kayaks and canoes.

The rental shop is run by a wiry, bearded guy named Jess and his assistant, Hank. Hank is around our age, tall and broad-shouldered, with curly hair and a sleepy smile. Molly flirts with him while we arrange the rental.

Because the river current is fast, part of their service is to truck the kayak upstream or to pick you up at a landing point downstream, if you choose to go that way. Molly wants to show me the source of the springs, so we'll be driven up there and then ride the current back. After we pay, Hank loads a two-seat kayak onto the back of a pickup. Molly makes a point of sitting next to him in the front seat.

Leaving the park, we cross a bridge and then follow a road up the west side of the river. Molly talks to Hank about school and the football team (I learn he plays linebacker). He jokes about her being the daughter of the chief of police, and about how boring the town is in the summer. He mostly keeps his eyes on the road, but every once in a while they slide sideways to check out our legs.

He turns onto a dirt road, and we drive past houses built in the woods and along the edge of the river. Some of them are big 1890s-style houses like the ones on Bliss Bayou. But there are also cracker houses, run-down cabins, and even some old trailers. Molly points out where Pete Hastings lives—the guy who was bitten by the cottonmouth. She says that several of the property owners along here are talking about selling. She's learned who they are from her interview with Fiona, which happened last night. She thanks me again for helping her arrange it and says she is still working on writing it up for her blog.

At the head of the springs is a little nature preserve. Hank parks there and carries our kayak down the trail to the landing spot. Molly and I apply sunscreen and put on our life jackets. Hank makes sure we've got them fastened snugly, and Molly takes the opportunity to flirt with him some more. Hank gives her his sleepy smile. He holds the kayak steady as we climb in. He hands us our paddles, then pushes the kayak off the bank. As we slip out into the current, he reminds us to be back by six thirty, when the shop closes.

Molly's in the front and takes the lead. We paddle against the current, up along the swampy shoreline. Oak and ash trees stick straight up on the banks, eighty or a hundred feet tall. The water is crystal clear, and I can see the bottom—sand and rock, with underwater grasses waving in the current. Molly points out a wide fissure marked by tiny bubbles escaping to the surface.

"I think that one is Love Spring," she says.

Each spring is a vent where water gushes up from the aquifer deep underground. I know from looking at maps that the headwaters are shaped like the joined fingers of a mitten. The four main springs still have the names the founders gave them: Love, Endurance, Balance, and Amity. The fifth spring, now Bliss Bayou, is at the end of its own channel downstream from here—the thumb of the mitten.

I saw the springs as a little girl, but never this close. "Wow. This is beautiful."

"I know," Molly says. "Definitely one of the cool things about living here."

I spot a big black bird standing on a rock with its wings spread, drying them in the sun. It makes me think of a guardian spirit keeping watch over the springs. Molly says it's an anhinga, a kind of cormorant.

We paddle around and look at the other vents. Molly points out a clearing at the top end of the shore, just visible through the brush. According to legend, the founders used to do magic rituals there. That makes me curious, and I tell her I'd like to see it. She says it's hard to get to from the water, but there's another clearing at the head of Bliss Bayou that we can check out.

As we glide down the opposite shoreline, I suddenly suck in my breath. A four-foot alligator is sunning on a dead log.

"They don't bother you if you don't bother them," Molly assures me.

I think about the alligator men I used to see in my hallucinations. I'm really glad Molly steers us well away from that log.

A little later, we pull into an inlet to rest. Molly insists that it's safe, so we climb out and drag the kayak onto a sandbar. We stretch out on the soft sand and crack open bottles of water. Molly asks me what I thought of Hank.

"Oh, he's fine."

Molly grins. "*Really* fine."

Lying there in the shade, we compare notes on guys and sex. Molly admits to having done it twice, with two different guys. Neither time was as thrilling as she had hoped, and the relationships didn't last very long.

I confess I've only gotten to second base, and that I've never gone out with a guy more than a couple of times. "They always want to go farther, faster than I do."

Molly laughs. "Most of them do seem to be engineered that way."

"Sure. But I want to feel I can trust a guy as well as like him, you know?"

"What does that mean, trust him?"

"Don't you know?"

"I don't know what it means to you."

That forces me to think about it. "Trust him not to hurt me, not to use me and then leave right away." I guess it brings up fear of abandonment...like my father abandoned me when he died. I file that away as something I should examine.

"I don't know," Molly says. "Depending on the guy, I might *want* him to leave right away."

We both laugh at that.

"Not Hank, though. Him I'd like to hang around for a while."

〜〜〜

We float downstream to the mouth of Bliss Bayou, then have to paddle hard to get out of the current. Once we enter the bayou there's almost no current, and the water is dark and muddy. I wonder out loud what could have caused Bliss Spring to close up all those years ago. Molly shrugs and says apparently it just happens sometimes.

We work our way up the bayou, passing the Alden house on the north shore and Grandma's and the other houses on the opposite side. At the head of the bayou, the land curves around in a half circle, with mucky pools and thick cypress trees. But there's a little stone landing and a raised path that Molly says was built in the founders' time. We tie up the kayak and follow the path through the undergrowth.

We emerge in a clearing about fifty feet wide, almost a perfect circle. There's a fallen tree along one edge, and a few small saplings, but otherwise the ground is clear, a carpet of pine needles and decaying leaves.

My eyes lock on the center of the circle, where three slabs of gray stone are set up like a table—or an altar.

"Weird, isn't it?" Molly says.

"Yeah. What keeps the forest from taking it over?"

"Every few years, the town pays someone to come in and clear-cut it. This end of the bayou was bequeathed to the town as a park on the condition that they keep this area cleared."

As she's talking, the edges of my vision blur, and I lose focus. I blink hard.

Then the world changes.

I'm staring at a scene that I know is from long ago. It's night, and the clearing is lit by candles in glass lanterns. Two girls are standing at the stone altar. I recognize them as the girls from my dreams. A guy is with them, a young man with slicked-back hair parted in the middle. The three of them are wearing robes with wide sleeves, their arms raised high over their heads. They're holding wands like the magic wand Violet used, and they're chanting, reciting words in English and some other language I don't know.

"Abby. Abby!" Molly is shaking my arm.

I blink again, and the vision is gone. But now I'm terrified—a physical sensation of pure terror that I can't explain and can't control.

"What's wrong with you? I've been calling your name for like a minute."

"Let's get out of here." I turn and look for the path. "This place is creeping me out."

"What happened?" Molly walks beside me. "You were totally zoned out!"

I don't answer her. I go down the path as fast as I can without slipping. I climb into the kayak, almost tipping it over.

"Slow down!" Molly says.

She steadies the boat, climbs in carefully, and unhitches the rope. As soon as she does, I push off with the paddle.

"What is wrong with you?" Molly is facing away from me now, and I'm glad she can't see my face. "Tell me what happened."

"I can't talk about it." I almost can't talk at all, I'm so scared. "Let's just get out of here!"

"All right! We're going!"

Numb and shaking, I'm not much good at paddling. Luckily Molly settles into an even stroke and doesn't press me with any more questions. I stare at my hands, trying to concentrate on paddling, trying to calm down.

But when we get near the Alden house, something forces me to look up.

Shadow Man is standing on the dock, watching us.

<center>~~~</center>

After we return the kayak, Molly insists that I sit down and collect myself. She marches me over to a bench beside the river. It's late afternoon, and we sit for a long time, just staring at the water.

Finally Molly says, "I've hung around the police station since I was a little kid. I've even gone with my dad on emergencies, when he got called suddenly and I happened to be in the car. But I don't think I've ever seen anyone as scared as I just saw you."

When I don't say anything, she goes on. "Don't you want to talk about it? I want to help if I can."

I'd like to tell her. I think about telling Violet and Kevin the other night, and how relieved it made me feel. But I'm so ashamed, so afraid she'll think I'm a freak. Besides, how could I tell Molly, of all people? Molly the ace reporter, the compulsive blogger.

"Abby, you can trust me."

"Can I?" My voice sounds small and whiny. "Anything I tell you will end up online."

"No, it won't. I promise."

I'm just not sure. "If I tell you, you have to swear you won't write about it."

-84-

"Write about it? Well, I *write* about everything. But that doesn't mean I have to post it. I've written tons of stuff no one but me has ever seen."

I shake my head.

"All right," Molly says. "This is tough for me, but I swear I won't write about anything you tell me—unless you give me specific permission. Okay?"

So I tell her. About the vision in the circle, about seeing Shadow Man, about my repeated drownings the other night. I *don't* tell her about Grandma, Violet, and Kevin doing magic. I have to respect their privacy, and besides, I take seriously what the Circle of Harmony manifesto said about keeping those things secret.

"I had hallucinations when I was younger, and they put me on meds," I explain. "But it was nothing like these past few days. These feel so real. I almost think they *are* real...somehow."

"I think that's possible," Molly says quietly. "It fits with the whole spiritualist history. What you saw in the circle sounds just like the kind of magic rituals they used to do up there. And the black shadow guy sounds a lot like what Laura Hilton and the Parkers saw. And the drowning—it could be you were reliving what happened to Annie Renshaw..."

She looks at me, and her eyes are moist. "God, Abby. I understand why you're so scared. I appreciate...I'm *honored* that you told me."

"You won't tell anyone else?"

"No, I promise. And I won't write a single word about it. But I'm going to do some more research. Maybe I can help you figure it out."

$$\approx$$

By the time I meet Grandma back at the shop, I've been able to compose myself. The tingling fear is still there, but I haven't seen any more visions, so I'm able to hold it down.

On the ride home, Grandma remarks that I'm awfully quiet. She asks if everything is okay.

I don't want to worry her if I don't have to. "Yeah, I'm okay. Just thinking about stuff. I need to decide about initiation."

"Right. So what are you thinking?"

I'm thinking the scary hallucinations will keep coming back, and if initiation might help me learn to protect myself, then I probably should go ahead. But taking that step feels really momentous, and frightening in a different way—like giving in to believing that the whole scary mess is real.

"What would you do if you were me?"

Grandma laughs. "I would probably ask my Grandma for advice. And she would tell me, once again, that it's a decision only I can make."

"Right..."

"I've pretty much told you all I know, Abby. If you have more questions, I think you should talk to Violet. She'll help you if she can."

After dinner, I tell Grandma I'm going up to my room to catch up on my homework. But instead I dig out my Tarot deck and ask the cards' advice: *Should I accept the offer and be initiated into the Circle of Harmony?*

The reading shows lots of fears and nasty obstacles. But the crowning card is the Magician. Holding up his wand under a bower of roses, he looks so calm and certain.

*The true magician.*

In the outcome position is the Queen of Pentacles. She sits on a throne, also under a bower of roses, with a blue stream running nearby. She gazes serenely at the pentacle in her lap, a five-pointed star in a circle of light.

*Like a gift. The gift of all the world.*

Maybe it's crazy, believing that my visions are real, that magic is real. That's what Franklin and my other friends would say. I don't even want to think about what Mom would say. Maybe I'm giving the secret Abby too much control, and it will lead me into trouble.

Except I'm already in trouble.

Crazy or not, my heart tells me this is what I need to do.

I go downstairs and tell Grandma that yes please, I would like to be initiated into the Circle of Harmony.

## 8. Unless you know my name, you cannot pass

"I'm so excited for you," Violet says, handing me a glass of iced tea. "And I'm excited for me. It's been a long time since we initiated someone."

I'm sitting on her sofa, the ceiling fan spinning overhead. It's a hot day, and I've walked over from the antique shop.

"I really appreciate your help, Violet. You and Kevin have been so kind to me."

"Not at all!" Violet is across the room, opening the creaky doors of an old armoire. She hunts through piles of folders and papers. "Now, let me see. I'll need to brush up on the Initiation Ritual with Kevin and your grandmother...Here it is." She sets a brown folder aside. "And we'll need all those instructions and essays for you to study afterward...they must be in here somewhere." She shuffles through all the shelves, selects a few loose pages, and finally gives up. "Well, I can find those later."

She carries the folder over and sits down beside me. "Okay. So you've read 'Admonitions to the Candidate.' Any questions about that?"

"I guess not. It makes sense, as far as it goes. Purity of intent, learning to watch your own thoughts, following the Five Principles—I get all that. But I'm worried about the actual initiation. I have no idea what I'm supposed to do."

She lays a hand on my wrist. "Not to worry. The ceremony is designed so that the candidate is guided through everything. You'll just follow your grandmother around and take your cues from her. In fact, most of the time you'll be blindfolded."

"Oh."

Violet has opened the folder and is glancing through the papers. "Yeah. We'll have to modify this a bit. In the old days, the ceremonies were conducted outdoors. But with only the three of us to officiate, that's too difficult—making sure it's private and all. I've spoken to your grandmother, and we've agreed to use her house. Have you ever done any meditation?"

"Umm. Yes, in yoga class. And we had a sports psychologist talk to the team once about visualization."

"Excellent. The training of a true magician begins with meditation and visualization." She taps a finger on her lips, thinking. "Now, we'll set up the magical chamber in your grandmother's living room. So first thing Sunday morning, I want you to clean that room slowly and carefully. Treat it as a form of meditation. It's symbolic, you see?"

"Okay."

"And no breakfast. You'll need to fast, starting at midnight on Saturday."

I nod.

"Now, let me see. After you clean the room, you take a warm bath. I'll give you a vial of oil to put in the water. Burn a single white candle in the bathroom. Relax in the water, breathe deeply, and meditate. Meditate on the Five Springs and the principles they represent—Love, Endurance, Balance, Amity, and Bliss. Can you remember all that?"

"Sure."

"Good. Then after the bath, you're to dress in the white gown that I'll give you. Then just relax and wait for us to start. If you get anxious, resume the meditation. Notice whatever thoughts and distractions come to mind, and just gently dismiss them and go back to the Five Springs. Got it?"

"Yes."

"Fine. Now, let's see, what else...what else?" She turns over a few more pages. "Oh yes, the oath. Very important. Before you can be accepted as a candidate, you must swear to keep three promises. First, that you will hold everything that happens in the Circle secret. That means secret from everyone except other initiates. Second, that you will follow the path of true magic to the best of your abilities. This basically means that you appreciate this is a gift and that you take it seriously. Now, the third is the most important: that you will use any occult powers you gain only to bring good and harmony into the world. Good and harmony as exemplified by the Five Principles. This means you swear to reject the temptations of vanity and evil magic. As I told you once before, Abby, this is harder than it sounds. Many who started down this path have gone astray to one degree or another. I believe that's what caused the decline of the Circle."

I think about Annie Renshaw and the vision I saw in the clearing, the man and the two girls with wands. "I've heard that some of them in the old days practiced evil magic."

"Oh, it never seems evil at first," Violet says. "A spirit appears, promises you power, appeals to your desires. It's so easy to be seduced. We all want to believe we're greater and more important than we are."

"So how do you guard against that?"

Violet points to her heart—"By listening here"—and to her brow. "And judging here. This path is designed to make you ever more conscious of your higher nature. As you advance, you will hear its voice in your heart. But you must always remember to use your intellect to judge: Does what you hear and desire conform with the Five Principles? Will it bring harmony into your life and into the world?"

It feels overwhelming. And Violet senses my anxiety.

"It's not easy, Abby. Other spiritual paths—religions—give you all the answers. And that's good—that helps people stay on a safe course and live good lives. But the path of magic is a path of growth. It forces you to find your own answers. It's hard, but it's the path some of us are called to."

When I hear that, something moves inside me, something rising in my heart. So when Violet asks me if I'm sure, if I'm ready to swear the oath and keep the three promises, I clench my jaw, squeeze down the flutter of panic, and answer.

"Yes."

"Good girl. Then stand up."

We both stand. Violet reads the three parts of the oath, and I repeat them. Each promise feels like a step into the darkness, like I'm already blindfolded. But I reach back to the answer that rose in my heart, and it gives me faith and strength. When we sit down again, I feel relieved, like I've just run a race and can now catch my breath.

Violet says, "Now, the only other thing is to choose your magical name. Each magician is known by a secret name that we use only inside the Circle. It can be whatever you wish. Some people choose animal totems or other names from the natural world, and some people choose mottoes based on one of the principles, sometimes in Latin or another language, to sound more exotic. Whatever you choose, it should represent the highest aspiration of your soul, the ideal that you aim for."

"Wow...I don't know. Can you give me some examples?"

Violet smiles. "No, dear. They're secret. I can't repeat any actual names until after you've been initiated. But you can take your time to think about it. Just let me know before Sunday."

"No. Wait, please." This feels super-important, and I'm just not sure how to choose.

When I hesitate, Violet speaks gently. "You might want to close your eyes and be guided by your inner voice. Ask yourself, what is your ideal? What have you found or done in this life that signifies you at your best?"

"All right." I close my eyes, take a deep breath, and ask. What comes to mind is me running on the track, with the Hudson Heights High logo on my shirt.

I open my eyes and ask, "Is—would Fighting Eagle be too silly?"

Violet looks delighted. "Not at all. I think it suits you beautifully."

≈

So two days later I stand in Grandma's hallway, barefoot in a white gown, with a black silk scarf tied over my eyes. I can hear Grandma and Kevin and Violet in the living room, talking in soft voices, moving things around.

Setting up the magical chamber.

I'm nervous, but not really afraid. Since that day I went kayaking, I've had no more scary visions or nightmares. My anxiety level has been up and down but manageable. I wonder if just making the decision to be initiated was enough to surround me with another sphere of protection.

I smell incense.

In a little while I hear drumming, a steady *thump-thump* like a heartbeat. This goes on for some time, and then it is mixed in with the sound of tiny bells—the shaking of a tambourine. Next I hear their voices chanting, intoning speeches in praise of the Circle of Harmony, of the venerated founders, and of the great spirit Lebab. I hear footsteps, then Violet's voice summoning the Elementals, the spirits of the four directions. She calls them "our friends" of air, fire, water, and earth.

"I now declare that the magical chamber is open."

Someone approaches me and takes hold of my hand. *Grandma.*

We take two steps, and then I hear her sharp knocking on the door jamb.

From inside, Violet's voice: "Who knocks at the threshold of our hidden chamber?"

Grandma answers, "A seeker of knowledge. A friend who would join our company."

Violet: "Has the seeker sworn to protect our secret knowledge?"

Grandma: "Her oath is duly recorded."

Violet: "By what name may we know this candidate?"

Grandma: "Her name is Fighting Eagle."

Violet: "Let Fighting Eagle come forward."

We take a step. But then I feel an arm blocking our way.

Kevin says, "Unless you are purified by the sacred waters, you cannot enter in."

A wet fingertip touches my forehead. It traces a pentagram inside a circle, then presses the spot between my eyebrows. *The third eye.* A sensation of energy washes through my brain.

Kevin: "Now you are purified. Pass on."

Violet: "Child of the world of confusion, welcome to our Circle of Harmony."

Grandma turns me to the right, and we walk slowly. The drum starts up again.

Violet: "Approach, Fighting Eagle, and learn the secrets of the Springs."

After we take a few steps, Kevin is there again, barring our way. "I guard the first Spring. Unless you know my name, you cannot pass."

Grandma answers, "Ignorance is your name. Deceit is your name. The deceit of the sensual world. The ignorance of those who perceive only surface appearances. By Love you are conquered, love of knowledge and of truth."

I hear Kevin step back. "You know me, then. Pass on."

We take three more steps and stop. I hear water pouring. Grandma lifts my blindfold, and I glimpse a picture of a fountain. It's painted in blue and rose colors and looks like an image on a Tarot card. The rim of a cup touches my lips.

"Drink from the Fountain of the Love of Truth."

I sip, and the tambourine rings. The water seems to sparkle on my tongue. Grandma takes the cup away and lowers the blindfold.

We move on around the room, the drum beating again.

A few moments later, Kevin blocks our way a third time. "I guard the second Spring. Unless you know my name, you cannot pass."

Grandma replies, "Fear is your name. Terror is your name. The fear of facing the immeasurable truths of nature. The terror of knowing one's own insignificance. By Endurance you are conquered—courage, strength of purpose, steadfast faith."

Again he steps back. Again I am shown a painting of a fountain, this one made of boulders, in grays and browns. Again the tambourine sings and the water tingles as I taste it.

We walk on. The blood in my body throbs in time with the drum.

Once again, Kevin stops us. "I guard the third Spring. Unless you know me, you cannot pass."

Grandma answers, "Pride is your name. Conceit is your name. The conceit of the glittering surfaces of the world, the pride of one inflated by a sense of growing power. Only by Balance are you subdued, the correction of harsh experience, the wisdom to align contending forces."

This time the painting shows two fountains, flowing one into the other, the colors blue and silver. I sip from the cup. The blindfold is replaced.

By now we must almost have circled the room, but it's hard to tell. I'm losing touch with everything except the changes I feel happening inside me.

Kevin stops us again. He is the guardian of the fourth Spring. He demands that we tell him his name.

Grandma says, "Greed is your name. Lust is your name. The terrible greed for power in the world, the lust for control over others. Only by Amity can you be overcome. That is compassion toward all beings and dedication to perfect harmony."

This time the painting is a fountain of gold, and it's a gold cup that holds the water I sip.

We move on. I'm only faintly aware of the drumming and of my body walking in darkness. Love, Endurance, Balance, and Amity are whirlpools spinning inside me. My mind is dazzled, stretching to comprehend them. I clutch Grandma's hand. It's all that keeps me from floating away.

"Let the candidate come forth and kneel," Violet says.

A few steps, and I am guided to kneel down on a cushion. I feel Kevin and Grandma standing beside me. Violet speaks from directly in front of me.

"Child of the world of confusion, I welcome you to Harmony. You have glimpsed the four Springs and tasted their sacred waters—the Springs that are Fountains and the Fountains that are waymarkers on the path of true magic. As you progress faithfully on this path, you will revisit the Fountains many times and learn their lessons. But now before you flows the fifth and ultimate Spring. Always remember that this Spring is the goal of your quest. It is Bliss. It is union with your own higher nature, that which is a fragment of the One Eternal Mind, the Spirit of the Universe. Remove your blindfold, Fighting Eagle, and gaze upon the waters of Bliss."

I lift off the blindfold. Before my eyes is a goblet of blue glass, the water inside swirling and full of light. I gaze at the circling water, then slowly raise my eyes. The walls of the room are gone; so is the ceiling. There's only the streaming light revolving and flowing, rising in spirals—higher and higher, the crystal-blue color of the Springs.

Then inside the spirals of light, I see shapes and faces. People in magic robes, or in Victorian clothes, and Native Americans in deerskin and feathers. *All people who have lived by the springs.* Then I see other beings—spirits. Dark creatures, like Shadow Man, shapeless and shifting like clouds. But also angels with eagle wings, goblins, fairies of the woods, sprites of the water.

None of it frightens me. I have no fear at all.

I am in the Circle of Harmony, protected.

I feel only bliss.

$$\approx\!\!\approx$$

After a time, I don't know how long, the vision fades.

Grandma and Kevin help me to stand.

Violet steps forward and gestures with her wand. "Arise, dear friend and companion of the quest, Fighting Eagle, True Magician."

She hugs me, and her energy helps bring me back to earth. I notice her robe—a deep, glossy purple, with gold and white symbols of the sun and moon.

"Now we may tell you our secret names," Violet says. "I am called Amor Verum, a motto which means 'love of truth.'"

Kevin embraces me next. His robe is gray, with red and black figures that look like African totems. "Welcome, Fighting Eagle. I am called Simano, which means 'wanderer.' It is a name chosen in honor of my ancestors."

I turn to Grandma, who beams and takes my two hands. "My dear Fighting Eagle, I am so proud of you. In the Circle I am known as Silver Bird—a name chosen because I love silver and birds."

Everyone laughs as Grandma hugs me.

They direct me to sit down and rest while they dismantle the magical chamber. First Violet walks around the room with her wand. She stops at the four directions and thanks and dismisses our "friends of the four elements." Then she and Kevin and Grandma put away the pictures and cups and other magic implements.

Later, after changing our clothes, we all sit in the dining room and share toast and tea, oranges, and strawberries with whipped cream. My nerves are still tingling from the energy of the Circle, but I feel calm and happy.

Violet shows me a folder full of papers, photocopies of typewritten pages. There are exercises to practice, records of visions received by the founders, and essays to read and study.

"This is the basic curriculum given to new initiates," Violet explains. "Or rather, all of it that I was able to find. Some of it has been lost over time, unfortunately. But I might have other bits somewhere in the house. I'll keep looking."

"I'll look at my papers too," Grandma says. "I still have them up in the attic."

Violet smiles at her. "I'm glad you're back with us, Kat."

"I am for now," Grandma says. "For Abby's sake. For myself, I'll have to wait and see."

Violet nods. "Anyway, Abby, you should study these and reflect on them, and come to us with questions. The main thing is that you practice this one, the Daily Ablution, every morning when you first wake up and every night before retiring. It teaches you how to visualize each of the Springs as centers of energy and move them around your body. The Five Springs have been awakened in your aura. Now they must be properly mixed and balanced."

"It's very important that you do this every day," Kevin adds. "It's the basis for all the other practices."

"I will."

Violet hesitates, then goes on. "When you visualize one or another of the Springs, you might meet a spirit or entity. This is rare for most beginners, but in your case I'd say it's very possible. Any being that you meet, treat with respect, but be guarded. If asked who you are, say that you are Fighting Eagle, initiate of the Circle of Harmony. Then demand their name in return. It's okay to ask them questions and gather information, but be careful you are not seduced. Do not follow them anywhere, and do not accept any gifts. If they threaten you, visualize the Five Springs in your body and let the waters gush out and wash them away."

"Okay..."

"Don't worry, Abby," Grandma says. "You can handle it. Remember, you're a true magician now."

## 9. Anyone ever tell you you're kind of strange?

Wednesday evening, Grandma and I eat dinner in town and then walk over to the Presbyterian church. Signs in the driveway announce the Save Harmony Springs community meeting, and the parking lot is filling up fast. We follow the crowd to the auditorium, which is a separate building behind the church.

Fiona Alden-Gathers stands at the door greeting people. She thanks us for coming and introduces us to her husband, Adam. Adam is tall and good-looking but seems uncomfortable. I sense that he feels this is Fiona's gig, and she's in charge.

Rows of folding chairs are arranged facing the stage. I spot Molly near the front. She's promised to save us seats. As we walk down the aisle, I see she's sitting with Ray-Ray and an older guy in a police uniform. They all stand up, and she introduces me to her father, Chief Arthur Quick. He's a heavyset man with a mustache and dark circles under his eyes. He seems serious and distracted as he tips his cap to us.

"And I think you've already met my brother, Ray-Ray." Molly smiles innocently.

"Right," Ray-Ray says. "The girl at the Parkers' house. The day of the skunk ape."

If feels like they're both teasing me, and I'm a little embarrassed.

"Actually it was the devil at the Parkers'," I correct him. "The skunk ape was another time." I don't like being teased.

Ray-Ray smiles and looks me over as we sidestep him to get to our seats.

I sit down next to Molly, who goes back to typing furiously on her tablet keyboard.

"The opposition showed up," she says, tilting her head toward the other side of the room. "This is going to be real interesting."

"Who are you talking about?"

"That group in the third and fourth rows over there. They're owners in favor of selling out. The blond guy in the blue sports coat is Phil Deering. He's a lawyer, and he owns a bunch of rental properties. And that guy next to him? I think he may be with the Texas-Brighton Land Company. I'm going to go find out right now."

She takes out her phone and opens the voice recorder app. When she jumps up, Ray-Ray grabs her wrist.

"Don't antagonize anyone. Please?"

Molly gives him a sweet smile. "Of course not! I'm just giving them the opportunity to state their side of the story."

She slides away, and Ray-Ray rolls his eyes unhappily.

"Irrepressible, isn't she?" I ask him.

"You've noticed."

I've also noticed there are two more police officers standing on the sides of the hall. "You're not expecting trouble, are you?"

Ray-Ray shrugs. "I hope not. But things could get heated. Lots of strong feelings around this."

As soon as Molly comes back, she starts typing again. "He's from Texas, all right. You should see the silver belt buckle. And inlaid boots! My god, he thinks he's a cowboy—a very oily cowboy, in my opinion."

The auditorium is almost full, and people are still coming in. When the seats are all gone, they stand along the side walls and in the back. There's a constant buzz of conversation.

Fiona and her husband come to the front of the room. They're walking with an older man in a black suit and minister's collar. He goes up onto the stage first and asks everyone to stand for a prayer.

After the prayer, the reverend welcomes everyone and thanks us for coming. He explains that the meeting was originally organized by Fiona Alden-Gathers to discuss development issues affecting the town, and to let everyone know about her organization, Save Harmony Springs. On hearing about the meeting, he says, Phillip Deering requested time to present an opposing view, representing some property owners on the springs. In the interests of fairness, the reverend felt he should allow this, and Ms. Alden-Gathers graciously agreed.

With that he introduces Fiona, and she comes up onstage. I admire how super-poised and confident she appears. She holds a clicker in her hand, and when she presses it a slide lights up the screen behind her. It shows a photo of the head of the springs, with the clear blue water, and the logo for Save Harmony Springs.

Fiona begins by talking about how she grew up in Harmony Springs, and what a special place it is. She then describes how she and her husband have been involved in many development projects.

"I am in no way against development," she says. "But I have seen how *irresponsible* development can destroy the very qualities that make a place desirable to live in. I want to show you some examples."

She clicks, and the screen shows a lovely rolling countryside with green hills and a farmhouse. Fiona explains that this was a site in Georgia that was targeted for development. The next slide shows the same site three years later. The farmhouse and trees are gone, the hills hidden behind close-built houses that all look the same.

"Awful," Grandma whispers beside me.

Fiona shows another example, a wooded riverbank with three widely spaced cabins in Tennessee. In the next picture, the woods have mostly vanished, and the river is lined with oversized mansions.

"Excuse me." Phil Deering has stood up and raised his hand.

"Sit down!" someone yells, and I see Chief Quick and Ray-Ray tense.

Fiona shows another slide. She says this is a project developed by the Texas-Brighton Land Company. The first image is an aerial photograph of farmland, a patchwork of open fields. The next picture shows the same fields, now covered with roads and closely packed houses.

"Excuse me!" Phil Deering shouts over the angry murmur of voices. "Ms. Gathers, this is quite misleading and dishonest."

"My name is Alden-Gathers," Fiona replies. "And there is nothing misleading or dishonest about it."

"Please! Please!" Phil Deering is holding up his hands. "No one involved in the proposed development is talking about clear-cutting the woods or building dense tract housing. And while we're at it, no one is talking about destroying endangered sea turtles or torturing puppy dogs."

This incites a lot more shouting, from people all over the room. Chief Quick jumps up and yells in a booming voice for everyone to settle down.

When the uproar subsides, Fiona says, "Frankly, we've tried repeatedly to get clarification from Texas-Brighton on exactly what they *are* intending. And to discuss if they are willing to accept restrictions on what can be built."

"No one's gonna tell me what I can do with my own land!" some guy in the back yells.

"Quiet!" Chief Quick says. "Any more interruptions like that, and you'll be escorted out. Let's have an orderly meeting here, folks."

"Thank you, Chief Quick," Fiona says. "At this point, rather than go on with my presentation, I think it well to let Mr. Deering take the floor. Perhaps he and his friends can tell us what they *do* intend. I yield the floor to Mr. Deering."

Phil Deering looks surprised but collects himself quickly. He and the guy Molly said is from Texas-Brighton shuffle out of their seats and walk to the stage. When they get to the podium, Phil blinks at the projector, which still shows the ugly tract housing in Texas.

"Can we turn this thing off, please?"

"Certainly." Fiona, who is standing to the side, nods to her husband. Adam leans over and switches off the projector.

Phil Deering introduces the man beside him as Elston Tyler, a representative of the Texas-Brighton Land Company. Then he describes how he was first contacted by the company about their interest in buying his properties. He's personally checked their financial statements and visited several of their projects. He believes they are a solid firm and that they build quality communities that people can be proud of. Most importantly, he's confident they will deliver on their financial obligations. Development is inevitable in Florida, he says. The town needs to be forward-thinking and choose a quality partner to work with.

Some people shout "No!" Others respond with "Quiet!" or "Shut up!" I glance at Grandma beside me. Her lips are tight and her eyes angry.

Elston Tyler addresses the meeting next. He's relaxed and soft-spoken, with a Texas drawl. He says it's premature to talk about restricting the number or types of houses. It will depend on how many properties the company is able to acquire. Of course, they will also need to obtain necessary building permits, which will be subject to normal government review. It will be a long process, and people in the community will have the opportunity to give input at every step.

He goes on to assure everyone that the Texas-Brighton Land Company wants to be a good partner with the town, and they will be happy to discuss their plans with "full transparency" as they move forward. Anyone who wants to speak with him can obtain his contact information from Mr. Deering.

After that, they open the floor to questions. Someone asks why they can't be more specific about their plans. Someone else wants to know *when* they will be able to say more. But Tyler and Deering just keep repeating that plans are "still fluid" and that they'll be "disclosed as soon as decisions are made."

"So much for full transparency," Molly whispers.

As the two men go back to their seats, there's scattered talking in the audience, and a few people applaud.

Fiona takes the podium again, shaking her head. "Thank you, gentlemen. I understand your reluctance to reveal specifics. Still, I know I speak for many of us here when I say that's just not good enough. You've provided absolutely no concrete information, just vague promises to let us know later. I'm very much afraid that if we don't act today to stop you, we will wake up tomorrow to find our beloved springs destroyed."

This causes another uproar. A few people gesture angrily and storm out. Molly jumps up and starts recording video on her tablet. Chief Quick and the reverend both stand and plead with everyone to calm down.

Eventually order is restored, and Fiona continues. The projector is back on, showing the first slide with the logo for Save Harmony Springs. Fiona explains that her concerns about preserving the springs inspired her to speak to other residents. She introduces the neighbors who have agreed to be part of her committee. They are sitting in the front row, and each of them stands up in turn. One of them is the reverend—Reverend Johnson—another is Elizabeth Hopkins, the town librarian. Two more are older gentlemen, owners of homes on the springs.

Fiona then outlines the group's proposal. First they intend to petition to have the property along the springs, from Founders Park north to the source, designated a National Historic District. This by itself would not provide protection, but it would make it legally feasible for the town council to place easements on the properties. Fiona says this is a proven mechanism for protecting historic places. Under easements, owners would still be able to sell their properties, but any new construction would have to be approved and stay consistent with the historic character of the springs.

As this idea sinks in, more discussion starts in the audience and quickly grows louder. A bunch more people get up to leave.

"No one's going to tell me what I can do with my land!" shouts the man who shouted this before. Chief Quick turns to glare at him, but the guy's already walking out.

When things quiet down, Fiona answers questions about the proposals. If easements are approved, she explains, a committee might be elected to review building permits, or the reviews could be done by the Florida State Historic Trust. She admits that these plans will take time to set up. In the meantime, the committee is prepared to pursue other avenues to delay development. These include demanding environmental and water purity assessments, lobbying the county commission, and filing lawsuits if necessary.

All of this is going to take effort and money. Fiona asks everyone who shares the committee's concerns to sign the petition for designating the springs a historic site. And she asks further that everyone pitches in—either with financial contributions or by volunteering time. A slide comes up showing the Save Harmony Springs email, phone number, and social media sites.

As the meeting breaks up, many people move to the front table to sign the petition. Others stand around in clusters, discussing or arguing. Ray-Ray and his dad wander off, to make sure it all stays peaceful.

Molly turns to me. "I'm going to volunteer. How about you?"

I'll only be in town another week and a half, but I want to do anything I can to help. "Sure."

Grandma says she wants to sign the petition and chip in some money. She joins us as we head to the front and mingle with the crowd surrounding the committee members. While we're waiting for our chance to talk with Fiona, Molly holds her phone in the air and takes pictures.

Something up on the stage catches my eye. Standing beside the curtain is a tall woman in a black dress. I squeeze my eyes shut and look again.

It's the woman from my nightmares, the one with the proud, glaring eyes.

No one else seems to see her, and she's not paying any attention to me. She's staring down at Fiona, who's busy working the crowd. I'm struck by a sudden, horrible suspicion.

She wants to kill Fiona.

I'd like to ask if anyone else can see her, but I'm afraid I already know the answer.

Then a glance at Molly gives me a crazy idea. I take out my phone and slip to the edge of the stage. I center the woman in the viewfinder and snap two pictures.

When I open the photos, they show no one. When I look up, Ghost Woman is gone.

*Damn.*

"Photographing the empty stage?" Ray-Ray is standing beside me.

I tense, then look stupidly at my phone. "Um...no, I was... checking the exposure?"

*Oh, what's the use?* I shove the phone in front of his face. "I don't see anyone in this picture. Do you?"

He stares at it, frowning. "Ah, no. Is this a trick question?"

I shake my head, smile, and put the phone away. "Nope. Exactly what I thought."

He peers down at me. "You're sort of a strange girl. Anyone ever tell you that?"

"Oh, yeah. I tell myself that at least nine times a day."

## 10. Occult forces seem to be converging—and I'm one of them

When I wake up the next morning, I sit in the middle of the bedroom floor and practice the Daily Ablution. I visualize the first Spring at the root of my spine, the brilliant blue water flowing into me, and I contemplate the Principle of the Love of Truth. After a while, the water rises up to the second Spring, around my solar plexus, and I contemplate Endurance. Then to the heart and the Principle of Balance, the throat and the Principle of Amity, and finally to the center of my head and the Principle of Bliss. From there I see the water gushing out the top of my head and falling in a shower to completely fill and cleanse my aura.

Then I get dressed and go for a run.

As my feet pound the hard-packed sand of Bliss Road, I let my mind roam. This morning it roams to Ray-Ray Quick. I imagine he's a really good kisser. But to kiss him, I'd have to stand on tiptoe, and he'd have to lean over. Or maybe he'd lift me up in his arms...

*Stop it.*

He thinks I'm a weirdo. Besides, I'm only going to be here ten more days. I'll find a real boyfriend back in New Jersey. Or maybe when I go to college...

Anyway, I have more urgent things to worry about. Like what I saw last night in the auditorium.

True, the vision didn't fill me with paralyzing terror the way they have in the past. I suspect that's due to the magical exercises. I've done the Ablution every morning and evening as Violet instructed. Each time I finish, I feel strength and bliss washing over me, just as I did at the end of the Initiation ceremony. That sensation fades as I tune back into the world. But as I go through the day, there's an ongoing feeling of calm and protection, of being *anchored*.

So seeing Ghost Woman last night came as a surprise. And I have to wonder if my intuition about her is accurate—that she's a threat to Fiona.

I'm not sure what to make of it. I need some advice.

～～<br>～～

Since the initiation ceremony, Grandma has seemed a little reluctant to talk about the Circle of Harmony and my magical studies. So when we get to the shop that morning, I phone Violet.

"I'm glad you called," she says. "I've been wanting to talk with you. How is your training progressing?"

Along with the Daily Ablution, my training consists of studying the Circle of Harmony writings that Violet and Grandma have given me. The papers are full of strangeness—accounts of conversations with spirits, descriptions of different realms that surround this world but influence it, stories of magicians who traveled to those realms through secret, invisible channels. Mixed in with all this are tantalizing hints about actually *using* magic—calling spirits, raising power, and casting it out into the world to *do things*. But only hints, no instructions.

"It's a little overwhelming," I tell Violet. "I've got all this stuff to read, but it seems like lots of details are left out. Like I'm assumed to know some things already, and I don't even have a clue."

"Your curiosity is awakened. That's good. You are meant to wonder."

"Well, I'm wondering. Listen, something happened last night..." I tell her about seeing Ghost Woman and sensing that she intends to harm Fiona.

"Hmm. And you have no idea who this woman is?"

"No, except that I've seen her before in my dreams and halluci—I mean, *visions*. What do you make of it?"

"Well...I wouldn't normally say too much to a newbie. But you are obviously very gifted. And more than that, you seem to be a focal point."

Prickling sensation. "What do you mean?"

She hesitates. "You see...I've had intuitions ever since this development thing started. My readings show there is more to it than meets the eye. Occult forces seem to be converging on the town. And I think *you* are one of them, that you have some important role to play."

The prickling becomes a flutter of fear in my stomach. "How can I—I mean, how can we figure this out?"

Violet sighs. "We just have to look for more signs and try to interpret them. That's how this works."

"That's not very reassuring."

"I know. Try not to worry about it. Just keep up with your training. And definitely let me know if you see any more visions."

≈

Saturday morning, three days after the community meeting, I go back to the Presbyterian church for an organizing meeting of the Save Harmony Springs volunteers. As I cross the parking lot, Molly runs up to me, bursting with excitement.

"Your black shadow guy's active again. This time he threw rocks!"

"What?"

"Yeah. He was seen yesterday at twilight, running away from Jonas Carter's house after a bunch of rocks hit the porch. And a little later a window was broken at another house nearby. Remember, Jonas is on the Save Harmony Springs committee. And the owner of the other house, Alice Dunbar, also signed the petition. What does that tell you?"

"Whoa. I don't know what." Somehow, I can't see Shadow Man throwing rocks. Not his style.

"I'm going up there later to talk with the homeowners. Are you in?"

Well, Violet told me we have to look for signs. "Sure, I'm in."

Inside the auditorium, the meeting is just getting organized. About a dozen people have shown up, most of them elderly. Molly and I are the only kids. Of course, Molly knows everyone, and she introduces me around. The fact that I'm a Renshaw automatically gives me some cred. Several folks ask after Grandma.

Fiona's not able to attend, so Reverend Johnson runs the meeting. He gives us an update on fundraising and on the application for expanding the Historic District. Part of the application will be the petition, so we need to get as many signatures on it as possible. He asks for volunteers to go door to door. Molly's hand shoots up. With her other hand, she takes my wrist and lifts it high.

Since we're the "young folks," the reverend assigns us the neighborhood farthest away, near the mouth of the springs. This dovetails nicely with Molly's investigation plans. The reverend gives us all copies of the petition and instructions on what to say. We rehearse our message—that our purpose is to protect the unique character of the springs without infringing on property owners' rights. Above all, we're to be polite and avoid confrontation. Reverend Johnson looks straight at Molly when he says that last part.

So, after lunch at the coffee shop and bringing Grandma a sandwich, Molly and I board her electric bike and head out of town. We cross the bridge by the park and then follow the road up the west side of the river. Near the mouth of the springs we turn left, into an area I haven't visited before. There are streets with ranch houses and well-kept lawns, but also dirt roads with cabins and run-down trailers.

We knock on doors and ring bells. Molly does most of the talking, so I just smile and act polite. Some of the people recognize Molly, but when they don't, she introduces herself and mentions that her father is chief of police. This puts some people at ease but seems to make others nervous.

Lots of people already know about the development issue. Some of them sign the petition right away. Others, Molly is able to persuade. But there are also people who refuse, and some of them are hostile. One old trailer has a Confederate flag hanging over the window. I expect the owner to maybe threaten us with a shotgun, but he's actually very polite. He signs the petition and thanks us for our efforts. His neighbor, on the other hand, threatens to feed us to his dogs if we even set foot on his property. Molly just laughs and takes it all in stride.

After a couple of hours, we cross back over the main road to the river side. We're close to the head of the springs, where the houses date back to the 1890s. One large house has a broken front window. This is the one owned by Alice Dunbar. Molly's hoping to interview her about the incident last night, but when we ring the bell, no one answers.

We have better luck two doors down with Jonas Carter. Jonas is a small, elderly man with silver hair and mustache. Very soft-spoken. He is on the Save Harmony Springs committee, so of course he's already signed the petition. He thanks us for volunteering.

Molly asks him about the disturbance the night before. He frowns and seems baffled. Just after sundown, he heard loud noises at the back of his house. When he investigated, he saw a slim man, all in black, running away toward the river. Several rocks had hit his back porch but luckily hadn't broken any windows. When Molly asks if he has any idea why someone would throw rocks at his house, he suggests it might be someone angry about the Save Harmony Springs committee. He seems sad and a little afraid when he says this.

Molly asks permission for us to go around back and look at his yard. He finds this an odd request, but says it's okay, and to watch out for snakes.

We walk around to the backyard. There's a buffer of tall grass and trees between his property and the river. Molly and I check it out. With the puddles and breaks in the foliage, we can't really tell whether anyone's run through here recently.

Molly turns to me. "Do you get any impressions?"

"Huh?"

"Well, you know, paranormal investigation teams sometimes include a psychic. So, with your abilities, I just wondered if you might have any psychic impressions about what happened here last night. I hope you don't mind me asking?"

"No. Why should I?"

"Well?"

I gaze around and consider it. I certainly don't see Shadow Man or any other apparitions, and I don't have any particular feelings about the place.

"Nothing. Sorry."

"Hmm. Too bad." She hesitates, as if she's deciding whether or not to ask her next question. But this is Molly, so of course she does. "Did you see something at the meeting the other night? Ray-Ray told me you took a picture of the stage and then asked if he saw anyone in it."

"Oh. Yes, that did happen." Now I'm the one who hesitates. "We're still sworn to secrecy about this stuff?"

Molly crosses her heart. "Promise."

"Okay." So I tell her about seeing Ghost Woman, and how I sensed she was a threat to Fiona.

"That's interesting." Molly twists her mouth. "Tall blond woman, black dress and pearls. Like a high-necked dress?"

"Yeah."

"That rings a bell somewhere...Listen, we've only got a few more houses to visit. Do you have time to stop at the library when we're done here?"

I pull out my phone and check. It's only three thirty, and Grandma won't close the shop till six. "Yeah, I can do that."

After we canvass the last of our assigned houses, we ride back into town. The library is on a side road off Main Street, three blocks down from Springs of Coffee. It's a dark old building, gothic style, with pointy windows and steep gables.

Molly hustles me to a tiny back room, where there's a microfiche reader. Most of the town's historic documents are stored on old-fashioned microfilm, and you use this device to read them. Molly goes through some drawers and pulls out little film cassettes. She pops one into the base of the reader and flips a switch. The screen lights up and shows an index page. We're looking at the Harmony Springs newspaper, the *Springs Sentinel*, for January to March of 1950.

Molly turns a knob, and the pages fly by in a blur. She stops every few seconds to look at pictures, shakes her head, and flies on. She changes the cassette and repeats.

In August of 1952, she stops. A dark rectangle covers a quarter of the newspaper page. The picture of a stern blond woman stares at us from the screen. She's dressed in a style older than the 1950s—fair hair piled in a bun, black dress with a high, frilly collar, and pearls.

"This is the one I remembered. Does she look anything like your Ghost Woman?"

The hair is bristling at the back of my neck. "She *is* my Ghost Woman."

"Okay!" Molly sounds triumphant. "Margaret Alden. Daughter of Albert Alden, one of the founders. She must be a relative of Fiona. A great-aunt or something."

We both read the article. It's the obituary of Margaret Alden, known as "Maisie." Born in 1892, one of seven children of Albert and

Helena Hennessy Alden. Never married, she was described as a shrewd businesswoman who managed to weather the 1929 stock market crash with her fortune intact. Later she acquired sole ownership of the Alden mansion on Bliss Bayou and bought up many other properties on the river and around the headwaters of the springs.

"She must be the one who bequeathed the land around the springs to the town," Molly says. "Including that circle at the mouth of Bliss Bayou..."

"Yeah. Where I freaked out." I'm remembering my vision in the church auditorium, and feeling afraid. "But if she was part of Fiona's family, why did I sense that she wants to kill her?"

"Good question," Molly says. "Definitely need more research. I will dig up everything I can about old Maisie, I promise you. This is *really* interesting."

∿∿

After getting ready for bed that night, I lay out the cards. I ask about my vision of Margaret Alden, and if it really means Fiona is in danger. At the covering position is the Queen of Swords, a stern and powerful woman, definitely Margaret. But the rest of the reading is hard to decipher. Indications of confusion, possibly deception, and much hidden from sight.

As if I didn't know *that* already.

All this has made me anxious—a nagging sense of something about to happen. So I settle down to calm myself with the Ablution exercise. I sit cross-legged on the rug and take deep breaths. As I relax, I visualize the first Spring at the base of my spine.

When I reach the second Spring, I have a vision. My eyes are closed, but I see myself beside a fountain with blue water tumbling over gray boulders. Standing in front of me is Margaret.

She looks about fifty, tall and erect—exactly as she has in my other visions and nightmares.

"You mistake me," she says, her voice deep and calm. "I mean you no harm."

I'm frightened, but I recall Violet's advice about what to do if I meet an entity during my spiritual exercises. "I am Fighting Eagle, initiate of the Circle of Harmony."

"I know who you are, Abigail."

*Whoa. Wasn't expecting that.* "And what is your name, spirit?"

"You know already. I am Maisie. Sometimes I am called back to this world. But I never meant to frighten you."

"Why are you called back?"

"When there is a need. I watch over Fiona. You see, I was a friend of Annie Renshaw's. Like others, I fell victim to her curse. Now I try to minimize the damage."

She holds out her hand. "Come with me, child. I will show you."

An inner alarm goes off. I remember Violet's warning about wandering away from the Fountains.

"I understand," Margaret says. "You follow the teachings of the Circle. That is good. Perhaps I will see you again. I hope that in time you will learn to trust me."

She turns and walks away, and her body fades into nothing.

〰︎

Next morning over breakfast, I tell Grandma about finding Margaret's picture in the library, then meeting her ghost in my vision. I'm actually kind of excited about it, but Grandma does not seem pleased.

"You'd best talk to Violet."

"Okay...are you angry with me?"

"No. I just don't know what to tell you." She stands up and gathers her dishes.

*Why is she so upset?*

She drops the dishes in the sink, then turns. "Listen, Abby. This worries me. I got you into practicing magic, but now I'm not sure it was the right thing. At the time, I didn't know what else to do. And it seemed to help you, but—"

"I think it's helped me a lot."

"Okay, but it's dangerous. Now you're talking to spirits. Bad things can happen, and I don't have the ability to protect you."

This makes me realize what a burden I've been to her these past two weeks. It feels awful. "I'm sorry, Grandma. I didn't mean to worry you."

"It's okay. Just please talk to Violet. Maybe she can protect you. I hope so."

Grandma is tense and gloomy the rest of the morning. She doesn't say much as we drive into town and open the shop.

When we get there, I call Violet on my cell. Unlike Grandma, she's intrigued by my adventure. "You did fine, Abby. I'm glad you remembered not to follow her away from the Spring."

"Do you think it was real—I mean, really the ghost of Margaret Alden?"

"I wouldn't be surprised. They used to say her house was haunted. And now they're renovating the place, right? That might have disturbed her spirit."

"Do you think she was telling me the truth?"

"That I can't say. Besides, it could be some other entity pretending to be her ghost. I wouldn't try to summon her back. But if you see her again, try to get her to tell you more. Ask *why* she needs to protect Fiona, and from what. See if she knows anything about the development people and what they are after."

"Okay, I'll try. Have you been able to learn any more, Violet?"

"Not much. My readings still say that forces are gathering. They all point to late July—probably the full moon. And you still seem to be a key player."

Well, that's scary. Besides, I won't even be here in July. "You know, I'm flying back to New Jersey in just over a week."

"Yes, I realize that. Maybe my impressions are wrong. Or else..."

"Or else what?"

"Or else you won't leave. Something will happen to change your plans."

## 11. A slight change in plans

Tuesday afternoon, I'm sitting in the back room of the antique shop reading, when my phone goes off—Mom's ringtone. We just had our weekly check-in call on Sunday, so I'm a little worried as I pull out the phone.

"Hi, Mom. Everything okay?"

"Hi, hon. Everything's fine. Can you talk for a few minutes?" Mom sounds breathless.

"Sure."

"Okay. So, you know we've been in London. Jim and I visited the office here last week, and, well, one thing led to another, and today they offered me a job. They want me to work out of the London office."

"What!"

"I know! Crazy, right? But it would mean a lot more money, and better than that, with the international experience, it would put me on track to make director in a few years. The first thing I said was they'd need to clear it with New York. And, Abby, they told me they'd *already* cleared it with New York. They really want me."

"Wow. That's great, Mom." *I guess...*

"I know, I know. I haven't given them a decision yet. I told them I'd have to talk it over with you. Jim's okay with it, of course. They told me they could arrange for private school for you over here. How does senior year in London sound?"

That sounds...*terrifying*. "Oh, I'm not sure. I'm pretty settled at Hudson Heights."

"I understand. But think it over. You might decide you really like the idea."

I *hate* the idea.

"The other option is—if I take the job—I could commute and spend one week a month in the States. Jim will still be home most of the time, and we could arrange for a housekeeper so you'd never be alone at the house. Do you think you could manage with that?"

I can feel Mom's heart soaring at this chance. It's like all her hard work is about to pay off. I can't let little Abby's insecurities snatch the gold ring away.

"Sure, I'll manage. Mom, I think you should take the job."

"Really? Oh, Abby. You're such a good daughter. Do you really think it's the right thing for me to do?"

"Absolutely. I'm proud of you, Mom."

"I love you, Abby."

"I love you too."

"Wow. Well, they want me to start in mid-July. Four weeks' orientation. After that I'll have some time stateside—I'll insist on that. I know we planned to look at colleges in July, but we'll have to squeeze that into August. I'm not going to let this interfere with my job as your mother. I'll meet you back home on Sunday as planned. I'll have a week to finish up in the New York office, then back to the UK. You'll come with me, of course."

"What, you mean to London, like next month?"

"Of course. It won't all be work, Abby. I'll make time to show you around London. And Paris is only a two-hour train ride away. We'll have fun."

Or I could end up stuck in a little apartment while Mom works eighteen hours a day. *Don't be such a buzzkill, Abby.*

"Sure, Mom. It'll be fine."

But after I hang up, I stand there stunned. Of course I'm happy for Mom. She sounds so excited. But being home for just a week, then flying to England for four weeks? Then rushing around in August to visit colleges. Big decisions to make and pressure to make them fast. And transplanting myself to a new school—in England, no less. Or else staying in New Jersey, but Mom gone three weeks out of four my whole senior year. My life feels like a roller coaster flying off the rails.

Then I think about what Violet said: "Something might happen to change your plans." But this can't be it. I won't be in New Jersey in July, but I won't be in Harmony Springs either.

"What was the phone call about?" Grandma's standing in the doorway. She just finished with a customer and must have heard part of it.

I tell her the news.

"Wow. Four weeks in England. You're certainly having an exciting summer."

"Yeah, I know."

But the more it sinks in, the more desolate I feel.

〜〜〜

To take my mind off my misery, I try to focus on schoolwork. Between studying the Circle of Harmony papers and everything else that's been going on, I haven't made any progress on the honors reading list. I finally bailed on *An American Tragedy* when I found out it was about a girl drowning—just what I *didn't* need. I'll have to make notes from the plot summary and fake it on that one. But I'm finding *The Grapes of Wrath* just as difficult to love.

I send Franklin a text, asking how he's getting on with the readings.

He answers in a few seconds: "Abigail Adams! I'm done with the Tragedy and skipping the Wrath. I recommend the movie version with Henry Fonda. A beautiful man!"

Me: "I'll consider him. Guess what? I'm going to London in July."

Franklin: "WUT?"

Me: "For real. My mom will be working over there."

Franklin: "*jealous*"

Franklin again: "You need to get the motherbot to take you to the theater. The London Stage!!!"

Me: "I'm coming home on Sunday. See you next week?"

Franklin: "For sure."

I put down the phone and stare at my tablet. Franklin is right—I ought to be thrilled about going to London. Any normal kid would be.

*Why can't I be normal?*

~~~

That night I make another futile attempt at the honors reading list. But after staring blankly at my screen for a time, I give up and stare out the window instead. The moon is almost full. Through the trees, I see little glimmers of moonlight reflecting off the bayou.

I don't want to leave this place.

Maybe Violet is right—unseen forces brought me here and I have some part to play, something to help save the springs.

Or maybe all that's a delusion, and Violet's as crazy as I am.

I don't know, but I *don't* want to leave.

In fact, the idea terrifies me—against all reason. It's not just going to England, or the thought of Mom being away my senior year. The whole thing has brought up this huge, suffocating dread. Dad died, and I felt abandoned. We left Grandma behind, and I was heartbroken. Mom worked all the time, and I was alone.

Then the nightmares and terrors started.

I wish I could stay here the rest of the summer. But it's been obvious the past few days how much my being here has strained Grandma. If I ask, she might say yes out of guilt. The last thing I want is to make her life harder.

But I'm so afraid of leaving...It feels like the abandoned and alone thing is happening all over again. I came here with the idea of facing my fears and growing up. I seem to have failed in spectacular fashion.

No, that's wrong. I've got tools for dealing with this now. I'm Fighting Eagle, initiate of the Circle of Harmony. I walk to the center of the room, sit down, and start the Ablution.

Concentration comes hard. At times, the visualization makes me shake. When finally the waters are gushing out through the top of my head, they feel like tears instead of bliss.

♒

The next day is not much better.

I didn't sleep well—kept waking up suddenly, frightened that Ghost Woman or Shadow Man might be lurking in my room. Then I'd toss and turn awhile before finally drifting off.

When Grandma mentions how quiet I am, I just tell her I've got a lot on my mind—flying home, going to England, all that. She nods and leaves it alone. She seems as grim and miserable as I feel.

In the afternoon I get a text from Molly, telling me to check my email. I open it up on my phone:

> Abby:
>
> I've verified that Margaret Alden did indeed leave the land at the head of Bliss Bayou to the town. Also, there were stories that her house up there used to be HAUNTED!!! For a long time after she died her GHOST was supposed to have inhabited the place. That's why it was abandoned for so long.
>
> I'd like to go in there and do a proper paranormal investigation, with video and sound recording, but I'm not sure how to pitch the idea to Fiona. Any thoughts?
>
> Also, I promised I wouldn't write anything about this stuff without your explicit permission. So now I'm asking. I WON'T use your name, and I'll let you REVIEW IT ALL and take out anything you're uncomfortable with.

So please let me know. This story is burning a hole in my brain!

Moll

What difference does it make now? I'm out of here on Sunday and probably won't be back for years, if ever. I reply to tell Molly it's okay—as long as I get to review it.

Less than two hours later, she sends me the story. Subject to my edits, this will be the first post in her *Quick Paranormal Investigations* blog. There's a headline in huge, bold font, and two subheadings:

### MYSTERIOUS EVENTS PLAGUE HARMONY SPRINGS
Manifestations of Malicious 'Shadow Man'
Has the Ghost of Margaret Alden Returned?

The story starts by reporting the first sightings of a mysterious "dark and wet figure, variously described as a skunk ape or devil," seen near houses along the springs. It then recounts the rock-throwing incidents and broken window that occurred last week. So far, the Harmony Springs police have found no clues to the perpetrators' identity. At none of the properties have footprints or other physical evidence been discovered—leading to speculation by some that the "shadow man" may be supernatural in character. Police Chief Arthur Quick will only say "the investigation is ongoing."

The story then reports on "sightings of a tall blond woman dressed in the fashions of one hundred years ago. This phantom has been identified as bearing an unmistakable resemblance to Margaret 'Maisie' Alden, whose ghost was said to haunt the Alden House on Bliss Bayou for many years." Molly goes on to recount Margaret's life story and to wonder if her appearance might in some way be connected to the shadow figure.

I notice with relief that she never mentions who reported seeing Margaret's ghost, or even that the sighting took place at the Save Harmony Springs community meeting. Nothing at all to link it to me.

The post concludes with the promise that our reporter will continue to investigate, and requests that anyone with information contact her.

I'm smiling as I text Molly back: "Story OK as written. Glad U didn't say 'police baffled.'"

In a moment, I get her reply: "LOL. THAT was in my first draft!"

〜〜

After supper, I'm lying on my bed reading *The Grapes of Wrath* when I hear a noise out in the hallway. It takes me a second to realize that Grandma has opened the locked door and is climbing the stairs to the attic.

I haven't been in the attic since I was a little girl, and even then only rarely. I remember it as huge and cluttered, full of trunks, boxes, furniture covered in bedsheets, all sorts of mysterious stuff— things left behind by generations of Renshaws.

I don't want to disturb Grandma, but I have to wonder what's up. The longer I hear her shuffling around up there, the more curious I become.

Finally curiosity wins out, and I step into the hall. Light streams down the open stairway—along with shadows caused by Grandma moving around. As I climb the stairs there's a breeze at my back. Grandma's turned on an exhaust fan, and it's sucking the cooler air from downstairs.

"Hey, Grandma. Mind if I come up?"

"No. Come ahead, Abby. I could use your help."

Bare light bulbs hang from the ceiling. The attic is musty and, even with the exhaust fan, hot from the sun beating on the roof all day. In a far corner, Grandma is leaning over a stack of boxes. She glances at me and smiles.

"I thought of something I need to give you—if I can find it. With you leaving in a few days, I didn't want to forget."

I step around the piles and join her. I help her shift cartons and old picture frames until she finds what she's looking for—a dusty cardboard box with "Rob's" written in black magic marker. Rob was my dad's name.

She sets the box on the floor and pries it open. "I hope it's in here. This is stuff your father left when he went away to college. He never got around to picking it up. I suppose I should have offered it to your mother, but it didn't occur to me at the time. She probably wouldn't want it anyway."

There's a touch of pain in her voice. She picks through kids' books, Boy Scout badges, coins in a plastic box. "Mostly junk. I guess I ought to try to sell some of this stuff." She hands me a picture and smiles sadly. "You might want that."

In the photo, Dad is about five years old, standing up straight and looking very solemn. It must have been a couple of years after Grandpa died. I don't really want a picture to remind me of how painful Dad's childhood was, but I take it and nod.

"Here it is!" Grandma's holding a little box of worn blue velvet. She opens it and shows me a gold ring. "I gave this to your father when he turned twelve. It belonged to Thomas Renshaw and was passed down through the family. It rightfully belongs to you now."

She places the ring in my hand, and I feel its energy, like a tiny electric current. The gold is formed into leaves and vines framing a cameo: the white-on-black image of a woman with wild hair, holding a torch.

I'm stunned. "Who is she?"

"Part of the magical lore of the Circle. She's the Great Goddess Who Shapes All Things."

"I don't recall reading about her."

"You will. You learn about her after you pass through the advancement rites and become an adept."

*If I ever get that far.* I'm leaving on Sunday and who knows when I'll be back? But that thought vanishes as I close my hand around the ring, imagining how Thomas Renshaw must have worn it when he and the others created the Circle of Harmony. I feel like all the magical power of the Renshaws is streaming through my blood.

"Thank you, Grandma."

Her smile turns wistful. "I've really loved having you here, Abby. I hope you'll come back."

"You *want* me back?"

"Oh, sweetie! Of course I do." She takes hold of my wrists. "I know. I know I've been cranky and...not very nice to you the past few days. Please forgive me. I've been trying to practice the spiritual exercises, and it's brought up a lot of pain—pain that I've repressed for a long time."

"I just thought I'd been such a burden to you."

"No! You've challenged me. But that's good. We all need that, especially when we get older. My life's been all closed up and lonely for so long. But to have you here, my granddaughter, who I love so much, and to be *needed* by you...that's the best thing in the world."

"I need you a lot." My throat is thick. "I wish I could stay here all summer. I really don't want to go to England."

"Then stay."

"Oh, I doubt Mom will go for that."

Grandma considers for a moment. "Listen. Your mom is doing what she needs to do for herself. But she loves you and wants what's best for you. You have to let her know that staying here for now is what *you* need."

"You don't know Mom."

"I know you. You're a lot stronger than you think. You just have to stand up for yourself."

"Well...maybe if you put it that way."

Grandma looks confident—and very happy. "We'll call her first thing in the morning."

Saturday is the Fourth of July. All the businesses on Main Street are closed. The owners, along with just about everyone else in town, are going to Founders Park for the big picnic.

Grandma and I arrive around three. She parks and we unload her minivan, unpacking lawn chairs, a cooler, and a picnic basket stuffed with goodies. Grandma's made sandwiches and macaroni salad. She's baked sugar cookies with red, white, and blue sprinkles. I had a great time helping her.

The park is already crowded. Kids are running on the lawns, throwing Frisbees, kicking soccer balls. The grown-ups mostly hang out in the shade, eating and drinking and laughing.

We set up our chairs in a grove overlooking the river. John and Emily Parker are nearby, sharing a picnic table with family from out of town. We visit with them, and when some of Grandma's other neighbors come by, we share our cookies and are offered hot dogs, chips, and cold drinks.

I leave Grandma chatting with the Parkers and go back to our chairs. I sip a root beer and stare at the white clouds drifting in the blue sky. I feel all peaceful and dreamy.

"So let me get this straight." Molly has walked up in front of me. "You're flying back to New Jersey tomorrow."

"Yes."

"But then you're coming back here after a week?"

"Yes."

"And you chose *that* over going to England for a month?"

"Yes."

Molly grins. "Yippee! You must really like us."

I grin back. "Yes!"

Mom took a lot of convincing. Grandma and I both talked to her three times before she gave in. She finally had to admit how little time she'd actually have to spend with me in London, and I think she began to see how lonely I would have been. She did insist that I fly home this week so we could see each other, but that was something I wanted too.

Molly and I stroll off through the trees, stopping by the park pavilion. The Save Harmony Springs committee has a table set up there, along with churches holding bake sales and raffles. We say hello to Reverend Johnson and to Fiona and Adam. They're collecting donations and distributing information. The petition to extend the Historic District has already been submitted— with over nine hundred signatures. Now Fiona is working with a lawyer on a draft plan for easements to restrict construction. She's going to present it at the town council meeting this Thursday.

As we wander off, Molly tells me there's a rumor Phil Deering has threatened to bring a lawsuit if any easements are passed. "It should be an exciting meeting. Be sure to read the *Quick Report* while you're away."

"I know I can count on you to keep me informed."

"I'd still love to get into Fiona's house and do that ghost investigation," Molly says. "I just can't think of a way to ask her that doesn't sound crazy."

Nothing paranormal has been reported in the last week, and Molly's sounding a little frustrated. She wonders out loud if her *Quick Paranormal Investigations* post might have been an overreaction.

"Don't worry about it today," I tell her. "Let's just enjoy ourselves."

"You're right, I suppose." Molly sighs. "Sometimes I think I'm too obsessive about my blogging. Do you think I might have a personality disorder?"

I laugh at that. "Molly, I've known people with psychological problems. Trust me, you're not one of them."

We walk back toward the river and end up on the path overlooking the swimming hole. It's crowded with kids wading and splashing. Some are running off the dock and jumping in. Others lie on a wood raft floating at the edge of the inlet.

"Wanna go swimming?" Molly asks.

"I didn't bring a suit."

"That doesn't matter around here, girl. I could get us towels out of my dad's Jeep."

For a second I'm actually tempted. I'm wearing cutoffs and a tank top, and I see kids in the water dressed like that. But I'm hesitant, shy. Then I have a moment of panic—the thought of jumping into cold water reminds me of my nightmares.

Molly picks up on it right away. "The idea of swimming here reminds you of your drowning visions?"

"Yeah...freaky, I know. I'm sorry."

"Don't worry about it."

The path takes us down to the edge of the dock. Three guys come up to us, dripping wet. I realize one of them is Ray-Ray. I almost didn't recognize him without his uniform.

"Hello, ladies," he says, smiling. "Coming in the water?"

I hesitate, so Molly answers. "We're gonna pass today."

"Oh, come on. The water feels great." Ray-Ray's looking down at me. Without his shirt, he seems even taller—wider in the shoulders, too.

"Nope," Molly says. "Passing." She starts to walk around him.

Ray-Ray steps right in front of me with a wise-guy smile. "You know, Abby, sometimes a person really wants to go swimming, they're too just shy. They need a little encouragement. Well, I'm here for that. Heck, I could even throw you in, if you want."

*Oh my god, he's flirting with me!* Now my feelings are rushing all over the place. Part of me wants to flirt back, even goad him into throwing me in. But another part of me is terrified.

So I stand there speechless, like an idiot, till Molly steps protectively between me and her brother.

"Back off, Ray-Ray! She doesn't want to go swimming, okay?"

He looks startled and raises his hands. "Okay. No problem."

He and his buddies turn away. They run out onto the dock and cannonball into the water.

I feel awful. "We hurt his feelings."

"Oh, don't worry about him," Molly says as we start walking again. "Sometimes he acts like he's still in junior high."

"He was trying to be friendly. Now he must think I'm a total dweeb."

Molly puts on a mocking, singsong voice. "Somebody likes my brother, Ray-Ray!"

Without meaning to, I smile. "Well, he does look good soaking wet."

Molly laughs. "I think he likes you too. Too bad he's so socially challenged about showing it."

"No, you're just being harsh...Doesn't he have a girlfriend?"

"He *did* have. He went steady the last two years with a girl named Laurel Atkins, a cheerleader, no less. She broke up with him just before graduation. I don't think his future looked grand enough for her."

"What about his future?" I know he just graduated, but Molly's told me nothing about his plans.

"He wants to go into law enforcement like our dad. Become a detective. He's going to Clermont State to study criminal justice. Laurel's going to UF in Gainesville to major in finding a rich husband."

"Whoa! You are snarky today!"

"Well, I'm sorry. I don't like the way she treated my brother. Ray-Ray was good enough for her when he played varsity basketball for two years. Then she dumps him right after senior prom. And the way she did it was so cold-blooded. By text! Ray-Ray tried not to show it, but it kind of broke his heart."

The thought of Ray-Ray with a broken heart makes me sad. "In that case, I agree with you. I don't like Laurel Atkins either."

Two more guys come down the path, shirtless and with towels slung over their shoulders. One of them is Hank, the guy from the kayak rental shop. He smiles at Molly as they pass.

Molly stops in her tracks. "You know, I think I might go swimming after all. Would you be okay with that?"

I give her a teasing look. "Sure. But I can't imagine what changed your mind."

I head back to our picnic spot and find Grandma sitting in the shade. She's been joined by Kevin and Violet. Violet is hard to miss. She's wearing a navy blue dress with white stars, and her long white hair is dyed with red stripes.

"You look just like the American flag!"

She spreads her hands. "Well, of course, dear."

Later I meet up with Molly again, and we buy drinks from the Springs of Coffee guys, who have a table set up near the pavilion. We take our cups over to the basketball court, where a pickup game is on.

Sipping my iced coffee, I watch Ray-Ray run up and down the court. He moves with a loping grace I did not expect. His personality on the court is surprising too. Serious, low-key police intern guy has morphed into a fiery, intense baller. The idea that this guy likes me enough to flirt is doing nice things for my self-esteem. When he scores on a breakaway dunk, Molly and I erupt in cheers.

After dark I sit with Grandma, Violet, and Kevin and watch the fireworks explode in the sky over the river. Across the park, little kids are running around with sparklers. It makes me think of fairies dancing in the woods.

*The enchanted forest.*

This was supposed to be my last night in Harmony Springs. I'm so glad I'm coming back.

〰
〰

When Grandma and I get home, I have to finish packing, since the shuttle is picking me up at eight in the morning. I set out my clothes for the trip, and on top I place the gold cameo ring. It is way too big for my fingers, but Grandma has given me an antique chain from her shop so I can wear the ring around my neck.

Downstairs, Grandma and I have a cup of herbal tea. Then we sit facing each other on cushions in the living room and begin the Daily Ablution.

We've practiced together several times in the past few days. It's interesting. I can sense Grandma's presence as we work our way up the springs. She is more experienced than I am, of course, and at times her influence steadies me. But concentration is hard for her, and sometimes it is me who helps bring her back to center.

This time it's really smooth. We've both had such a happy, relaxing day that the deep harmony is easy to reach. At the end, I open my eyes and see bliss reflected on Grandma's face.

Something flickers at the edge of my sight. My gaze swings to the doorway, and for an instant I think I see Shadow Man.

Then the dark thing is gone. I think I must have imagined it.

Still, I have the feeling he was there watching us, and that he ducked out of sight because I discovered him.

"Something wrong, sweetie?" Grandma asks.

"No, I don't think so."

I look in the hallway, just to be sure. Nothing there.

Grandma asks again, so I tell her I thought I might have seen my evil shadow creature. "But he's not here now."

"Maybe you're anxious about the trip," Grandma says, stretching her arms. "I was always nervous before flying. Still, just to be safe, I could do a banishing ritual for you in the morning. A little protective magic never hurts."

"That would be great, Grandma. Thanks."

I don't think I really saw Shadow Man in the hall. Still, I'm worried and sleepless most of the night.

And it's not just because I'm flying the next day.

## 12. How was Florida? Did you get in any surfing?

But in the morning Grandma does her banishing magic, and everything seems fine.

She fixes me a big breakfast and gives me a hug just before I climb into the van. I ride to Orlando, navigate the airport, get on the plane. I wear Thomas Renshaw's magic ring under my shirt, and it makes me feel strong and protected.

Mom is waiting for me outside the security gate in Newark. She's all smiles and tells me how glad she is to see me. She says I look like I've grown two inches. I assure her I'm still five seven, and that I'm happy to see her too.

Mom and Jim arrived home just yesterday, and Jim is busy catching up on work. So Mom takes me to dinner at my favorite café, on Hill Street in Englewood. I notice dark circles under Mom's eyes and realize she is suffering from jet lag. She tells me a little about Paris and Venice but mostly talks about the new job in London. She's super-excited for the opportunity, but under the surface I feel apprehension. Of course, it's a huge change in her life, and right now she has a million details to handle.

"But London is going to be great," she says. "Are you sure you don't want to come with me next week? It's not too late to change your plane ticket."

"Now, Mom—"

"Seriously, Abby. I don't want to force you, but I *would* like you to reconsider."

"Mom, we settled this."

"I know. I know I said it was okay. But I've had more time to think about it. I'm just not comfortable with you going back to Florida for a month."

This makes me explode. "I can't believe you're bringing this up again. I've got myself all set on it, and now you're jerking me around!"

She looks embarrassed. "Abby, keep your voice down. Let's try to have a rational discussion."

I just stare at her, waiting for her to start the *rational* segment of our talk.

She gets the message. "All right...I'm having a hard time reconciling myself to your being away from me for another whole month. Maybe I'm being silly and overprotective. I know you're almost grown up and that I'm going to be away a lot this year—that is, if you don't change your mind about going to school in London..."

"Not happening, Mom."

"All right." She holds up her hands. "But Florida—Harmony Springs. I just don't get the attraction. Maybe if you'd tell me more about how you're spending your time down there..."

*Well, Mom, I've initiated into a secret magical order. And I'm riding around on a motorbike with a crazy girl blogger, hunting for ghosts.*

*Better skip those parts.*

I take a deep breath. I tell her about working in the antique shop, meeting Grandma's friends Kevin and Violet, and having "interesting conversations about the history of the town." And about making friends with Molly and meeting Fiona and working with them on Save Harmony Springs.

"Fiona's really nice," I tell her. "She said you two were good friends."

"Well, more business acquaintances, really," Mom says. "I forgot you were helping her with that. You sound really passionate about it."

"Yes. It feels really important to help save the springs."

She sets down her wine glass and looks at me thoughtfully. "You know, when you first decided to go down there, I worried that seeing the place again would bring back bad memories—about losing your dad and all. But I think the opposite has happened. Confronting the place has done you good."

"I'm glad you think so too."

"Okay," she says, "I admit I was wrong. And I'll stop haranguing you about it. But I want you to know, I'm really going to miss you when I'm in London."

So now it hits me. This is not about Mom controlling my life, and only partly about her being protective. The other part, maybe the bigger part, is about her missing me. And not just having me around, but having my emotional support.

It sounds all wrong. She's always been the strong one, and me the fragile child leaning on her. Yet right this moment, she looks vulnerable.

"I'll miss you too, Mom. But Harmony Springs is where I need to be right now, just like London is where you need to be."

She smiles sadly and reaches for my hand. "I understand. And I'm proud of you, Abby. You definitely know who you are."

*Really? I do?*

〰〰

That night I dream I'm running through the woods around Bliss Bayou. This time no one is chasing me. Instead the woods are on fire, and I'm rushing to get to Grandma's house because I know she and Violet are trapped there.

When I arrive, the house is burning.

I sit up in bed, gasping, possessed by a hopeless, smothering fear.

I get up and walk around my bedroom, doing stretches and deep breathing. Finally I sit back down and do the Daily Ablution. That settles me enough that I'm able to go back to sleep.

~~~

Next day is Monday, and I meet up with Franklin for lunch. I go to the men's clothing store where he's working, and we walk down the block to the Sweet Shoppe. We both order grilled cheese sandwiches and double-thick shakes. Franklin tells me he's on a diet but is making a special exception in my honor. He has weight issues, but I've long ago given up encouraging him to exercise.

Franklin has sandy hair, bushy eyebrows, and a face that always looks like he's about to say something ironic—which he often is. He pulls out his phone and sends me an email. "I looked up what's playing in London. These are my top five theater recommendations."

"Yeah, about that. I'm not going to England after all."

He slaps his forehead with his palm. "I'm crushed! Mommabot's job fell through?"

"No, she's still going. I just decided not to."

Now he slaps both palms against the sides of his face. "I'm crushed *and* confused. What are you doing instead?"

"Going back to Florida for the month. I know that sounds boring—"

"A *fella* is involved?" He gives me a smirk.

I think of Ray-Ray. "No, not really. That's not it."

"Then Abigail, what *is* your motivation in this scene?"

I tell him about spending time with my Grandma and about working for Save Harmony Springs. Franklin looks skeptical, like he can tell I'm holding back. I actually consider telling him more, maybe explaining about the nightmares and hallucinations and how being in Harmony Springs is helping me work through it all. But anything I say about that will just lead to more questions, and when I mentioned the metaphysical stuff to him last time, he joked about needing to put me on meds. No way I'm going there again.

I hate keeping so much of my life a secret from him. I can see how following the magical path is going to isolate me more and more from my friends.

But I guess that goes with the territory.

"Maybe it sounds lame," I tell him, "but saving Harmony Springs is important to me."

Franklin shrugs expressively. "I suppose Abigail Adams must have her causes. Just remember to duck when the musket balls fly."

I nod sagely. "Excellent advice, which I shall take to heart, Mr. Franklin."

∿

I do the spiritual exercises several times a day now, and they help me stay centered. That's good, because things around the house are pretty hairy. Mom's at the office ten hours a day and comes home exhausted and frazzled. Some mornings she gets up at five o'clock to teleconference with London.

I hardly see Jim, but when I do, he's gloomy. He encouraged Mom to take the UK job, but now it must be sinking in how little she's going to be around. I've never known them to fight, but this week I hear impatience and raised voices whenever they're together.

I work hard to keep things on an even keel, to support Mom in the midst of the storm. I fix some meals, do the laundry, keep the house neat. Mom and I are supposed to go to the movies one night, but she looks so tired that I convince her we should just watch something at home instead.

In the mornings I jog over to the high school and run on the track. I say hi to kids from some of the different sports teams who are working out there, but my friends from track are all out of town. Bridget's at camp in the Catskills, Lori's in California looking at schools, and Karen's on vacation at Long Beach Island on the Jersey shore.

Luckily Karen gets back midweek, so we're able to arrange a night out. She picks me up at six thirty in the Mazda her parents bought for her seventeenth birthday, back in April.

I won't have my license till August. Mom was supposed to take me driving this week on my learner's permit, but it doesn't look like that will happen now.

Karen sits up straight, both hands on the wheel. She drives slowly and talks fast. She's all excited about some guy she hooked up with down the shore. He took her surfing, and they made out late at night on the beach. She says there's a scratch on the roof of her car where he tied on his surfboard.

"How was Florida?" she asks. "Did you get in any surfing?"

"Not exactly. The place I stayed is inland. I did get to go kayaking, though. They have some really beautiful natural springs."

"That sounds cool. Did you meet any guys?"

"Well...sort of. Maybe."

Karen gives me a sly look. "Come on, Abby."

"Well, I did meet a guy that I kind of like. And he flirted with me a little. But it didn't go beyond that. He thinks I'm strange."

"Strange can be devastatingly attractive," Karen declares. "Besides, everyone knows you're strange, Abby. Once they get to know you."

"Thanks. I think."

We go to the Cineplex at the mall to see the latest superhero movie. We both like fantasy and sci-fi, and I haven't seen any of the summer blockbusters yet. The movie is good, though kind of repetitive with earlier ones in the series. As I watch the energy fights and zooming CGI effects, I remember something Grandma said:

"Magic is not like what you see in the movies."

She got that right.

〰

The blaze of the forest fire reflects off Bliss Bayou. I climb out of the boat I'm in and rush across the dock. The Alden house is burning. Fiona is trapped in there, and it's up to me to save her.

But as I reach the edge of the road, Shadow Man looms in front of me, all slimy and shiny black. From his face-with-no-mouth comes the evil voice: "So glad you are here. Now the curse can be fulfilled."

I wake up, rigid with terror. I scan the room. It's all quiet and empty.

The nightmares are getting worse.

〰

Friday afternoon, two days before I'm due to fly back to Florida, I get a text from Molly: "Check out the *Quick Report*. The whole town is going nuts!"

I pull up Molly's blog and see she's got a new post, published a few minutes ago.

Turmoil Erupts in Harmony Springs
Near Riot Outside Town Council Meeting

From what I read, the meeting last night was even wilder than Molly had expected. Fiona presented her plan to require easements on new construction. Phil Deering promised that any easements passed by the town would result in litigation. People from both sides disrupted the meeting repeatedly, and the police conducted some of them out of the hall. The meeting ended with the council referring the matter for legal review. Outside, the police broke up a fist fight and arrested four men and one woman.

But that's not all. During the night, rocks were thrown at several houses on the springs, and a pickup truck was set on fire. People on both sides of the controversy are accusing each other of vandalism and are threatening reprisals. The police have increased night patrols around the springs, but so far there have been no arrests.

Reading all this gives me a weird, prickly feeling—like somehow I'm to blame. Like my leaving Harmony Springs has stripped the town of some magical protection. This feeling links right in to the nightmares in which I desperately try to save people—and fail.

*I have to get back there. I should never have left.*

As nutty as that feeling is, I can't shake it the rest of the day.

〰

Soaking wet and slimy, I stumble into the clearing at the mouth of Bliss Bayou. It's night, of course, and a bonfire has just been lit. Grandma and Violet are tied to stakes in the middle of the pile of fuel. Shadow Man is holding a torch.

He turns to face me.

I lift my arms and attempt to banish him. Energy beams shoot from my palms. He just stands there as the energy disappears into his bottomless blackness.

With a chill, I realize my mistake. He's absorbing the energy—and growing stronger.

I wake up with a gasp. My heart is racing, and it takes a long time for deep breathing to slow it down.

It's five in the morning. I switch on the bedside lamp and do the Ablution exercise.

After that, I'm still too restless to sleep, so I break out my cards. I ask the meaning of my nightmares and about this crazy urgency I feel to get back to Harmony Springs.

The reading is full of chaos and destruction. The crowning card is the Moon. In the picture, the moon hangs in the sky between two towers. A path emerges from a pool in the foreground and twists off into distant hills. Three animals—a wolf, a dog, and a lobster—rear up from the water and look at the moon. The card signifies illusions, fears arising from the Unconscious, perilous mysteries.

For a while I stare at the face of the moon. *What are you trying to tell me?*

Then the moon opens its mouth, and I hear a hollow voice clearly in the room: "Harmony can be restored—if you have the courage to walk the path."

I shiver and blink and come out of the trance.

The picture of the moon is just a picture again.

Was the vision truthful? Can saving Harmony Springs really be up to me?

Or have I just watched too many superhero movies?

## 13. Violet is through messing around

On Sunday I fly back to Orlando.

I'm kind of hoping the shuttle driver will be Timothy again, my friend from Belarus who drove me to Harmony Springs the first time. But it turns out to be some other guy. No matter: this time I can give the driver exact directions to Grandma's house.

And this time, Grandma fulfills my fantasy by rushing across the front porch as soon as the van arrives.

Only instead of a sunny afternoon, the weather is dark and threatening.

In the summer, ferocious thunderstorms often flare up in Florida. I've heard rumblings ever since we got near Harmony Springs. As I climb out of the van, the sky is black, and wind whips the upper branches. Grandma hugs me and says we'd better get inside. I tip the driver and pick up my suitcase and backpack. While we're crossing the front yard, there's a flash and a loud thunderclap. Just as we reach the steps, the rain starts pouring.

We sit in the kitchen and have a cup of tea. Grandma's opened the windows and screen door so we can watch the storm and feel the cool air blowing in. Sheets of rain dance across the backyard. The voice of the storm is a loud hiss, like air escaping a punctured tire. Sometimes it turns into a groan that makes me think of a sick woman in a hospital bed. Once, the thunder cracks so loudly it makes my shoulders jump, and Grandma's too.

We look at each other and laugh. Grandma says, "I'm so glad you're back, Abby."

∼∼∼

I wake from a dream of drowning in black water.

I sit up straight in bed. The room is icy cold, with a strong, swampy smell. The terror starts at the base of my spine and rushes up to squeeze my heart.

He's standing at the foot of the bed, visible in the faint light that comes from under the bathroom door. When I first saw him, he was a flowing black cloud fresh from my nightmares. On the dock at Bliss Bayou, I saw him as a slumping man-shaped thing a head shorter than me.

Now he's six feet tall.

"Yes...I am getting bigger."

I shove down my panic and say as forcefully as I can, "Go away!"

"I too am glad you are back, Abby Renshaw."

I remember the banishing magic. I trace a five-pointed star in the air with my finger. "Be gone from this place and leave us in peace!"

His head moves a little, but that's all.

I stand on the bed and take up a self-defense pose. "I am Fighting Eagle, initiate of the Circle of Harmony. I have tasted the waters of the Five Springs. In the name of our founders, I banish you from this place."

He leans back but does not go. "Abby...your fear comes from within. I am not your enemy."

This attempt to reassure me only makes me more terrified. Desperately I try to think what else I can do. Thomas Renshaw's ring lies on my bedside table. I snatch it up and hold it to my chest. I imagine the Springs flowing through my body. I visualize the Spring of Balance near my heart.

*Stay close to the Fountains, Abby.*

"I am Fighting Eagle of the Circle of Harmony, spirit. I demand to know your true name."

The shadow stiffens, as if I've surprised him. But then he settles again.

"What if I told you my name is Lebab?"

That shocks me. No, it feels all wrong. "I would say you are a liar."

He actually snickers. "What do you really know, Abby Renshaw, about the magic of these springs? In past times, young people sacrificed themselves for the good of all, drowned themselves in the waters as offerings to me, Lebab. *That* is where the power comes from. Magical power is never free. You are but one in a long, long line."

Maybe that's it. It all adds up—my nightmares of drowning, the crazy unrest that's gripped the town, my sense that it's up to me to set things right, my suspicions since I was a little girl that I am cursed...

He holds out his hand to me. "But there is another choice. If you join me, you can live. I will share my power with you, teach you as I taught your ancestor."

My shoulders relax. *If he could save me from dying. If he really is Lebab.* My hand wants to reach toward him.

Then I remember what Violet advised me. I seek the voice of my heart.

My heart tells me this creature is evil, that it's not Lebab. It is a *deceiver*.

This time he takes a step back, as though I've stung him a little. But he says, "I am patient. I grow stronger. I will stay till you are ready."

〜〜〜

We stare at each other for a long time.

Finally I sit down and wrap myself in a blanket.

I'm awake the rest of the night, repeating the Ablution exercise, breathing slowly, trying to stay calm.

Each time I open my eyes, he's there watching me.

Over and over I think about drowning in Bliss Bayou, the agony and blackness. And the pain it would bring to Mom and Grandma. What if I'm wrong? What if he really is Lebab and the way to save myself is to trust him?

Awhile after sunrise, I hear Grandma moving around. I jump up and run into her room. She's just put on her robe.

"Abby. Is something wrong?"

I rush to her side and grip her hand. I tell her the evil entity is back, and I can't make him leave. I try to sound calmer and stronger than I feel. As I'm talking, he follows me into the room, and it's suddenly colder.

"Oh my god!" Grandma says. "I can feel it. It's horrible." She clutches me tight and yells in the direction of the door, "Get out of here! I will *not* let you harm my granddaughter."

I steal a peek from the corner of my eye. He stands in the doorway, not moving.

"Don't worry," Grandma says. "I'll get Violet and Kevin to come over. There are things we can do."

We go downstairs, and even though it's only seven, Grandma telephones Violet. She tells her the spirit that attacked me before has returned, and we need her help. They discuss it for a few minutes. When she puts down the receiver, she smiles at me reassuringly.

"Violet and Kevin will be over in a little bit. We'll make it go away, don't you worry. I think Violet is relishing the challenge."

I glance over at Shadow Man. I swear he now looks *seven* feet tall. I hope he's not too big of a challenge.

Grandma makes breakfast, but I'm too upset to eat. Shadow Man lingers in the kitchen. His silent presence makes me feel desperate, like I'm half a step away from losing my mind. Maybe this is how

Annie Renshaw was driven to drown herself. I try not to think about it.

Grandma and I go out to the back porch and sit on the swing. It feels a little safer out in the daylight, although Shadow Man has followed me again. He waits by the screen door, motionless, like a black hole in the middle of my reality.

Violet and Kevin show up at eight thirty. They carry shopping bags packed with gear—robes, candles, pictures, and a big book bound in leather, with brass hinges. Gold lettering on the cover gives the title: *The Book of Lebab*.

"We're going to do a Profound Expulsion," Violet says. "I am through messing around with this thing."

Grandma looks solemn, but Kevin winks at me. "Don't worry, Abby. When Violet is through messing around, she is *through* messing around."

In spite of my fear, I smile.

They sit down with me in the living room and ask me to describe everything that's happened. When I tell them that Shadow Man is growing, Violet and Kevin glance at each other and seem worried. When I tell them that he identified himself as Lebab and offered to save me, Violet is outraged.

"Don't believe that for a second. The little bastard is trying to confuse you."

I glance over at Shadow Man. He doesn't look so little.

"It's a common ploy," Kevin says. "Malevolent spirits try to trick a magician through lies. In the writings of the Circle, they call such creatures *deceivers*."

"That's the word that flashed in my mind when I asked my inner heart."

"Good," Violet says. "It's very good that you sought advice and received that answer. The Circle of Harmony is protecting you."

They get to work setting up the magical chamber. They arrange pictures of the Five Fountains around the room, with candlesticks and vessels for holding incense and spring water. Violet fills a large silver bowl with water and sets it down on the coffee table.

"I have a task for you, Abby," she says. "We want to drive this creature away from this earth if possible, but especially away from you and your grandmother. I need you to take this bowl outside and sprinkle water at the four corners of the property. Move in a clockwise direction, beginning with the east. As you sprinkle the water, concentrate on the Spring of Balance at your heart and visualize that Spring and the water in the bowl as flowing from the same source. Okay?"

I feel scared, but I nod and pick up the bowl.

"Maybe one of us should go with her," Grandma says.

"No." Violet is definite. "She needs to claim her own power over this. You'll be all right, Abby. Go ahead."

East is at the side of the house that faces the Parkers', so I go out the front door. Shadow Man follows me as far as the porch but stands in the shade, watching. Maybe he's like a vampire, and direct sunlight will kill him.

*Yeah, right.* I wish it were that easy.

I sprinkle the water at the front corner by the road, then follow the property line around to the back. I try to keep my mind focused and my feet steady. I sprinkle the two corners of the backyard, then return to the front of the house.

When I get there, I find Molly climbing off her bike.

"Hey, Abby. Welcome back! I texted you yesterday, but—what are you doing?"

*Panicking, that's what.* I can't have her here now. And I don't know what to tell her.

"What's with the bowl? Why is the Palmer's Books car here? What's going on?"

"Molly, I can't tell you. I'm sorry."

A statement like that is guaranteed to make Molly more curious. "What do you mean, you can't tell me? What is it that you can't tell me?"

My hands are shaking, so I set the bowl on the ground. "Please—"

"Is this some sort of magic thing?" She eyes the bowl.

"I can't tell you!"

Now I've screamed at her. Molly looks stunned, then wounded. "I thought we were friends."

"We are." I speak with slow desperation. "But I can't explain. And I need you to leave—right now."

Molly stares at me. Her mouth turns down, and I can tell that I've really hurt her. She glances at the front door then turns and walks back to her bike. She doesn't look at me again or say a word, just starts up the engine and rides away.

I feel wretched.

As I bend to pick up the bowl, I see Shadow Man standing behind me. I sense that he witnessed it all—my panic and confusion, Molly's pain—and loved every second.

My focus is shot now, but I go through the motions of sprinkling the water at the last corner. When I get back inside, Violet, Grandma, and Kevin are dressed in their robes and are ready to begin.

They place me in the center of the room. Violet walks around and traces the magic circle. All of us visualize the blue waters of the Springs revolving around us.

Shadow Man stands in the doorway. I sense that, once the circle is established, he cannot cross the boundary. He watches us steadily, showing no reaction.

The Profound Expulsion contains long speeches that Violet reads from *The Book of Lebab*. Some of it is in English and some in another language that might be Latin or Greek or something else. Violet calls these parts out in loud, vibrating tones.

We turn and face each of the Five Fountains one by one, visualizing their waters flowing into our circle. Kevin beats a drum, deep and loud like a giant heartbeat. Grandma and Kevin and I repeat certain phrases as we're prompted by Violet:

"We conjure you."

"We command you."

"We abjure you."

"We expel you to the outer darkness whence you came."

With each repetition, I feel the power in the circle growing.

And Shadow Man begins to fade, gradually changing from black to a dim, shallow gray.

Just before the expulsion reaches its climax and he disappears completely, I hear his creepy whisper in my ear: "You should not have involved these others. Now if you do not join me, *they* will suffer and die."

〰〰

When it's over, Violet sits down, all white and panting. Kevin looks concerned and checks her pulse. She rests on the couch while Kevin goes around the room, releasing the energy of the circle. Grandma and I help him pack everything away.

After that, Grandma goes to the kitchen and fixes a fresh pot of coffee. By now Violet looks better—still exhausted, but with a spark of exhilaration in her eyes.

No one asks me if I still see the evil spirit. They all know he's gone.

But now I have a new worry. His last words stick in my mind. When Grandma asks how I'm feeling, I hesitate, then tell them what he said.

"Oh, don't be alarmed about that." Violet waves it off. "Empty threats. They'll try anything to scare you."

"Yeah, the little creep," Kevin says. "Just talking trash as we kicked his ass out the door."

But I'm not sure they're as confident as they're trying to sound.

〰〰

Well, at least he *is* gone for now. The house is filled with peaceful, protective energy. After Kevin and Violet leave, I eat some toast, then shower and change clothes. I ride into town with Grandma to open the shop.

It's a quiet Monday morning. As soon as we're settled in, I work up my courage and text Molly: "Sorry about this morning. Please forgive me."

She doesn't answer right away, so I try again in an hour.

Still no reply. I cringe, picturing the way she looked at me this morning. I've probably ruined our friendship forever.

But I don't know what else I could have done.

I suppose that if you have to keep secrets from people, it's inevitable that you'll hurt them sooner or later.

That's a painful and lonely thought.

## 14. Renshaw and Quick, ghost hunters

Next day, I feel a whole lot better.

It's a beautiful, breezy morning in Harmony Springs, and I'm grateful to be alive. There's been no further sign of my shadow adversary, and the house feels full of light. When I do the Daily Ablution, the visualization is strong and clear. I lose myself completely in the waters of Bliss.

As soon as we get to the antique shop, I send Molly another text: "I'm so sorry about yesterday. Please meet me at 11 at Springs of Coffee. I'll tell you the truth about the magic." I know Molly well enough to be certain that even if she hates me, her curiosity won't let her resist that offer.

Sure enough, in a few moments I get her reply: "OK."

When I walk into Springs of Coffee, I spot her at our usual corner table, bent over her keyboard. Lewis, the barista, takes my order, then motions me closer so he can whisper. "Good luck talking to Molly."

"What do you know?"

He rolls his eyes. "She came in here yesterday with steam blowing out of her nostrils. Your name was featured: 'You think a person is your friend, dot dot dot.'"

"I know. She's got a reason to be pissed at me. But it really wasn't my fault."

Lewis smiles. "Be kind. She's a lot more sensitive than she likes to show."

I collect my nerve and walk over to the table. Molly looks at me with an indifferent expression.

"Hi, Molly."

"Hi."

"Listen. I'm really, really sorry about yesterday. When you showed up, I was in the middle of something—"

"Yeah. Something you wouldn't tell me about, something you didn't feel you could *trust* me with."

"I know. If I hadn't been so crazy, I would have handled it better. You have a right to be angry with me. But I need to know that what I tell you now is going to be kept secret."

Molly looks peeved. "I think I've proven I can be trusted."

"You have. I wouldn't be here if I didn't trust you. I just need to make sure we still have the same understanding—absolute secrecy."

"Okay. We do."

"Good. The truth is, when I saw you yesterday, I was under psychic attack. Remember I told you about Shadow Man? The night I flew back from New Jersey, he showed up in my bedroom. And I needed help to get rid of him."

"Who helped you? How?"

I hold up my hands. "I'm sworn to secrecy about most of it—as in, *a binding oath on my soul*. But I have gotten permission to show you this much."

I unzip my backpack and take out the Circle of Harmony manifesto and "Admonitions to the Candidate." Violet gave these to me before I was initiated, so I figured it was okay to share them. I verified this with Grandma this morning.

"I'm in touch with a small group of people here in town who practice magic—the same kind of magic taught by the founders. These are the papers they gave to people who were interested in joining their secret society."

I hand over the pages. Molly devours them with her eyes. "Wow...holy crap...this is fantastic!"

Lewis calls out when my order is ready. I go to the counter and pick up my food while Molly keeps reading. As I eat, she continues to pore over the documents. Finally she sets them down and peers at me.

"How did you get in touch with them?"

"Well, when I got into trouble my first week here, my Grandma knew someone to call."

"Right. I saw Mr. Palmer's car there yesterday. And he lives with that lady who does the palm reading and stuff..."

"I can't reveal any names. And you mustn't, either. There's a reason it's called a *secret* society."

"I get it. I promise." She glances down at the stack of pages. "This is so cool. Can I get a copy of these?"

"I'll have to check on that. I only got permission to show them to you."

"All right. I understand." She straightens the pile of papers and hands them back to me. "Thanks, Abby. Having you for a friend is amazing."

"So...we're friends again?"

"Oh!" Molly looks surprised, then pained. "I'm such a selfish idiot! Here you were being attacked and terrorized, and I just made it worse. I'm so sorry."

"That's okay. You didn't know."

"Did the magic work? Did they make Shadow Guy go away?"

"Yeah. He's been expelled. At least for now."

"*Expelled*...wow." She considers for a moment. "So, you still think he has something to do with all the trouble in town? And maybe, if he's been expelled, things will go back to normal?"

"Could be. But there's also a chance he'll return."

"God, Abby, you have such an interesting life!"

"Yeah." I laugh. "Sometimes not in a good way."

Molly squeezes my hand. "You're doing fine. I think you're wonderful."

"Thanks." I choke up a little. "I'm so glad you're not mad at me."

Molly brightens. "Listen, I had an idea about how we can get in to investigate Margaret's house..."

≈

When I return to the shop, Grandma is in the back talking with Kevin. They both look at me as I walk in. Their faces are strained.

"Glad you're here, Abby," Grandma says. "We were just talking about you."

I see a bunch of papers spread out on the glass countertop.

"Violet sent you these," Kevin explains. "They're part of the advanced curriculum for the Circle of Harmony. We think it would be a good idea if you studied them."

"Sure...but why so serious?"

They glance at each other. I can sense disagreement. Kevin says, "Violet will explain more in a few days, once she's feeling better."

"Is she sick?"

"More worn out," Kevin says. "The ceremony took a lot out of her. And then she stayed up half the night doing trance work and readings."

"Violet tends to overdramatize things sometimes," Grandma says.

Kevin frowns at her. "That might be fair, Kat. But that entity, whatever it was, felt pretty real—and nasty. At least I thought so."

Grandma nods grudgingly. "I did too."

"So you think he's coming back?" I ask. "Does Violet think so?"

"It's possible," Kevin says. "It's also possible other things may...come up. Violet senses the potential for a lot of weird stuff to happen over the next month. She just wants to prepare you to protect yourself as much as possible."

"And I think that's fine," Grandma says. "Studying is fine. Reading the advanced curriculum is fine if Violet thinks she's ready for it. I just don't want Abby frightened needlessly. You know as well as I do, Kevin, fear by itself can lead to obsession—and worse."

"I'm not frightened," I say. *At least, not too much.* And after witnessing the ceremony yesterday, I'm more convinced than ever that the magic of the Circle is real. If I can use it to protect myself, then the sooner I learn, the better.

Kevin shows me the papers and booklets he's brought. There are scripts for five rituals, called advancement ceremonies. The idea is that the initiate advances to each Spring one at a time and learns its lessons in detail. There are also lectures to study after each advancement ceremony, plus detailed instructions for constructing magic tools. Kevin explains that one tool corresponds to each of the first four Springs—the wand for Love, the dagger for Endurance, something called a seeing stone for Balance, and a cup for Amity.

I notice a page that says a candidate must wait at least three months after initiation before the First Advancement, and a similar time between each of the other rites.

"That's how it was done back in the day," Kevin says. "But in your case, Violet thinks we should accelerate the program."

Grandma lifts her eyebrows at this. She does not look happy.

∼∼∼

On Wednesday Molly and I show up at the church auditorium for the Save Harmony Springs volunteers meeting. Nine other people are there, including Reverend Johnson and Fiona Alden-Gathers, our fearless leader. Fiona looks tired, like she hasn't been sleeping well. Her excellent makeup doesn't quite hide the shadows under her eyes.

But she takes charge of the meeting with her usual aplomb. From talking with her lawyers, she says, she's confident that any lawsuit against property easements will not stand up, especially if the easements are passed by a town referendum. She plans to propose the referendum at the next town council meeting. Meantime, there's been no word of further moves by Phil Deering or the Texas-Brighton Land Company. Fiona thinks it's possible that just the mention of easements may have caused them to reconsider the project.

Reverend Johnson expresses concern about the violence that followed the last town council meeting. Fiona seems a touch defensive about it. She points out that the increased police patrols have been successful in quieting things down. There have only been two incidents of vandalism reported since the big night of trouble last week.

For now, Fiona says, the crucial thing is that we all stay "on message." Whether there is new development or not, our goal is to preserve the quality of life and historical character of Harmony Springs. She discusses plans to seek grants from two different historic preservation societies, with the money to be used to fund Save Harmony Springs and possibly to set up an endowment for restoring historic houses. She asks for volunteers to help her with the grant applications, and two of the older women speak up.

Before closing the meeting, Fiona publicly recognizes Molly and thanks her for her work on the Save Harmony Springs website, which "now has a lot of content and looks great." Molly beams as she receives a round of applause.

When the meeting breaks up, Molly and I go to the front to speak with Fiona. Fiona says she's glad to see me back in town. Molly says she has a new idea for the website.

"We want to show people the history that we're trying to preserve, right? I know you've done a lot of work restoring your own house up on Bliss Bayou. I thought a photo essay about the house would be really effective."

"Oh, well, that's a thought." Fiona considers. "They're not quite finished with the work, though. They're still painting and doing trim on the outside."

"That's okay," Molly says. "Pictures of the workers could be part of the story."

Fiona looks at us cautiously for a second, but then she shrugs. "I guess it's all right. And I think it's a great idea for the website. Let me know when you want to go up there, and I'll tell the foreman to expect you."

〜〜〜

Next day, Molly picks me up at Glenda's Antiques at three in the afternoon. Along with her phone and tablet, she's brought a video camera, a digital thermometer, and an audio recorder with tape cassettes.

"Sometimes spectral sounds are picked up on tape but not other media," Molly explains. "No one seems to knows why."

Molly's been studying paranormal investigations. As we ride her electric bike out to Bliss Bayou, she describes our plan of attack.

"We basically go into each room and turn on all the recording devices. I call out for any spirits to make themselves known. Then we wait and see what happens. As the team psychic, you let me know any impressions you receive. Everything gets logged. Everything."

I'm having mixed feelings about this. The past couple of days, things have been quiet on the occult front, so I'm reluctant to go kicking any hornets' nests. On the other hand, Shadow Man might return at any time, and we still don't know what his connection is with Margaret Alden. If investigating her house can shed any light, then it seems like we ought to try.

Besides, Molly's so enthusiastic. I don't want to rain on her picnic.

Vans and pickup trucks are parked in front of the Alden house. Two guys on ladders are hammering in new boards along the roof line. We walk all around the outside of the house, and Molly snaps a lot of pictures.

"Any impressions so far, Abby?"

Nothing except a queasiness in my gut. "Not really."

"Let's try inside."

We climb the steps to the front porch and go in through the open door. The entryway has a new tile floor and a crystal chandelier. I remember the polished wood columns and the arched doorways with stained glass. Everything looks spotless and lovely. Molly takes pictures as we wander around, soaking it in. We find the painting crew at work in the dining room. Molly tells the foreman we want to stay out of their way, so we'll start upstairs.

We go up the grand staircase to the second floor. There are six bedrooms off the central hallway, and we start with a bedroom in the front. It has a fireplace with a marble mantel, and tall windows to let in the light.

Without furniture, the room feels all brand new and empty. But underneath that I get a sense of a long, unhappy history. My queasiness grows.

Molly turns on the tape recorder and video camera and sets them on the mantel. She steps in front of the camera, then speaks into her phone. "Audio redundancy," she explains.

"Alden house investigation, July 16, 3:52 p.m. Investigator, Molly Quick. Associate investigator and team psychic, Abby Renshaw. We are in the northwest bedroom on the second story." She checks the thermometer. "The temperature is 88 degrees." She raises her voice. "To any spirits who are present, we greet you and ask that you make yourselves known."

We wait five minutes. Nothing happens.

"Any impressions, Abby?"

If anything, the room feels emptier and deader than when we came in. If there are spirits around, my guess is they're avoiding us. "I'm pretty sure there's nothing here."

Molly nods and turns off the recorders. "Too bad we don't have an EMF."

"An EMF?"

"Electromagnetic field detector. It measures fluctuations in electromagnetic energy, which are caused by spirit activity. You can get one for fifty bucks on Amazon."

"Oh."

"Of course, something may show up on the tape that wasn't audible to us. Let's try the next room."

We investigate the other two bedrooms on the west side of the house but get the same results. Molly is starting to look disappointed.

"Ghost hunting takes a lot of patience," she says. "I wonder what this is..."

She's already opened a couple of doors in the hall that turned out to be closets. But this one leads to a narrow stairway.

"Ah, the attic. Let's look up there."

Warm, musty-smelling air flows down the stairs. With it comes a burst of creepy energy that tilts me back on my feet. *I don't think this is a good idea.*

But Molly's already halfway up the steps, so I squish down my fear and follow.

"Whoa! Look at this!" Molly says.

The attic room is dark and stifling. No windows. A little daylight slants in through vents near the ceiling. Molly turns on the flashlight on her phone to get a better look. She searches for a light switch, but doesn't find one. Apparently electric lights were never installed up here.

I fish out my phone and turn on the flashlight. We're standing in a large central room under the high attic ceiling. The room is shaped like a polygon, with eight—no, nine—equal sides. The nine walls are all about five and a half feet high, with a black door in the center of each.

"I don't think they've renovated this part of the house," Molly says, declaring the obvious.

The ceiling has a dim mural, a Victorian-style painting with streams of blue water and figures seated on clouds. The walls and floor have faded drawings and diagrams—glyphs—like I've seen in the Circle of Harmony documents.

"They did magic here," I whisper.

Molly tries to open a couple of the black doors but finds them locked. "Too dark for video," she says. She turns on the audio recorder and logs where we are and what we can see. She notes the time and temperature, then calls out for any spirits present to make themselves known.

My vision starts to spark and blink. I see candles, dozens of them, floating in the air. Then I see they're not floating but set on tall wooden holders that are carved in fantastical shapes. The candles are arranged in a spiral, forming a path that curls to the center of the attic. There I see three people in ceremonial robes, two girls and a young man—the same ones I saw before, in the outdoor circle at the top of Bliss Bayou. This time I feel certain that the girls are Margaret Alden and Annie Renshaw.

The three of them are chanting and gesturing with their wands. As they continue to chant, a shadow rises in their midst. It grows and darkens, and so does my fear.

Shadow Man stands in the center of the spiral. Margaret and Annie and the guy keep chanting and pointing their wands at him. They chant louder and louder, and Shadow Man seems to bask in the attention.

*That's it!* They think they are drawing magic power from him, but in fact he is drawing energy from them.

*Deceiver.*

"Molly, Abby? Are you up there?" Someone is climbing the stairs.

The vision flickers out. My head is swimming, and my knees buckle. I hear Molly speaking my name. She's grabbed my arm to prevent me from falling.

"What are you two doing up here?" Fiona appears at the top of the stairs. "This part of the house hasn't been remodeled yet."

"Yeah, we figured that out," Molly says. "Sorry. Come on, Abby."

I'm a little unsteady as I follow her to the stairs. Fiona is staring at us. In the dim light, her face looks grim.

"We weren't expecting you to be here," Molly says as she leads the way down the steps.

"I just thought I'd check in," Fiona answers, "to make sure you got what you needed."

"Yeah, I think so," Molly replies. "We got some great pictures of the outside. And the hallway downstairs looks fabulous."

Fiona accompanies us back to the ground floor. Molly asks her some questions about the woodwork and glass, and whether she plans to move in when the renovations are finished. Then Molly takes pictures of Fiona standing by a pillared doorway and in front of the staircase.

All the while, I sense that Fiona is afraid. I recall my impression from the first Save Harmony Springs meeting, the thought that the ghost of Margaret Alden meant Fiona harm. I start to wonder if Fiona might be under psychic attack. Maybe she too was targeted by Shadow Man, to drown herself in Bliss Bayou.

Then I think back to the vision I saw in the attic, and another idea comes to me.

Molly thanks Fiona and promises to post the story for her to review in a few days. We say good-bye, and Molly leads me quickly outside to her bike. As we drive away she starts hitting me with questions.

"What happened in the attic? I could tell you were having a vision. What did you see?"

I describe it: similar to what I saw in the outdoor circle, except this time Shadow Man was there, and I could feel him absorbing their energy.

"Interesting," Molly says. "Still, it doesn't tell us what the ghost of Maisie wants, and if she's a friend or foe of the shadow monster."

"I know." I hesitate. "There was one other thing. Just an impression."

"Tell me. Everything should be logged."

"Well, my vision showed people doing magic like a hundred years ago. But I have a feeling people have done magic in that attic recently. Like within the last month."

~~~

Before going to sleep that night, I do my Ablution exercise. When I get to the Second Fountain, Margaret Alden is waiting for me—the middle-aged Margaret, in her black dress and high collar. She looks upset.

"You should not have disturbed my house. You are meddling recklessly. It will only make things worse."

Her intensity is scary. But I get hold of my nerve, determined to get some answers. "I'm sorry. But that *was* you and Annie I saw, wasn't it?"

Her eyes focus far away. "Annie raised the curse. Otis and I merely followed. We were swept up in the current of evil. But our intentions were always pure. We were innocent." She sounds anxious to convince me—or perhaps to convince herself.

"The spirit I saw you with, that's the same spirit that is haunting me now, isn't it? The thing that smells like the swamp and looks like a shadow."

She hesitates, then whispers, "Yes."

"And he is the one causing all the trouble in town?"

Her face is frozen, but she gives a fraction of a nod.

"Someone is doing magic in that attic in the present time, aren't they? Is it Fiona?"

That name seems to snap Margaret out of her trance. "Fiona is in danger. You must protect her."

"How can I protect her?"

"If you can do protective magic, do it for her. And for yourself."
With that answer, she fades away.

My eyes blink open. I want to call her back, but I remember how
Violet warned me against doing that. Conjuring spirits is way above
my grade level.

So I'm left wondering how much of what Margaret told me was
the truth—about Fiona, about herself. Was she as innocent as she
claimed?

Or is she another deceiver?

## 15. He feeds on fear and rage. He is formed of human evil.

The following day, Grandma drops me at Violet's on our way into town. It's been four days since the Profound Expulsion, and Violet is feeling well enough to see me. In fact, Kevin said she urgently wants me to visit.

After stopping in the driveway of the little cracker house, Grandma puts a hand on my wrist. "Remember, sweetie, you don't have to commit to anything you're uncomfortable with. And if you want my advice about something, we can talk."

"Sure, Grandma. I'll be fine. Really."

She's still wary about my plunging too deeply into magical studies, and after what I've put her through—my first few days in Harmony Springs, and again earlier this week—I can understand the concern.

Which is why I haven't told her about all the stuff that happened yesterday.

Which is why I'm all the more anxious to talk with Violet.

When I knock on the screen door, Violet calls out from the kitchen for me to come in. The ceiling fan is going, but the house is stifling. The air smells humid and dusty, with a whiff of incense. Violet's dressed in a wrinkled housecoat, her white and red–dyed hair hanging loose and wild. Her eyes are bleary, like she hasn't been sleeping much.

She motions me to sit down at the table. She sets a glass of ice water in front of me, then sinks into a chair.

"How are you feeling?" I ask her.

"Oh, fine. Fine. Did you have time to read any of the documents I sent over?"

"I read them all. But before we talk about that, there's something else." I tell her about my ghost hunting adventure at the Alden house, the vision I saw in the attic, and my visit last night from Margaret's ghost.

Violet listens, a finger on her lips. At times her eyes grow wide. When I'm finished, she blinks and clears her throat.

"Well, I'm not surprised that our black entity is linked to the founders' families. He certainly feels like he's been here a long time."

"Feels? You mean, he's still around?"

"Yes, I'm afraid so." Her mouth bends into a frown. "And you believe it wasn't just a vision from the past, that magic has been done in that attic recently?"

"That's just a feeling. Not based on anything I saw. Except...Fiona seemed very uncomfortable to find us in the attic. But that may have been nothing. I find it hard to believe Fiona is involved. If she was the one who raised Shadow Man, why have I sensed that *she's* the one in danger? And why would Shadow Man be attacking people who are on Fiona's side, *against* the development project?"

Violet shakes her head, looking as confused as I feel. "It's all murky. Maybe you've been misled about Fiona. Maybe the ghost of Margaret is lying to you. Or maybe Fiona really is in danger, and some other group, working *for* the developers, raised the entity. Fiona could also be doing magic to protect herself from this other group."

"Right...so lots of possibilities. Where do we go from here?"

Violet peers into my eyes, like she's looking there for the answer. Then she nods, as though she's found it. "I'll do a reading. Maybe with what you've told me, I can get a clearer picture."

She heads off to a bedroom and returns in a few moments with a pack of cards. When she unwraps the silk handkerchief, I see it's a different deck than the one she used the first time she read for me. This is more like my own Tarot deck, with pictures on every card.

"You shuffle," Violet says. "Ask the cards to reveal what the entity is and who summoned it."

I touch the cards, and I swear I can feel their magical energy through my fingers. As I shuffle, I concentrate, asking about Shadow Man.

Violet cuts the deck three times, then lays out the cards. She uses a spread I'm not familiar with—five rows of five. I have no idea what the positions signify.

In the pictures, I see anger and confusion, crossed swords and wands, along with images of streams that remind me of the springs. At one end of the top row is the Magician—which, strangely enough, I feel represents me. In the center of the spread is the Devil, who strongly reminds me of Shadow Man.

Violet stares at the reading, her eyes vacant. Seconds tick by. I want to ask what she sees, but I'm afraid to break her concentration.

I gaze at the Empress card in the top row near the Magician. I saw her in the reading I did back in May, the one that told me to come to Harmony Springs. In that reading, I identified the Empress as Grandma. Now I'm reminded that she represents a great goddess, seated beside the Stream of Life. But as to what she means in this reading, I have no clue.

Suddenly Violet stretches out her hand and touches the Devil card. Her whisper comes from someplace dim and far away. "Alden, Renshaw, Feaster...brought him here...unaware of what they did. Now—now his purpose is hidden." She picks up the card, her arm trembling. I realize she's gone into a trance. Her voice rises into an anguished, strangled groan. "He feeds on fear and rage. He is formed of human evil!"

She drops the card, and her wrist thumps down on the table. Her head slumps to her chest. For a moment I think she's fainted. Then, for a crazy instant, I'm afraid she's dead.

But next moment her head pops up, her eyes wild, and she shivers. "What happened? What did I say?"

I repeat her words as best as I can remember. Violet reaches for my ice water and takes a big gulp, which makes her cough. She sets down the glass and shivers again.

She stares at the reading for another minute, then says, "Pick up the cards, will you, dear? I don't think they'll tell us any more."

As I scoop up the cards, I ask her, "Do you know who Feaster is?"

"Who?"

"You mentioned that the entity was summoned by Alden, Renshaw, and Feaster. That might be the young man I saw in my vision with Margaret Alden and Annie Renshaw."

"No idea. It doesn't matter."

"Okay." I fold the silk handkerchief over the deck. "You also said, 'He feeds on fear and rage and is formed of human evil.' Does that make any sense? What does it mean?"

Violet sighs. "Yes. It makes sense. You know from your studies that there are many kinds, or tribes, of spirits: Elementals, of course, and nature spirits. Every tree and flower, every stone has a consciousness that can be summoned and spoken to. But there are other entities who dwell in the spirit world—what we call the inner planes. These entities are remnants of thoughts and emotions. Every thought and dream and desire leaves a trace of energy, and those too are conscious. Sometimes these entities can...coalesce into long-lived beings. And if they come into contact with a magician who traffics with them, they can gain power in this world."

A chill has crept into my belly. This does not sound good at all. But it *does* sound exactly like Shadow Man.

"So where does that leave us, Violet? What can we do?"

"We can prepare ourselves to oppose him. As true magicians, that is our duty." She takes hold of my hand. "Like it or not, you're a focal point for these events, Abby. Fiona might be one too, but you definitely are. We need to get you up to speed as soon as we can."

I just stare at her, unsure what she means.

"I need to ground myself," Violet says. "Something to eat. Then we'll get to work."

<center>~~~</center>

Violet fixes a pot of green tea and some toast, which she eats with blueberry jam. I pour my tea over ice and mix in a dab of honey. While I sip, I scan the Circle of Harmony papers, which I brought along in my backpack. I question Violet about some of the points I found confusing.

The Elementals, for instance, "our friends of the elements"—fire, water, air, and earth—are they really the primal forces of creation?

"Yes," Violet says, "in an esoteric sense."

I'm not sure what that means—or how it fits with what I know about physics. Then there's the question of the magic tools. There is one for each of the first four Fountains—wand, dagger, cup, and seeing stone.

"What exactly is a seeing stone?"

"Don't worry too much about the tools." Violet waves a hand. "They are just symbols for the mental skills that you acquire. At the end of the day, all magic takes place in the mind."

*Magic.* I want to ask her about actually doing magic. From the narratives I've read, it always seems to involve calling on spirits and then raising and releasing power. Before I can formulate my question, Violet goes on.

"At this point, you don't need to make tools in the physical world. After you go through each advancement, you can visualize receiving the tool. This will actually create it on the astral plane, and that's really good enough."

"Hold on. You're talking about me going through the advancement rites? How can I do that? Aren't you supposed to wait several months between each one?"

"Yes, that's the traditional way. But in this case, Abby, we just don't have time. I need to prepare you as best I can to protect yourself."

I'm only getting more confused. "So..."

"So, in the history of the Circle, some magicians have been *self-advanced*. By reading the ceremonies and visualizing them, you can gain a form of advancement. Sometimes guides appear to add their energy and help the candidate realize the full power of the Spring. Hopefully that will happen for you."

This sounds overwhelming. Or maybe it's the grim urgency coming from Violet that's making me so anxious.

"I'd like you to do the First Advancement as soon as possible," she tells me. "This evening, if you're up to it. Then call me tomorrow and let me know how it went."

She's gazing at me with such force that I lower my eyes. "Okay. I'll try."

"Good." She relaxes a little. "Let's walk through it now, so you can practice."

〰〰

At nine that night I go up to my room and close the door. I take out the script for the First Advancement and place it in the middle of the rug. Next to it, I light a candle and burn a cone of incense in a brass bowl.

I walk slowly around the room, tracing a circle of imaginary blue fire. I do the same banishing ritual Grandma used the first time she chased Shadow Man away. Lacking a wand, I use my hand, keeping the middle and index fingers pointed as Violet showed me.

I sit down in front of the candle. I close my eyes and do the Daily Ablution. When that's finished, and I'm feeling calm and strong, I pick up the pages and begin.

> The Advancement to the Eternal Spring of the Love of Truth. Each Spring is a Fountain, and each Fountain a waymarker on the Path of True Magic. These things are secret and must not be taken lightly.

I read the ritual all the way through. Then I set down the papers and stare at the candle. I visualize myself standing at the edge of a circle surrounded by forest. It is night, and the clearing shines with lanterns. People in white robes stand within the circle. I imagine one of them walking toward me—my guide.

Then the vision goes dark, and I'm staring into inky blackness.

I blink and focus my eyes. I'm back in my room, the candlelight fluttering.

I look down at the page and try again.

This time the visualization is sharper—lanterns winking, white robes bright. When my guide approaches, I can see that it's a young woman.

Then it all goes black again.

When I open my eyes, I see only blackness. I blink furiously, shake my head.

*I'm blind.*

I press down the feeling of panic, reminding myself that I'm safe in my room. I force myself to breathe slowly. I stretch out my hand to the papers, the candle.

My fingers touch nothing.

I squeeze my eyes shut, then try looking again.

Blackness.

*Breathe, Abby. Get hold of yourself.*

For a long time I sit blind and alone in the Universe, straining to hold on to my nerve. Eventually I remember the Daily Ablution. I work hard to focus on the first Spring. Although I see nothing, I *imagine* I can see it. My mind settles into the familiar pattern. I draw the waters up from center to center along my spine. At last I feel the waters of Bliss flowing out the top of my head.

I open my eyes and see my room. The candle has nearly burned out.

So much for my first self-advancement.

## 16. Blood on the ground, and watermelon

On Saturdays there's a farmer's market on Palmetto Lane, just off Main Street. Along with booths selling food and local produce, there are tables with crafts and flea market stuff. Save Harmony Springs has a table under an old live oak, between the Friends of the Library and a stand selling watermelons. This morning, I've volunteered to mind the table.

It's sweltering hot, and the crowds are pretty slim. Only a few people stop by the booth, mostly asking if there are any updates. When there's a lull, I take the opportunity to phone Violet and fill her in on what happened when I tried the First Advancement.

I sense from Violet's tone that she's a little baffled, but she tries not to show it. "You did very well, Abby. Always remember: return to the Springs. Nothing can harm you there."

"Yeah, I'm glad I did remember that. So what do you advise now?"

"Hmm. I think you should give it a day or two, then try again. I know it's difficult, but you need to work it through. This is important."

I really don't relish the idea of going back to that terrifying blindness. But there's a stubbornness in me that says Violet is right. Maybe it's courage. Maybe it's dumb foolishness. I hear myself telling her, "Okay."

My fellow volunteer at the table is Jonas Carter, one of the leaders of the Save Harmony Springs committee. He's a quiet, low-key guy in his sixties, but this morning he's agitated. Rocks were thrown at his house last night, the third time he's been targeted. This time two back windows were broken. It was well after dark, but he's had floodlights installed in the backyard, and he got them turned them on in time to see a guy dressed in black running toward the river. He's got a pretty good idea of who it was.

I ask if he reported it to the police, and to my surprise he says no. He has no proof, so what good would it do? This makes me wonder how many other acts of ugliness might have been committed and not even reported.

The morning wears on, and the traffic stays light. I hand out a few leaflets and explain the current status of things—the committee's plan to propose a town referendum on setting up easements. I spend most of the time on my phone, researching what different occult sources have to say about entities like Shadow Man—beings that are formed out of human thoughts and feelings but that take on a life of their own. It's pretty mind-boggling.

I'm startled out of my reading when Jonas suddenly jumps up and yells into the crowd. "I see you smirking over there, Casper Wainwright! I know it's you and your boys who threw rocks at my house."

Everyone stops dead still. Then one figure moves. A scrawny old man walks toward us from across the street. He's dressed in shorts and a dirty tank top. His skin is like wrinkled brown leather, and his long hair and beard are white. He stares at Jonas with a face full of hate.

"Don't go accusing folks you know nothing about! You and your uppity tree-humpin' friends."

"Oh, I know all about you. We'll catch up with you ignorant crackers sooner or later."

Casper smirks at that. "Ignorant crackers? You candy-ass turd!"

I can't believe this is happening.

Jonas rushes around the table and stands chest to chest with the other man. "Call me that again."

Casper sneers. "I just said what you are, you candy—"

He doesn't get to finish. Mild-mannered Jonas Carter has sucker-punched him hard in the nose. Casper staggers back and lands on his butt.

He looks shocked for a moment, blood flowing out of one nostril. Then he shakes himself and climbs to his feet. A crowd has gathered around them now, and someone yells, "Git him, Daddy!"

Casper Wainwright charges, tackles Jonas, and drags him to the ground. Now they're rolling around on the pavement, heaving, punching each other. Everyone just stands there, looking stunned— except for a few guys who are cheering them on.

*What should I do?* I saw a police car parked at the barricade at the end of the lane. I should run down there and find a cop. But I shouldn't leave the booth unattended. And Jonas is not exactly in a good place to be watching it right now. I take out my phone and call 911. I'm connected to a dispatcher in a call center somewhere. She asks for my name, then asks me to spell it, then asks for my exact location, then asks me to describe what's happening.

"Two white-haired old men are rolling around on the ground punching each other. For god's sake, please send the police!"

As she's patching the call through, a Harmony Springs officer shows up and pushes her way through the bystanders. She yells at the two men to stop, then drags them apart. Both guys have scrapes on their arms and knees. Casper has blood dripping out of his nose and a swollen eye. Jonas is trembling like he can barely stand. I hurry over to prop him up.

The officer asks how this got started. Casper and several people from the crowd start answering. While the officer shouts for them to be quiet, Jonas frees himself from my arm. Before anyone knows what's happening, he's picked up a watermelon from the booth behind us. He lifts it over his head, staggers forward, and flings it at Casper.

In best-case scenarios, a watermelon is not much of a weapon. Here, the officer sees it coming and blocks it with her arm. The watermelon drops and smashes on the street.

"That does it!" the officer says. She forces Jonas' arms behind his back and puts him in handcuffs.

Casper, still bleeding, taunts him. "This isn't over, you puny wimp."

"Don't come near my house, or you'll regret it!" Jonas tells him.

"That's enough out of both of you," the officer says.

She uses her walkie-talkie to call for backup. Casper's two sons, skinny guys in T-shirts and caps, examine their dad's wounds and congratulate him on the fight. Jonas stands next to me, shoulders slumped. He looks bewildered.

"I don't know what came over me," he says.

But I think I do. *He feeds on fear and rage. He is made of human evil.* Hot and sweaty as I am, I shiver.

Two more officers arrive shortly after that and take statements. Everyone agrees that Jonas threw the first punch. Casper insists on pressing charges, so the officers have to arrest Jonas. They lead him away, still wearing the handcuffs and looking confused. I ask, and the first officer promises to see that Jonas gets medical attention at the station.

I go back and sit behind the Save Harmony Springs table. I wonder if I should call someone on the committee to tell them what happened. But it's twelve thirty, and more volunteers are due in about twenty minutes to help pack up. The farmer's market is already starting to shut down, and the lane is almost empty.

For a while I stare at the smashed watermelon on the pavement, wondering who's going to clean it up. Finally I realize no one is, so I get two paper plates from a food stand and use them to scrape up the mess.

I have the feeling it's going to be another bad Saturday night in Harmony Springs.

Unfortunately, my psychic antenna is right on target. Grandma and I hear police sirens several times after sundown, coming from both sides of the river. The atmosphere seems full of urgency, anxiety, and helplessness. Bad things are happening, and there's nothing we can do.

Around eleven, I'm lying in bed reading when I hear what sounds like a gunshot close by. I jump up and go into the hallway, where I meet Grandma.

"That sounded like it came from the Parkers' house," she tells me, pulling on her robe.

I follow her downstairs to the kitchen. Out the back window, through the woods, we can see the porch light is on over at the Parkers'. Then I spot another light—someone is moving around the backyard with a flashlight.

"I better call," Grandma says.

We go to her study, and she gets Emily Parker on the phone. From the side of the conversation I can hear, I gather Mrs. Parker is upset.

"Have you called the police?" Grandma asks her. Then: "No, don't worry, Emily. I'll hang up and call them right now."

She explains to me as she's pressing the buttons. "Someone threw rocks. John chased them off with his shotgun. He fired both barrels."

Grandma puts in the call and explains what's happened. Ten minutes later, we hear the police siren coming up the road. It stops at the Parkers'. By now we've put on clothes and shoes. Grandma takes a flashlight from the kitchen drawer, and we head out the back door. Now that the police are here, she's confident no one will shoot at us. With only John Parker and his shotgun patrolling the property, she wasn't so sure.

I'm still not sure. But Grandma is determined, so I figure I'd better go with her.

When we get to the Parkers' backyard, they are talking with a heavyset police officer. It takes me a second to recognize that it's Chief Quick himself, Molly's dad. He's none too happy to see us.

"Ms. Renshaw," he says, "please go back home. You two really shouldn't be out here."

"I just want to make sure my neighbors are all right," Grandma answers.

"I assure you, everything is under control," the Chief says.

The Parkers do look perfectly fine. A second officer is moving around the back of the yard, examining the ground with a flashlight.

"Hey, Chief," he calls. "Fresh blood back here."

Chief Quick grimaces in Mr. Parker's direction. "Well, John. Seems you hit something."

∿<br>∿

When Grandma and I get to the shop Sunday afternoon, my phone has three texts from Molly.

From last night: "OMG. Tell me what happened at the Farmer's Market!"

From this morning: "Tell me what happened last night at the Parkers!"

Then later: "We need to talk. Call me."

I touch the phone icon, and she answers on the second ring. "Hey, I'm at the police station. Things are poppin'."

"Like what?"

"I'll have to call you back."

An hour and forty-five minutes later, she rings me. "Whoosh. I'm outside the station. This has been a *really* interesting day."

"Talk to me, Molly."

"Right. They arrested Cletis Wainwright—one of Casper Wainwright's sons. Get this: he has a gunshot wound in the upper thigh and buttocks. And the footprint in the mud at the Parkers' house matches a shoe they found in his closet. They're running a match on his blood now. That should be back from the lab tomorrow. Now get this: in the same closet they found not one but two black nylon bodysuits with ski masks. Sound like anyone we know?"

"Shadow Man."

"Exactly. My dad thinks Cletis and his brother, Wendell, are responsible for most, if not all, of the vandalism."

"Wow..."

"I know."

I remember Casper Wainwright fighting with Jonas Carter yesterday. I also remember him speaking up loudly at the first Save Harmony Springs meeting and cursing at me and Molly when we carried the petition around.

I say to Molly, "So the Wainwrights are *for* the developers and *against* Save Harmony Springs. That would explain the vandalism against Jonas and the other anti-development people. But what about the vandalism on the other side?"

"Yeah, my dad has two theories. One, someone on the Save Harmony Springs side took reprisals. Or two, the Wainwrights got carried away and acted indiscriminately. That family is bad news. They've been in trouble before. And they've had other feuds with their neighbors."

"I guess that makes sense."

"Yup. So far Cletis has refused to say anything to implicate his brother, but Dad thinks if they work on him long enough, he might crack. Right now they got Cletis over at the hospital, picking the birdshot out of his butt."

"Eww."

"I know. Serves him right, though. Anyway, Dad's hoping he can put both Cletis and Wendell in jail for a while. And that *that* will calm everybody down."

"That would be great." I'm turning it all over in my mind. "What about Mr. Carter? Will this help with his case?"

"It might, since he allegedly started the fight because he believed the Wainwrights vandalized his house. He's at home now, released on his own recognizance till the hearing."

"That's good. I feel so sorry for him."

"Yeah, fill me in on what happened. I only know what the officers told me. How did it start?"

I give Molly the details, up to and including the watermelon.

"That's so strange," she says. "What could have made Mr. Carter go off like that?"

"I don't know."

"Evil spirits?"

"Well, it's a theory."

"Yeah," Molly says. "But if the Wainwrights *are* behind all the Shadow Man sightings, I don't know where that leaves our whole paranormal investigation."

I've been thinking that too. Except it sure wasn't the Wainwrights who I saw expelled by magic from Grandma's house or who made me hallucinate about drowning over and over. I just say to Molly, "I don't know."

"Right. We'll have to look for new leads on that," she says. "I gotta go nose around some more. Don't forget about tomorrow."

"Dinner at your house."

"Right. See you, girl."

~~~

I was invited for dinner at the Quicks' house because Molly's mom wanted to meet me. I'm flattered. I'm also in a quandary as to what to wear. I have to admit this is mostly because Ray-Ray will probably be there. I finally decide on my yellow sundress, and to leave my hair down. In the Florida heat, I've taken to wearing it up or in a ponytail with a baseball cap, but today I brush it out and wear it loose past my shoulders. I even consider eye makeup but decide against it.

*Let's not get carried away.*

Molly picks me up at the shop, and we ride over on her bike. The Quicks live a few blocks from downtown, in a neighborhood of mostly brick houses with small front lawns and wooded backyards.

We go around to the back and enter the kitchen. Molly introduces me to her mom, Beatrice, who is energetically chopping vegetables. Mrs. Quick is large and heavyset, a lot like her husband. Unlike Chief Quick, she has a wide mouth and sparkling, amused eyes. She feels like the kind of person who never lets anything trouble her too much.

Mrs. Quick wipes her hands on her apron and then shakes my hand. "Welcome, Abby. Molly's told us a lot about you. I'm really glad she's found such a good friend right here in town."

"Thanks. It's been great for me too. Can I help you fix anything?"

"Well, you *are* different from Molly. Cooking's not exactly her strongest interest."

"I can cook," Molly says, handing me a glass of ice water. "I'd just rather serve up tasty writing."

Mrs. Quick laughs, rolling her eyes. "You girls go hang out in the cool. Dinner will be ready in a half hour. Hopefully the boys will be home by then."

The "boys" are Chief Quick and Ray-Ray. I know from talking with Molly that they're not always able to get off work according to schedule. The Harmony Springs police force has only eleven employees—nine sworn officers and two administrative staff members. It's not easy for them to police the whole town 24/7. Molly's told me that a lot of rural towns in Florida have given up their police forces in favor of contracting for law enforcement from their county governments. It's an ongoing challenge for Chief Quick to keep the town satisfied with the force, and to keep his job.

Of course, all the recent troubles have made that harder.

We chill out in Molly's room, and she updates me on the latest news. The police were never able to get Cletis to incriminate his brother, but it turned out not to matter. They pulled in Wendell for questioning and let him drink from a bottle of water. Then they told him they were going to match the DNA on the bottle to evidence found in one of the black bodysuits. That was enough to break him down. With Wendell under arrest, Cletis confessed too. In exchange for reduced sentences, they admitted to every act of vandalism the police tossed out at them.

"So you think they really did them all?" I ask.

"Apparently."

"But what about the fact that they never left a trail or footprints?"

Molly shrugs. "Most of the time they worked from a canoe and cut right back to the water. As my dad said, they're backwoods boys and pretty crafty about not leaving trails when they don't want to. Cletis only got careless and left prints after he was shot."

Chief Quick and Ray-Ray show up at ten minutes before six, right on time. Ray-Ray smiles like he's happy to see me. He goes to change out of his uniform. Chief Quick flops down in a recliner and puts his feet up. It's the first time I've ever seen him relax.

He asks after my Grandma, and if I've seen John and Emily Parker since Saturday night. I tell him I haven't. Then I ask if Mr. Parker will be in any trouble over the shooting.

"None at all," he says. "He was defending his property. The law's completely on his side."

Mrs. Quick brings in a plate of sliced carrots and celery with dip, and Molly follows with a pitcher of iced tea. They both go back to the kitchen, and then Molly returns with a bottle of beer, which she hands to Chief Quick.

"You can take off your shoes, Dad," she says. "Abby won't mind."

"Don't do it, Arthur!" Mrs. Quick calls from the kitchen. "We have company."

Chief Quick had started to reach for his laces. Now he actually looks sheepish.

"Please go ahead," I tell him. "I really don't mind. You should be comfortable."

He smiles. "Molly, I like your friend."

Ray-Ray comes in, wearing shorts, flip-flops, and a tank top. He plops down in a chair and reaches for the iced tea.

"I see Dad's shoes are off already," Ray-Ray says. "You know what that means, Abby?"

"Uh. No."

"You're officially no longer a guest. Now you're part of the family."

They all smile at me, and it touches something in my heart. "Well...that suits me fine."

Awhile later we go into the dining room. Ray-Ray and Molly help Mrs. Quick carry in the dinner. There's grilled pompano with lemon, rice garnished with almonds and orange slices, green salad, and homemade cornbread. Everything is light and really tasty.

As we're eating, Mrs. Quick asks me about my mom and her job, and what it's like in New Jersey. She's impressed that Mom works for an investment bank, and even more that I turned down a chance to spend a month in London. I explain that Mom would have needed to concentrate on her work, and besides, I'm really enjoying Harmony Springs.

They ask about my plans after high school, and I admit I haven't decided on anything yet. "Unlike Molly and Ray-Ray. I really admire how they have their acts together."

I get a little smile from Ray-Ray for that, and it makes me braver. "So, there's something I've been wondering about," I say. "If you don't mind my asking, where does the name Ray-Ray come from?"

They all think that's funny. Mrs. Quick says, "Well, we have Molly to thank for that. His real name is John Raymond. But when Molly first started to talk, she would only call him Ray-Ray. For some reason, it stuck. He's been Ray-Ray ever since."

"The first of many, many problems Molly has caused in my life," Ray-Ray says with mock gravity.

He's capable of irony. Who knew?

Of course, so is Molly. She looks solemnly at her brother. "I'm so sorry...John Raymond."

## 17. True magic is never an easy road

The following night, I gather my courage and try the First Advancement ceremony again. Same result—the lights go out just as I'm getting started. At least now I know what to expect, so I'm less afraid. I immediately begin visualizing the Fountains and am able to work my way out of the darkness and back to my room.

I try again two nights later. Same, same.

Apart from these snags on the inner planes, the week is perfectly quiet—no fights, no spooks, no vandalism. The July weather is broiling and humid, with a few afternoon thunderstorms cooling things off. I help Grandma in the shop, work on my summer reading assignments, continue my magical studies. After all the fear and turmoil, Harmony Springs feels unnaturally peaceful. I wonder if the arrest of the Wainwright brothers might really have brought a close to the troubles.

Or is this the lull before another storm?

Molly is wondering too. While she's published two posts in the *Quick Report* about the arrests and people's reactions, her *Quick Paranormal Investigations* blog is at a standstill. With no further sightings of Shadow Man or Margaret's ghost, I've had no news for her. She's asked for copies of the Circle of Harmony papers that I showed her, and permission to publish them, but Violet said definitely not.

Molly texts Friday morning and asks if she could maybe interview a member of the Circle. We're at the shop, so I ask Grandma about it.

She just laughs. "No way that's happening."

I text Molly back: "Sorry. No interviews. They feel secrecy is necessary."

Molly: "OK. I knew it was a long shot."

Molly again: "Do you think we've heard the last of Shadow Monster?"

Me: "I wish I knew."

Molly: "If there are no more sightings, does that mean it really was the Wainwrights all along? Nothing supernatural about it?"

Questions along those lines have been needling me too. Did Shadow Man inspire the Wainwrights to act for him? Does he ever actually manifest on the physical plane? Is it possible that Grandma and Violet and Kevin only sensed his presence because they were picking up on *my* perceptions? Does he even exist outside my insane imagination?

Molly: "I didn't mean to imply your visions weren't real, Abby."

She tactfully does not say, *Maybe you're just delusional, Abby.*

I text her back: "I understand. You'd like proof it's not all in my head."

Molly: "Independent verification would be helpful."

All in my head...what was it Violet said about this? At some level, hallucinations and true visions are just different forms of the same thing.

But where does that leave me—apart from confused?

〜〜〜

When I talk to Violet that afternoon, she's not happy that I still haven't gotten past the First Advancement. The full moon is coming in another week, and she's convinced something extreme is going to happen. She decides to take matters into her own hands and arranges for Kevin to drive me over to their house the next day on his lunch break. She warns me not to eat any lunch myself until after we've met.

So Saturday at noon, Kevin and I leave the shop and go out to his beat-up old RAV. It's got silver tape holding the seats together, and it smells like the inside of the bookstore.

After buckling his seat belt, he turns to me. "Listen, Abby. I wanted to talk to you about something. I'm not quite sure how to bring it up."

He seems worried, and my intuition tells me it concerns Violet. "Is Violet okay?"

He looks at me sharply. "You *are* quick on the uptake. Actually, I'm worried about her. Ever since we did the expulsion at your grandmother's house, she's been going really hard." He hesitates, then starts the car and backs out of the parking space. After putting it in drive and stepping on the gas, he continues: "Violet and I have done magic together for over forty years. But I've never seen her like this—up at all hours of the night, constantly brooding. I'm afraid she might have gotten obsessed with banishing this entity."

*Obsession.* It's warned against in the Circle of Harmony writings. It seems that, if you practice spiritualism and magic, it's easy to mistake your own emotions and hang-ups for real forces, and to become lost in constantly focusing on them—or fighting them.

"But the shadow entity is real. You said so yourself, Kevin."

"Yes. I definitely felt that way at the time. But after we expelled him, it seemed to me that he was truly gone. And this week in particular, since they arrested the Wainwright boys, it seems that things have calmed down around here, that the evil influences have waned. What do you think?"

"I've been wondering that too, honestly. But Violet doesn't think so?"

Kevin shakes his head. "Violet doesn't think so. That's why I'm worried that it may have become an obsession. I've tried to talk to her about it, but she's sure I'm wrong. She's always been more advanced in occult work than me. I don't know, maybe I *am* wrong. I certainly don't want to interfere with any magical work that you two need to be doing—especially for your protection. I don't know what I'm asking here, Abby. Except maybe that you keep an eye on her, try not to strain her too much?"

"Wow. I'll try, Kevin. I wish I were more advanced so I could...know better what to do."

"I know. It's never an easy road, is it? Most people think that if magic was real, they could just solve all their problems. But true magic...they have no idea how hard it is."

≈

When we get to the house, Violet greets us at the door. She looks tired, but actually better than when I saw her last week. Her hair is combed out, and the creases around her eyes less pronounced. She's wearing her magical robe—deep purple and sewn with gold and white badges of the sun and moon.

We sit in the kitchen, and she chats with Kevin while he fixes a sandwich to take back to work. When he's ready to leave, he kisses her on the cheek and begs her not to tire herself.

Violet watches him walk out the door. She has a fond, wistful expression. "Isn't he a beautiful man?"

Well, I haven't really thought about that...

"Forgive me." Violet laughs. "It's just that, for a woman my age to have a lover like Kevin—I feel so lucky. Do you have a boyfriend, Abby?"

"Nah. No one special."

"Well, you should. Find one as soon as possible. Love is good for you. It's good for your health, and it's good for your magic. Take chances. Love recklessly. If your heart gets broken, that's all right. Cry, patch it up, and do it again...well, that's my advice on *that* subject."

"Okay. I'll remember it."

"Good. Now, regarding your little problem with the First Advancement. This is what I'd like to do..."

She proposes doing the ceremony with me. She'll play the parts of both the guide and the guardian, which will be a little awkward. But she feels this is the best way to get over the hump.

I suspected she had something like this in mind, and I thought I was prepared to go through with it. But now I'm not so sure.

"Are you game?" Violet asks me.

I feel a little grimace fly across my face. "Well, are you sure it's necessary? I mean, that it's really this urgent?"

Violet looks deflated, then suspicious. "You've been talking to Kevin?"

There's no hiding stuff from Violet."Yes. He seems to think that the shadow creature is not so much of a threat anymore. I think my Grandma feels the same. I'm just wondering if we need to be in such a rush."

"Hmm." Violet rubs her chin. "We all have different levels of sensitivity, Abby. Kevin and Kat perceive things on the spirit planes more clearly than most people, but I think less strongly than you and I. I'm pretty psychic; you are even more so." She stares into my eyes. "What have you noticed lately in the atmosphere around town?"

"Well...since they arrested the Wainwright brothers, it's all felt really peaceful."

"Yes. Now, I want you to look inward. Close your eyes and ask your intuition: *why* has it seemed so peaceful?"

I hesitate, then shut my eyes. As soon as I center my attention on my heart, the answer is there waiting for me. "Because the evil forces have gone underground. They're building."

"Exactly as I see it," Violet says. "It makes me think the entity is gathering itself—or else someone is containing it by magic to build its power. Either way, it does not bode well."

The truth I sense in her words is frightening. I try to make my voice sound brave.

"Okay. I guess that makes up my mind, then."

∽

Twenty minutes later, I'm standing at the door of Violet's spare bedroom, where she does her magic. I'm barefoot, dressed in a plain white gown, a copy of the First Advancement in my hand.

When Violet calls out from inside that she's ready, I knock three times.

The door creaks open, and Violet's face appears. "Who seeks entry to the chamber of our hidden knowledge?"

"I am an initiate of the Circle of Harmony, and I seek advancement to the First Fountain."

"By what secret moniker are you known?"

"In the Circle, I am called Fighting Eagle."

Violet pulls the door wide and bows to me. "You are welcome, Fighting Eagle, dear friend and magician. Herein is the circle of the First Advancement to the eternal Spring of the Love of Truth. Each Spring is a Fountain, and each Fountain a waymarker on the path of true magic."

The room is smoky-sweet with rose incense. Votive candles, arranged in a circle on the floor, make a shivering light. Across the room on a small table is a gold cup. Above it hangs the blue and rose painting of the First Fountain.

Violet sprinkles water on my forehead and traces a design with her finger. Now I am purified.

"Come."

She takes hold of my sleeve. We walk slowly in a clockwise direction on the outer edge of the circle of candles. After a few paces, we stop. Violet turns to me and pulls on her hood. Now she is the guardian.

"Unless you know my name, you cannot pass."

I look down at the paper and read aloud: "Ignorance is your name. Deceit is your name. The deceit of the sensual world. The ignorance of those who perceive only surface appearances. By my love of knowledge and of truth, I banish you."

I point my hand, index and middle finger extended. She bows and steps back.

Now Violet removes her hood and takes hold of my sleeve again. I follow her as we circle the room three times. At last we stop in front of the painting.

"Behold you the Spring of the Love of Truth," Violet intones. "A true magician gives herself to the full power of this love, for it is the motive force for your magical work. The soul is a cauldron of will and desire, ever seething and bubbling. Only by binding your desires to the love of truth can you nourish your magic and your life."

She lifts the gold cup to my lips.

As I drink, pulsing waves of light and darkness seem to wash over me. When I look up, I glimpse another figure standing at Violet's shoulder. She wears a white blouse and a straw bonnet. Her hair is in black ringlets, and her dark eyes are luminous. She smiles at me.

I blink, and she's gone.

〜

After the ceremony, I help Violet clean up the magical chamber. Rather than tired, she appears elated by the ritual. I'm relieved that it hasn't strained her. I tell her about my glimpse of the dark-haired young woman.

"I've seen her before. I think she's Annie Renshaw."

"That's good. Very good," Violet says. "As I told you, spirits sometimes appear to lend their energy to the candidate. I think we've made a breakthrough here."

〜

I have plenty to think about on the long walk back to Grandma's shop. I ponder what it means to be a true magician—to bind the desires of your soul to the love of truth. It means being different from other people. It means giving up what everyone else finds safe and certain.

Maybe Kevin and Grandma are right about Violet. Maybe she has gone off the deep end. Maybe I'm insane to believe in her perceptions.

Then I remember the other thing Kevin said—true magic is never an easy road.

But easy or not, insane or not, it's my road.

I think I know that now.

## 18. Her fashion sense was retro, that's for sure

That night, I sit down in my bedroom to perform the Ablution.

She is waiting for me in front of the First Fountain, her dark eyes shining. She feels kind and friendly, but I've learned to be careful.

"I am Fighting Eagle of the Circle of Harmony," I tell her. "What is your name, spirit?"

Her lips bend in a smile. "In the Circle I am called Enfant de Lune. But you know me by another name."

"Annie Renshaw."

"Yes, my friend, my courageous Abigail. I have been trying so hard to reach you. Now, at last, your aspiration to the love of truth has broken through the barrier."

"What do you want with me?"

"To do you service. The evil force is indeed growing, as it did before in that life when I was Annie Renshaw. I have knowledge that can help you."

As she speaks, she and the fountain start to shimmer and fade.

"Do not be concerned," she says. "This vision is passing. But the connection between us is firm now. I will contact you in a different way."

~~~

In the morning, after my run and shower, I dress as usual in shorts and a T-shirt. When I pick up my phone from the night table, I notice there is a message.

*Weird.* There is no service out here in the woods, and I'm positive there were no texts when we got home last night. I open the message. It gets a whole lot weirder.

From Unknown: "I will meet you at your coffee shop at 11 this morning. - Annie"

I squeeze my eyes shut and look again. I try pinching myself, closing the message app, rebooting the phone. Each time, the message is there, real as any text on any screen.

Well, she said she would contact me in a *different* way...

I think about telling Grandma or calling Violet. But I'm not sure just what to tell them. If I have totally broken the insanity barrier, they'll find out soon enough. I decide I'll just show up at Springs of Coffee at eleven and see what happens.

At five to eleven, I tell Grandma I'm going to run over to the coffee shop.

Literally, I *run* over to the coffee shop.

As soon as I walk in, I see her sitting at a corner table. She's wearing the white blouse, the long skirt, and lace-up shoes. Her sun hat sits on the table. She meets my eyes and smiles.

"What can I get you, Abby?" Lewis asks me.

"Oh. Uh, just a bottled water for now."

I pay for the water and clutch it as I walk toward the ghost of Annie Renshaw. I gaze into her calm, luminous eyes as I slide into the chair.

"I see you got my message," she says with amusement.

"How did you..."

"I was given to communicate with you in a way you would find meaningful."

She looks totally solid and real. Either I am *deeply* hallucinating, or...

"The power of your magic, from the ritual yesterday," she says. "It allowed me to open this channel, to manifest for a short time in your world."

"But why? Why here?"

"So you would know for certain that I am real. That all these things are *not* just your imagination."

I don't know what to say. Maybe I should take out my phone and try a picture.

"I cannot stay long, Abigail, so listen closely. The evil spirit is strengthening. In the sky, the planets Mars and Saturn are moving into alignment. The full moon under this aspect is a time of great potential. All of the occult forces will converge on that night. It was the same 103 years ago, when I—when I passed out of your world."

"When you drowned in Bliss Bayou?"

"Yes, Bliss Spring. Even now, it hurts to remember. *He* was to blame. We thought we could control him, make him do our bidding. But all the time, he was subtly growing stronger, gaining control over us and our magic. There were three of us—Maisie, Otis, and myself. We were so young...and foolish. When I realized what was happening, I tried to stop it, put an end to our conjuring of him. But it was already too late."

"What happened? The story I heard is that you drowned yourself."

She looks startled. "No—"

"And that you put a curse on the Renshaws."

She smiles sadly. "I promise you, I did not. There *is* a curse on our blood, but it is none of my doing."

Fear is crawling through me, my mind lurching back and forth between believing her and not.

She presses my wrist—a completely human touch. "I understand. It can be hard to know whom to trust. I could tell you who made the curse. But you will believe it better if you hear it from another. If you want to know the truth, go to the Harmony Springs cemetery late at night. Find the grave of Otis Feaster. He is buried near the northern wall, under a cypress tree. Pour a libation on his headstone—beer, if you can manage it. Otis was fond of beer. Then call him. Speak your name, Abigail Renshaw. Say you are a relative of Annie, who loved him very much and loves him still, and that you need his knowledge. He will come to you, I am sure. He will tell you what occurred."

She withdraws her hand. "Do you have the courage for this?"

I'm not sure I do, but I swallow and nod my head.

Annie smiles, like she's proud of me. "I knew you would. You have a valiant heart. Now, two more things I must tell you. The true name of the dark one is Raspis. Knowing this will give you some power over him. But when you confront him, as I think you must, do not cast magical energy at him. That is a mistake. It is given to his kind to absorb all human power sent against him. Instead, cast your power into the Springs. By the forces of Harmony Springs, he can be vanquished." She stares hard into my eyes. "Now say his name, so I know you'll remember it."

"Raspis."

Annie nods. "It is well."

I've been totally focused on listening to her, but now suddenly I'm aware of my surroundings again. Some people have entered the shop. I hear them talking to Lewis at the counter. Instinctively I turn to look. One of them is Molly.

I turn back to Annie.

She's vanished. I'm all alone at the table.

*Great.*

〰〰

I pick up my water and go over to the counter.

Molly says, "Hey, Abby. I didn't expect to see you here this early. Who was that girl you were with?"

I stop, my legs turning to stone. "What? You *saw* her?"

"Sure. Black hair, dressed in white. Awfully hot for that long skirt."

I'm almost tongue-tied. "You—you really saw her?"

"Yes!" Molly looks over at the corner, puzzled. "I didn't see her leave, though...Hey!"

I've grabbed her wrist and am pulling her toward the back of the shop. We go down a short corridor, past the kitchen, and out the screen door that leads to the porch. There are a few outdoor tables there, but at the moment the porch is empty.

I face Molly and grip both of her arms. "Listen, Molly. This is really, really important. Did you just see me at the corner table talking to a young woman with black hair and dressed all in white—like in *clothes from a hundred years ago*?"

Molly's face has a "why are you asking such stupid questions" look. "Yes. I. Did.... Who *was* she?"

I sigh, incredibly relieved. *I am not insane.* "That was the ghost of Annie Renshaw."

Molly's mouth drops open. Her eyes grow wide. "Oh my god! Oh my god! OH MY GOD!" She squeezes both of my upper arms and starts squealing and jumping up and down. "I saw her! I saw her! Annie Renshaw! Oh my god!" She stops jumping. "Wait! Independent confirmation!"

She grabs my wrist and hustles me back into the shop. Lewis has just finished taking an order. "You want some lunch now, Abby?" he asks.

"Lewis," Molly says. "This is important. Did you see Abby over at the corner table a little while ago, sitting with another girl?"

"Sure."

"And how was she dressed?" I ask.

Lewis snorts. "Well, her fashion sense was retro, that's for sure."

"Eeeeeee!" Molly's bouncing up and down with excitement.

"What's this all about?" Lewis says.

I take Molly's arm, and we head back toward the porch. "Thank you, Lewis! You are a great friend!"

"Jeez," Lewis calls after us. "You know, she never ordered anything. Kind of rude."

Outside, Molly turns to me. "What did she say? Tell me everything!"

"I will. But the first thing is, I need your help tonight. Are you up for some more ghost hunting?"

## 19. Just a night in the graveyard

Back in Jersey, I knew kids who would sneak out of the house at night. Sometimes they went drinking or to make out. Sometimes it was just for the thrill. Nothing very bad. Typical teenage behavior.

Never done it myself, of course.

Until now.

I hate deceiving Grandma. But I can't exactly tell her I'm going down to the cemetery at midnight to raise the dead. How could I explain *that* in a way that wouldn't worry her? Besides, Annie Renshaw made me feel like it's my job to deal with this.

Luckily I have my reliable sidekick.

At 11:35, I'm sitting on the front porch steps, waiting for Molly. I'm dressed in jeans and a long-sleeved button-down shirt. Molly's warned me to cover up—there are mosquitoes and other nasty critters abroad at night.

The moon is white, floating high over the trees. Waxing. Full in another five days.

*When all the forces will converge.*

I see Molly's bike gliding up the road. That quiet electric motor does come in handy. I trot across the front yard to meet her. I have my backpack, with a candle and some matches, a water bottle, and a flashlight.

"Hi, partner," Molly whispers.

"Did you have any trouble getting out?"

"Naw. My parents go to bed early. And Ray-Ray's working the night shift. They're letting him drive a patrol car on his own this week. I brought the beer. I hope Otis likes Budweiser."

I laugh as I climb onto the seat behind her. "I'm sure it will be fine."

As we motor down Bliss Road, Molly tells me what she's learned about Otis Feaster. "I found his obit—1918. Not a lot there; he died too young. Like Annie and Maisie, he was a child of one of the founders. He grew up on the west shore, near the head of the springs. He enlisted in World War I and was killed in France, age twenty-four. His body was shipped home for burial."

"So it fits, that he could have been friends with Annie and Maisie."

"Oh yeah. It fits."

The cemetery is near Founders Park, a few blocks north of Main Street. The road is narrow, lined with oak trees draped in Spanish moss. Old clapboard houses stand back in the shadows. Part of the cemetery is bordered by a broken-down chain-link fence, part by an old brick wall. Molly turns into the entrance, past a historical marker, which it's too dark out to read.

"Where did Annie say he's buried?" Molly asks softly.

"Near the north wall, under a cypress tree."

We cruise down a winding path of hard-packed sand and crushed dead leaves, past gravestones and monuments, some well-tended, some overgrown. Black branches reach over us like twisted fingers. Maybe it's my imagination, but I can sense all the spirits sleeping around us.

Molly stops the bike at the edge of the path. The moon has passed behind some clouds, so we take out our flashlights. The graveyard is dark and very quiet. We hunt until we find an ancient, leaning cypress, and beneath it a granite headstone.

Otis Feaster
1893 – 1918
Corporal, US Army Expeditionary Force
Killed in action January 15, 1918
Beloved Son of Peter and Susannah
*Nobilis Sol*

"I wonder what Nobilis Sol means," Molly whispers.

"Probably his magical name."

"Oh, wow."

I light a candle in front of the headstone and ask Molly for the beer. She opens the can and hands it to me. Then she takes out her phone.

"Okay to record this?"

"Um...I guess so. But don't say anything once I start."

"Okay." She takes a step back from the grave. "Ready."

I pour the beer three times over the top of the headstone. Annie told me to use my own words, so here I go: "I call upon the spirit of Otis Feaster, buried in this place. I am Abigail Renshaw, relative of Annie. Annie loved you very much in her lifetime and loves you still. Please show yourself to me, Otis, Nobilis Sol. I have great need of your knowledge."

I pour him three more drinks and wait.

Nothing happens. Except...I have a feeling that Otis is here, that's he's gathering himself.

For the first time, I feel afraid.

I gasp, and so does Molly. A car has turned into the cemetery. It catches us for a moment in the headlights.

"Oh, shit!" Molly says.

The car pulls slowly around the path, pins us in its headlights, and stops. I see now that it's a police car.

"Damn," Molly says. "We're busted."

A guy in a uniform gets out of the driver's seat. A tall guy. He shines a flashlight on us.

"Right! I should have known it would be you two," Ray-Ray says.

~~~

Ray-Ray walks over to us, keeping the light on our faces. "What do you think you're doing? Don't you have any sense at all?"

"Wait." I'm shielding my eyes from the light. "What's wrong? We haven't broken any laws, have we?"

"No? How about creating a disturbance, for starters? Guy across the street called us. With everything that's gone on lately, you're lucky somebody didn't get scared and start shooting."

"I hadn't thought of that," Molly admits.

"Yeah. Two underage girls messing around a graveyard after midnight." His flashlight beam finds the beer can in my hand. "And drinking, too."

"No!" I protest. "That wasn't for us."

"Yeah, right. Get in the car and don't give me any more arguments."

"But..." I look at the grave. *I need to stay and talk with Otis.*

"Better not argue," Molly says. "When he's like this, he won't listen to reason."

"Reason?" Ray-Ray barks out. "Just wait till morning, Molly. Dad will give you some reason."

I've never seen Ray-Ray so angry. Reluctantly Molly and I pick up our stuff and follow him to the car.

"I need to get my bike," Molly says.

"No, you don't." Ray-Ray's opened the back door and is waving us in. "You can *walk* over here tomorrow and pick it up. If it's still here."

"Damn, Ray-Ray," Molly says. "You're such a pain." But she gets in the car as ordered, and I slide in beside her.

Ray-Ray climbs into the driver's seat and switches on the radio. He reports that he's in the cemetery and that the situation is in hand. He catches my eye in the rearview mirror. "Just a couple of idiot kids fooling around. I know them both. I'm going to drive them home."

"Okay on that, Ray-Ray," says the voice on the radio. "Check in when you've dropped them off."

"Ten-four."

He puts the car in gear and drives slowly up the cemetery path. Molly and I sit silently in the back seat, fuming.

I'm thinking: *Well, this is typical. The first time I ever sneak out at night, and I'm picked up by the cops.*

And I'm thinking: *This has spoiled my big chance to talk with Otis. How am I going to contact him now?*

And I'm thinking: *Ray-Ray is now certain I'm an idiot. But he doesn't understand what I'm going through. How could he?*

I catch him looking at me again in the mirror.

"Can I ask what you thought you were doing out here?" he says.

I grimace and shake my head. What can I say?

"Research," Molly answers. "Paranormal research."

"Oh, right." Ray-Ray turns onto the road outside the cemetery and accelerates. "Abby, I expect this kind of stunt from my sister. But I would have hoped you would be a little more sensible."

Now he's making me mad. Who does he think he is, my father? "I think Molly's one of the most sensible people I know," I tell him. "She's smart, she asks questions, and she decides things for herself. What's more sensible than that?"

"Why, thank you, Abby," Molly says. "I think all of that about you too."

Ray-Ray shakes his head. "Wonderful."

He drives past Main Street, in the direction of the Quick house. I thought he'd take me home first, but he's dropping Molly off instead. I guess he wants to get her home as soon as possible.

When he pulls up in front of the house, he turns to Molly. "I'll watch you go in. Try not to wake Mom and Dad."

"You're not going to tell them, are you?" Molly says.

"Not this time. But only because I don't want to upset them. You pull something like this again, Molly, you're on your own."

"Thanks, bro." Molly grins. "You are the best." She climbs out of the car, then leans in with the door still open. "I notice you're dropping me off first. Do you want Abby to sit in the front seat with you?"

Ray-Ray's jaw drops. He glares at her and points sharply to the house.

"Okay, okay." Molly smirks. "Just a suggestion."

She shuts the car door quietly and steps up the walk. After opening the front door, she gives us a little wave before going inside. Ray-Ray sighs and steps on the gas.

"I'm sorry," I tell him. "I didn't mean to put Molly in danger. I mean, from scared citizens with guns."

"Something like that could have happened," he says. "Or you could have been attacked by some maniac. Harmony Springs is usually pretty safe. But two girls roaming around alone at night aren't exactly safe anywhere."

"I hear you."

We're both quiet as he drives back through town and turns up toward the springs. I'd like to explain, to make him understand why it was so important to go to the graveyard. But how can I? All the occult stuff is completely outside his version of the world.

In other words, he's *normal.*

Must be nice.

We ride past the last houses on the outskirts of town. As we turn onto Bliss Road, I glimpse a figure in the headlights. A man walking on the side of the road, in a striped jacket and straw hat—like men wore a hundred years ago.

In a second, the headlight beams pass him, and he's gone back into the dark. Ray-Ray jams on the brakes.

"Did you see him?" he asks. He grabs his flashlight and leans out of the car, sweeping the beam through the woods behind us. "Who's there?" he yells. "Harmony Springs police. Come on out."

I see no one. After a few seconds, Ray-Ray switches off the light and gets back behind the wheel. "Some vagrant hiding out in the woods," he says, not sounding too certain. But he drives on. "Another example of why you need to be careful at night."

"Dressed kind of strange, wasn't he?"

"Yeah." He's quiet for a bit, then: "Listen, Abby. I'm sorry I called you an idiot kid."

"That's okay. You had a reason."

"I worry about Molly. You'd think, growing up in a police family, she'd be more cautious. But she just charges into things, never thinking about what trouble she might get into."

"Yeah. She's pretty brave." Come to think of it, so is he. I'm impressed with how he's driving around on patrol without a gun, doing the job of a regular cop.

"You're like her best friend ever," Ray-Ray says. "But she also looks up to you."

"Really?" I hadn't noticed that.

"Sure. Coming from New Jersey and all. You're like a breath of sophistication in our little hick town. Anyway, my point is, it would be nice if you could sort of...keep an eye on her?"

"Well...I can try."

"I know it's hard to rein her in. Believe me."

He pulls around the last curve and stops in front of Grandma's house. "Listen, if you *do* get into trouble—with or without Molly— you can always call me. I'll give you my cell number, okay?"

"Sure." I take out my phone and punch in his number as he says it. "Thanks."

He turns on his flashlight and walks me to the front door. I take out my house key and place it in the lock. He switches off the light then and stands still in the moonlight.

For a second I have the crazy idea he's going to lean down and kiss me goodnight. Instead, he pats me on the arm. "Take care of yourself, Abby."

"I will. Thank you."

I go inside and close the door—as quietly as I can.

This night did *not* turn out as I expected.

~~~

I walk slowly up the stairs and across the hall, trying to step so the floorboards don't creak. I get to my room and shut the door.

Well, my first time ever sneaking out of the house: Busted by the cops, but at least I didn't wake Grandma.

I brush my teeth and change into my nightclothes. Then I sit down on the floor and do the Ablution exercise. When I finish, I open my eyes, and my head jerks back.

The man in the striped jacket and straw hat is standing in my room, luminous and gray like a ghost in a video. He looks...confused.

"This is Annie's room," he says. "But who are you?"

I'm not completely surprised. Since spotting him in the woods, I figured we would meet sooner or later.

"Are you Otis?" I speak gently, so as not to frighten him. *Don't frighten the ghost, Abby.*

"Yes...you are her relative, the one who called me?"

"That's right."

Otis takes off his hat. *He's a well-mannered ghost.* "Why did you summon me?"

"Annie suggested it. She said you could tell me what happened to her—how she died."

A look of awful pain comes over his face. "They killed her."

"Who did?"

"Maisie and the shadowy one."

"Raspis."

"Yes. That was his name. We believed we could compel him to do our bidding, but in the end, he turned us into slaves. He wanted us to bind the Spirit of the Springs. On the night of the full moon, Annie rebelled. She tried to prevent the rite. But Raspis was already too strong. He channeled his power through Maisie and broke Annie's will and mine. He cursed Annie and all of her blood. Then they made Annie walk out on the dock and throw herself into the spring. The noise of the splash brought me back to myself. I ran and jumped in to try to save her. But the current was swift and the water cold. I never...her body was found downstream three days later.

"Oh, my sweet Annie." He stares down at his fists. "I loved her so. We all three were in love, in love with each other and with our magic. But it all went so wrong."

I can feel his torment in my own heart. But I have to know the rest. "What happened after that? Why was Annie blamed for the curse? Why did everyone believe she drowned herself?"

He looks at me, bereft. "Because I failed her. When I crawled up on the bank, Maisie was there, and Raspis standing behind her. She was changed, totally in his power—or his power in her. They took away my will once more. They made me lie, say that Annie had become hysterical for no reason and thrown herself into the spring. After that, I gradually regained myself. Maisie still wanted me, but I could no longer abide her presence. The very sight of her was loathsome—she and her evil companion. I slipped into a kind of madness. I drank. I drove my car aimlessly. I tried more than once to drown myself. Then our country entered the war. I found a merciful death from the German guns. As I lay in the mud, bleeding, I felt Annie come and take my hand. She led me to the place of peace."

I stare at him, unable to answer. Finally I say, "I'm so sorry, Otis."

"He is back again, isn't he?"

"Yes."

"I do not know how to conquer him. I would tell you if I did."

"Annie said that the only way was to use the power of Harmony Springs. But I don't know how to do that."

Otis lifts his ghostly eyebrows. "Yes, that might serve. If you could channel the power of the Springs themselves. If you could raise Lebab..."

## 20. ...And a day in the emergency room

After Otis goes back to the graveyard, or wherever ghosts go when they're not summoned to the mortal world, I'm totally exhausted. I go to bed and sleep like I've been drugged. I have no dreams that I remember.

But I wake up tense and fearful. I sense all kinds of psychic momentum, everything converging, focusing on Bliss Bayou and the coming full moon. I know I'm destined to play a role, but I have no plan. If that's not pressure enough, I sense that whatever happens will determine the rest of my life—or even if I *have* a rest of my life.

I go for an extra-long run. As usual, this calms me and helps me feel centered.

When I get home, I trudge up the steps all sweaty and panting, and open the front door. Grandma is lying in the hallway at the bottom of the stairs.

She looks up at me, grimacing with pain. "Abby, I fell."

"Oh no!" I kneel beside her. "Grandma, what happened?"

One leg is underneath her, the other stretched out. That leg is bruised and swollen around the ankle. I've seen sports injuries, but nothing like this. Grandma is almost weeping from the pain.

"I fell on the steps. I think I broke something."

"What should I do?"

"Call 911. Get an ambulance."

I rush into her study and punch in the call. They take the information and promise to send an ambulance right away. I tell them Grandma is conscious and that her ankle is swollen. They suggest I get her to sit up, then elevate the ankle and put ice on it.

I go back to the hall and tell Grandma what they said. I help her sit up on the bottom step.

"Never mind the ice," she says. "Listen. I was coming down the stairs, and...*it felt like someone pushed me*. I think our evil entity is back."

"Oh god."

"I want you to go up to my room. My dagger is in the top drawer of my dresser. Bring it to me. I'll try to cast some protection around us." As I start up the steps, she adds, "Abby, be careful!"

Climbing the stairs, I half expect Raspis to jump out at me. I don't see him, but now I think I can feel his presence, smell him. On my guard, I walk into Grandma's room. I find her dagger and bring it to her.

She takes it and tries to sit up straight. She starts to chant, but her voice is weak and broken. Finally she gives up and hands me the dagger.

"You'd better do it, sweetie. Draw a circle of protection around us. Trace pentagrams at the four directions. Then command all evil to be gone."

I push down my fear and stand straight. I trace the circle and pentagrams, visualizing them as blue fire. I point the dagger at the ceiling and then at the floor: "I command all evil spirits to leave this place." Then I add, "I know your true name, Raspis. By the power of the Springs, I command you to be gone!"

Grandma stares at me, dull surprise mixed in with the pain. I visualize blue protective water flowing up and filling the space around us.

After thirty minutes, the ambulance arrives. The med techs, a guy and a woman, check Grandma's vital signs and examine her leg. They explain they're going to take her to the emergency room, and suggest I get her insurance card and anything else she might want.

I run upstairs and get her purse. Then I go into my room and take my backpack and phone. By the time I get downstairs, they've wheeled in the stretcher and are lifting Grandma onto it. She grunts a little as they lay her down.

I ride in the back of the ambulance and Grandma holds my hand most of the way. She asks if they can give her something for the pain, but they tell her she needs to see the doctor first. The hospital is seventeen miles away, on the outskirts of a town called Weaver. Even with the siren going, it takes almost twenty minutes to get there.

They wheel Grandma through the emergency room and into a curtained waiting area. A nurse takes her insurance card and ID, then comes back a while later and has her sign papers. Grandma asks again for pain meds. The nurse says they'll be with her as soon as they can.

Forty minutes later I'm at the front counter complaining, begging them to send someone to help my Grandma. I try to channel my inner power, and it seems to work. Or maybe they just finally get around to seeing her. A doctor and nurse come in and check her. The doctor's an Asian woman and the nurse is a tall man with blond hair and a beard. They give Grandma a shot for the pain, then wheel her down the hall for an x-ray.

By now I'm feeling woozy. While Grandma is having her x-ray done, I find the vending machines and get a protein bar and a coffee with cream and sugar. I take them into the waiting room. The place is filled with injured and suffering people wearing hopeless, dazed expressions. Two TVs are playing with the sound up high, perhaps to drown out any moaning or complaining. It feels suffocating, so I go outside and sit on the edge of a planter.

I'm sticky with sweat and I smell awful, but at least the nourishment ramps up my blood sugar. For the first time, I have a chance to think. My brain zeroes in on what Grandma said: someone tried to push her down the stairs.

Raspis said that Grandma and Kevin and Violet would have to die. Now he's trying to make good on the threat.

I take out my phone. There's a text from Molly, asking if I'm okay after last night, and what's our next step in the investigation. I leave that for later and call Violet. She picks up on the second ring.

"Abby, I knew it was you. Is everything all right?"

I blurt out that we're at the medical center in Weaver and that Grandma may have broken her ankle or foot. That Raspis pushed her down the stairs.

"Slow down, dear. Who is Raspis?"

I get a grip and start from the beginning. I tell her about my meeting with Annie at the coffee shop and my conversation with Otis last night.

"Abby, that is fantastic," Violet says. "I knew you were gifted, but what you've accomplished here is terrific."

"It's not terrific, Violet! We're in danger. All of us."

"Calm down, dear. I understand about the danger. But you've given me much more to go on. Knowing the entity's true name helps a lot. And I was right about the full moon. But Mars conjunct Saturn—I never would have thought. I never was much of an astrologer..."

"What are we going to do?"

"I'm not sure yet." She pauses. "You just take care of Kathryn. Get her home safe, then throw a lot of protection around the house. Leave the rest to me."

"Violet, be careful. Remember what Annie said: you can't cast magical energy at him. He just soaks it up."

"Yes, I understand. Don't worry about me, dear. And go ahead with the Second Advancement. You're doing fine."

She hangs up, and I stare at the phone shaking in my hand. I'm more worried than ever. Violet does not seem to understand how grave this is.

Or maybe she does, and she's just trying to keep me from losing it.

〰

I think about calling Molly but decide I'd better go check on Grandma. I find her in another curtained alcove, where they've parked her to wait for the x-ray results. She's in less pain now and talks to me about her fall.

"I was halfway down the stairs when suddenly I sensed someone behind me. Then I felt a push in the small of my back. If I hadn't been able to grab the banister, I might have broken my neck."

I take a deep breath and tell her about my talk with Annie Renshaw, and what she said about Raspis—and how it's all coming to a head.

When I finish, Grandma's face is white. "It really is true. He said he would kill us all, and now...Abby, this is bad. We have to warn Violet."

"Already did. She said I should just get you home and then surround the house with protection."

Grandma nods vacantly, a look of shock on her face. She reminds me of a child who's been traumatized. I squeeze her hand. "Try not to worry, Grandma. It will be okay."

*I hope.*

〰

Three hours later, we're camped out in a waiting room in a medical building across from the hospital. The x-rays showed a small fracture and some ligament tears. The ER doctor fitted Grandma with a walking boot and prescribed pain meds. She also said Grandma needed to make an appointment with an orthopedist.

Since Grandma won't be able to drive for at least two weeks, she asked if she could get an appointment today. It took us both a lot of begging and haranguing at the front desk, but finally they got the orthopedist to agree to fit her in at two thirty. We had lunch in the hospital cafeteria, and then I wheeled Grandma across the parking lot and up an elevator.

My phone chirps, and I see another text from Molly—just a row of question marks. I step out into the hallway and call her.

"Where you been, girl?"

"Weaver. At the medical center."

"*What!?*"

I explain how my day has gone.

"Oh my god. Is your grandma okay?"

"She's in a walking boot. We're waiting to see a specialist now."

"How are you going to get home?"

"I'll have to call a taxi."

"No, you won't. I'll get Ray-Ray to pick you up."

"Oh no. Don't bother him."

"He'll want to. He doesn't start work till eight. He's just sitting around."

"No, really."

"Abby, *he'll want to*. What time is your grandma's appointment?"

"Two thirty."

"Text me the doctor's name. We'll be there."

〜〜

The orthopedist sees Grandma at a quarter to three. He says the x-ray looks pretty clear but suggests it might be worth having an MRI, just in case. Grandma says she'd rather not. She really just wants to go home. The doctor frowns but agrees to skip the MRI, provided that Grandma calls him if the pain gets worse, and that she makes another appointment for next week. Grandma starts to argue about that, but I tell her not to worry: I'll get her here next week no matter what.

Outside the doctor's office, we find Ray-Ray sitting in the waiting room.

"You didn't have to come all the way out here," Grandma says.

"Not a problem, Miss Kathryn." He looks at me. "Molly wanted to come too, but my truck only seats three. She offered to ride in the bed, but of course that's not happening."

"I really appreciate this." I'm afraid my voice sounds weepy—I'm so glad to see him.

"Not a problem."

We take Grandma back to the ER and trade in her wheelchair for a pair of crutches. After making sure she's okay on the crutches, Ray-Ray goes out to get his truck. I walk beside Grandma, ready to support her as she slowly makes her way through the emergency room.

Ray-Ray's pickup is about ten years old. The body's a little battered, but the motor hums solid and steady. I slide into the front seat, and Ray-Ray helps Grandma get in beside me. She's grimacing a little but says she's okay. Ray-Ray gets behind the wheel and drives out of the parking lot.

"Sorry it's not a luxury ride," he says.

I use his line: "Not a problem." I'm self-conscious about sitting close to him, given the state I'm in. "Sorry I didn't get a shower this morning."

He laughs and pats my knee.

As we near Harmony Springs, it starts sinking in for Grandma how she's going to be incapacitated for a while. "I don't know how we're going to manage, Abby. Do you think you can run the shop by yourself, maybe just a few days a week?"

"Sure, Grandma. I can walk into town or maybe get a ride from Molly."

"You don't have your license yet?" Ray-Ray asks.

"Just a learner's permit. In New Jersey you have to be seventeen."

"Can you drive your grandmother's car?"

"Yes. She's given me a couple of lessons."

"You'll be all right, then," he says. "Just stay off the county roads. Given the circumstances, I'm sure your friendly local police will give you a pass."

Ray-Ray pulls the truck up close to Grandma's front porch. We help her up the steps and into the living room. She sits on the couch, and I prop up her foot on a pillow.

Ray-Ray asks if there's anything else he can do. Grandma says no, but wouldn't he like something to eat or drink?

"No, thanks. I ought to go. I'm sure Molly will be out to see you both later today or tomorrow. But if there's anything I can do, please don't be shy about calling me."

He looks at me when he says that last part. I think about how I've liked him for a while...but never so much as this moment.

~~~

When Ray-Ray's gone, I walk all over the house, checking out the psychic energy. Then I take Grandma's dagger and cast a circle of protection around the entire house, raising up as much power as I can.

With that done, I go upstairs and finally get my shower. I stand under the hot water for a long time. Tears come, and I let them, sobbing until they're all gone.

After that I fix us dinner, then clean up the kitchen. I help Grandma with a sponge bath and make up the couch with sheets and pillows. She's going to be sleeping downstairs for a while—no way she's making it up to her bedroom on those crutches.

Grandma and I are both worn out, so at nine thirty I head up to bed. I tell Grandma I'll leave my door open so she can call me if she needs anything.

After undressing, I'm too tired to read or even to do the Ablution exercise. I collapse into bed.

But my brain is too wired for sleep. I'm scared, and it feels like no one can help me. Grandma is injured. Mom's on the other side of the ocean. Violet is trying, but I'm afraid she's out of her depth. Molly and Ray-Ray care about me, but they live in a different universe.

Whatever is coming with the full moon, I'm going to face it alone.

## 21. I'm a zombie sponge of magic power, that's what

Violet stands in a sphere of light. Thick gray smoke pours into the light from below. She wears her purple robe and holds a wand—a stout old woman with wild hair, her arms raised in the broad sleeves. She is chanting.

In the smoke, a black figure appears—Raspis. He grows and grows until he stands twice Violet's height. She lowers her wand and speaks words of power. Blue light rises, like shimmering water. For a moment Raspis vibrates, engulfed in the light.

Then from his chest comes a silent explosion of blackness. It knocks Violet back and she falls, hitting her head. She doesn't move.

I sit up in bed, gasping.

*Violet is dead.*

Was it only a dream? *Was it?*

〰

I scarcely sleep the rest of the night. In the morning, I still don't know if what I saw was real or just a nightmare. I go downstairs and call Violet's house.

No answer. I leave a message begging her to call me back. A little later I try Kevin's cell, but again there's no answer.

After fixing Grandma breakfast, I tell her about it. She looks stricken with fear, but she doesn't know what to suggest. Maybe I shouldn't have told her. I don't *really* know if anything's happened to Violet, and Grandma's got enough troubles.

We just sit there in the living room, not eating, not talking.

After nine, I try Violet's and Kevin's numbers again. Still no answer. Grandma suggests I call Jenny Nesheim at the craft shop. I get Jenny on the phone. She hasn't seen Kevin and is wondering if she should open the antique shop and the bookstore or just leave them locked. I tell her to leave them locked for now, and ask her to call me if Kevin shows up.

I ask Grandma if maybe I should drive over to Violet's house to check on her. Grandma seems anxious about letting me go, but then decides that I should.

I leave her with her foot propped up and make sure that the phone and some books and a pot of tea are within reach. I take her car keys and go out to the Honda Odyssey. It's much bigger than the car I used for driver's ed, but compared with everything else, my fear of driving it is miniscule. I back slowly out of the driveway and head down Bliss Road toward town.

When I get to Violet's house there is no one home, and Kevin's car is gone. More than that, I sense a dark, creepy energy—like I might expect to feel at the scene of a murder. I'm shuddering as I get back behind the wheel.

I drive down to Main Street. Luckily there's almost no traffic, because I have to pull in and out of the parking space twice before I get inside the white lines. I open the antique shop, then go next door and talk to Jenny. She still hasn't heard from Kevin. I try his cell again and get nothing.

I call Molly and let her know what's going on, telling her I'm afraid Violet may have actually been attacked, and that I'm really worried.

"Too early to file a missing persons report," Molly says. "But maybe I can get Janie to make some calls." Janie is the police dispatcher. Molly is going to ask her to check with the nearby hospitals and law enforcement agencies.

I phone Grandma and tell her what I've learned. Grandma says she's doing okay and wants me to stay at the shop for a while, in case Kevin shows up. If Kevin calls her at home, she promises to let me know right away.

So I hang out at the shop and try to stay busy. I dust the shelves and wait on a customer who comes in. I call Kevin again, but still no luck.

Around noon, Molly calls me. "Janie just got back to me. Violet Morgan was admitted to Weaver Medical Center and is in critical condition. That's all they're allowed to say."

"Oh god."

"I'm sorry, Abby. Do you want Ray-Ray to drive you over there?"

"No. There's nothing I can do. Besides, I'd better stay close to my Grandma."

I hear Molly exhale. "First your grandmother, now Violet. This is getting really scary."

*Tell me about it.*

After I hang up, I see I just missed a call from Kevin. I hit redial, and he answers on the second ring.

"Abby?"

"Yes. How's Violet?"

"She hit her head. We're at the hospital. She's in a coma. They don't know yet what's going to happen."

"I'm so sorry, Kevin."

"She was doing magic. She had the door sealed. It went on and on for hours, but I was afraid to interrupt her. If only I'd gone in sooner..." He chokes up and is quiet for a few seconds. When his voice comes back, it's hoarse and weak. "I tried to warn her...but she wouldn't stop. She was on a mission."

"I know."

"Take care of your grandmother, Abby. Are you at the shop?"

"Yes."

"Just keep the bookstore closed. I'll...reopen in a day or two, unless...You should probably go home and stay with Kathryn."

"I will. Call us at the house when there's news. Or if I can do anything."

"Sure."

During the call I realized someone was in the shop—although I never heard them open the door. Now I look up.

Margaret Alden is standing there in her black dress and pearls. She glares at me, furious. "This is all your fault!"

I'm as terrified as the first time I saw her, in my bedroom up in New Jersey. "What do you mean?"

"If you had worked with us instead of against us, Annie, we could have shared the power. We could have all been together."

*She's crazy. She thinks I'm Annie Renshaw.* "You know better than that," I tell her. "You should have listened to Annie. You should never have conjured Raspis!"

The name makes her gasp. And then I understand what Otis was talking about—Margaret is possessed by Raspis. His *presence* is in her. I perceive his slimy energy hovering around and behind her like a damp, poisonous vapor.

From far away I hear myself screaming, "Get out of here!"

~~~

My knuckles are white on the steering wheel as I drive back to Bliss Bayou. The dread is relentless, a steady throbbing inside me. What can I do? *What can I do?*

When I get home, I tell Grandma the news about Violet. She stares at me with a deer-in-the-headlights expression. I sense how frightened and hopeless she feels. She says maybe I should just stay at the house, not go into town anymore.

I tell her to try not to worry. Then I go and fix us some lunch.

As we eat our sandwiches, I turn over in my mind everything that Violet and Annie have told me. The more I think about it, the more it all adds up to just one thing—and the more clearly I see the path in front of me.

I have to go ahead with the advancement rites as quickly as possible. I need to become as powerful as I can to face whatever is going to happen.

That's all there is now—the only thing to do.

At least it's a plan.

≋

That night, after settling Grandma on the couch, I go up to my room. I set out the candle and incense and trace a circle of protection. I go through the Daily Ablution, then pick up the pages of the Second Advancement.

> The Advancement to the Eternal Spring of Endurance.
> Each Spring is a Fountain, and each Fountain a waymarker on the Path of True Magic. These things are secret and must not be taken lightly.

I read the ritual all the way through. Then I stare into the candle flame and begin the visualization.

I wait at the edge of a clearing, surrounded by forest. Lanterns are arranged in a spiral leading to the center, where a fountain of clear water spills over rocks. A guide appears. Her face is hidden by a hood, but I believe it's Annie. She purifies me with water, then leads me onto the spiral path.

After some steps, the guardian appears. "None may pass this way who cannot vanquish me. Know you my name?"

My guide hands me a dagger, and I point it at the guardian. I recite the words which I've committed to memory: "Fear is your name. Terror is your name. The fear of facing the immeasurable truths of nature. The terror of knowing one's own insignificance. By Endurance you are conquered—courage, strength of purpose, steadfast faith."

The guardian bows and fades back into the darkness.

We walk on to the center of the maze. We stop before the fountain made of gray boulders, the water pouring down in steps from level to level. Annie pulls back her hood and smiles at me.

"We stand before the Spring of Endurance, the second waymarker on the path of true magic. Only by trial and courage is the spirit tempered and endurance attained. Each fear and doubt must be met, examined, and released. Only one who is brave and steadfast of purpose can advance farther on the path."

She hands me a cup of dull gray metal, like pewter. I drink, and the taste is metallic.

Then darkness rushes up at me. I've plunged into freezing black water. For a second, I'm seized by terror, remembering my visions of drowning.

But this is different.

Wave after wave of blackness and fear wash over me, rocking and shoving me like I'm caught in rough surf. But I can breathe, and I struggle to keep my breath steady, to let the waves pass through me and disappear.

After a while, I don't know how long, I'm back in front of the gray fountain, leaning on my hands and knees. I stand up. Annie is gone, replaced by...

I suck in my breath. I can't believe it.

"Dad...Daddy!"

The luminous gray ghost of my father stands before me—wide shouldered, curly haired, and with a worn, sad face.

"Hello, baby."

I want to hug him, but I'm afraid he'll vanish into nothing. *Like when he died.*

"Dad. I've missed you so much." I'm on the verge of sobbing, and so is he.

"I know, Abby. I'm so sorry. I screwed up."

"Why did you leave us?"

"Because I was weak. I couldn't face living. Living is hard...but it's even harder to be dead and have so much regret."

I stare at him, trying not to cry.

"I know I can't make it up to you," he says. "But I want to give you what little help I can. It's only this: don't run away, like I did. Once you start running away, it gets harder and harder not to run. Pretty soon, running away becomes who you are."

As I listen to this, I realize how desperately I've wanted to run away these past two days, ever since Grandma fell. I didn't let myself think about it much, but now I do. I could call Mom tomorrow, get her to book me a flight. Leave all the terror behind. It might work...or I might go completely insane.

But there's another way out. I could just give up, let Raspis have his way, drown myself in Bliss Bayou. The temptation is surprisingly strong—pain for a few minutes, then peace forever. Living *is* hard.

*But it's even harder to be dead and have so much regret.*

"I understand, Dad."

"One other thing," he says. "Be kind to your mother. She's a good, strong person, much better than I was. You're sensitive like me, but you have her strength. You must thank her for that and not resent what she is."

He's right again. I have resented Mom for being so tough and driven, for caring more about her career than me, for leaving my senior year to go to England. I need to let that go.

"Abby," Dad says. "I love you. It would mean so much if you could forgive me."

I see a tear sliding down his cheek. "Yes, Daddy, I forgive you. I love you too."

The ghost of my father steps close and wraps his arms around me. He does not feel like a ghost at all, but a solid, living man—the one I've loved and missed for so long.

I clutch him, shaking, until I lose all track of time, of who and where I am.

When awareness comes back, I'm lying on the floor in my bedroom. The candle and incense have gone out. My face is wet from crying.

〜〜〜<br>〜〜〜

*Wednesday, two days before the full moon.*

When I get to the shop around noon, I send a text to my mother: "Just saying Hi. Hope U R OK."

We've gotten out of the habit of texting every day, so I guess she's surprised to hear from me. She replies in a few minutes: "Busy, but fine. How R U?"

"OK. Grandma fell and broke her ankle, but I'm helping her out."

"Oh no! Anything I can do?"

"We got it covered. She'll be on crutches for a while."

"Sure you're okay?"

"Sure. I'm proud of you, Mom. Don't work too hard."

"I'm proud of you! Let me know if you need anything."

I feel better having gotten in touch with her. If something bad happens to me, at least she'll know I was thinking of her and that I felt good about what she was doing.

I spend the afternoon in town, keeping both the antique shop and Kevin's bookstore open. Kevin called this morning to let us know there was still no change in Violet's condition. He had come home to sleep but was heading back to the hospital. Grandma suggested it would be a kindness if I opened the bookstore for part of the day.

Grandma seemed better this morning. Like she's gotten over some of the shock and is adjusting to being confined. We haven't talked more about Raspis or the threat hanging over us. I want her to put that out of her mind as much as possible, and to rest. I know she appreciates my taking care of her. Thinking about it, I suppose no one has taken care of her at all since my grandfather died.

As for me, I'm in a kind of zombie mode. I'm handling all the outside reality—driving the car, talking to customers, selling books—

but my mind is elsewhere. I feel calm and numb. When I think about it, I realize I'm digesting the magical energy raised by the advancement rites, absorbing power like a sponge.

That's me: a numb zombie sponge of magic power.

♒

In my vision, I see a fountain with two columns of shining stone, one white and one black. Clear water tumbles from the tops of the columns into a gray pool at their base.

Annie Renshaw pulls back her hood. "Before us lies the Spring of the Sacred Balance, the third waymarker on the path of true magic. All the many worlds are formed by contending forces. Only at the point of balance does contention cease. Only by finding your inner place of balance can you wield the purest magic."

She hands me a goblet of cobalt blue glass.

When I drank from the second Spring, I was plunged into darkness. This time I'm blasted by light, brilliant and blinding. I squint and shade my eyes.

When the pulses of light diminish enough, I see a tall woman. She has wild black hair and glittering eyes. Torches of many colors flash in the air around her. I know her from the image on Thomas Renshaw's ring—the Great Goddess Who Shapes All Things.

I'm awed and terrified. Instinctively I bow. But then I hear my own voice asking, "What is your name, spirit?"

She notices me for the first time and looks almost surprised. Her voice is soft and hollow. "I am known by many names."

She lifts something in her hand—a Tarot card. As I recognize the High Priestess, the card grows huge and sucks me in. Then I'm standing before the throne of the High Priestess, but I know it is still the Goddess.

She stares at me, calm and gentle. "What would you ask of me?"

I didn't expect that. "Umm. There is an evil spirit who wants to kill me—and other people who are dear to me. I must learn how to banish him or...defend us from him."

She considers before answering. "Behind me are the hidden sources of creation. The river of the Universe flows at my feet. I sit at the gateway between two pillars—light and darkness, love and strife. The contention of these forces causes all things to be. To wield the highest magic, you must station yourself at this gateway, the point of perfect balance. Then your will can shape what flows into manifestation. So all things are possible."

I've focused hard to understand her words. My impulse is to ask how—how can I do that?

But in an instant, like the blink of an eye, the vision is gone and I'm back in my bedroom.

I lie flat on my back and breathe.

∿

*Thursday, the day before the full moon.*

I'm cleaning up the breakfast dishes when I hear the brass knocker on the front door. Grandma calls me, but I'm already running from the kitchen. I pull open the door and see Molly.

"Hi. Just checking in to see how you're doing."

I'm really glad to see her. I fix her an iced coffee, and we talk while I finish the dishes. I let her know Grandma is doing okay, and that there's no news on Violet. Also, no further occult events—at least not in the attack category. I explain that I'm working on magic every night to make myself stronger because I believe things are coming to a head.

The one piece of news Molly has is about the Wainwright brothers. They've been released on bail. No one knows who gave them the money, which was a lot more than they should have been able to raise. Chief Quick is unhappy. He was hoping to keep them locked up till they went to court.

"Oh, and Ray-Ray is off the night shift. He's working days again. He asked me to say hi, and to tell you to call him if you need anything."

That gives me a little glow as I stand over the kitchen sink. "Tell him I...that I said thanks for caring about me."

That sounds dorky even to me. But Molly just nods.

We go to the living room and sit with Grandma. She tells Molly about the novel she's reading, and we have a gabfest about different books and movies. Grandma likes romance and classic British novels. Molly favors mystery stories, while I'm into urban fantasy. Too bad all this reminds me of how far behind I am on my summer reading list.

Well, I've been a little busy.

When it's time for me to drive into town, Molly offers to go with me or to stay and keep Grandma company. I tell her I'd be happy either way, but Grandma's been alone a lot, and if she doesn't mind staying...

Grandma tut-tuts about imposing on Molly, but I can tell she's enjoying the company.

Molly says she'll be glad to stay. "But if I get annoying, Miss Kathryn, you just tell me to buzz off."

When I get to the shop, I call Kevin. He's hanging out at the hospital, and there is still no change. He thanks me for keeping his store open and says that waiting and doing nothing is starting to drive him nuts. So he'll probably come in to work tomorrow, and he would be happy to cover Grandma's shop as well.

I close up at five and drive back home. Molly's waiting for me on the front porch. Grandma started to look tired, so Molly left her to take a nap.

"We talked all afternoon, Abby. I didn't mean to interview her about the Circle of Harmony, but it sort of turned out that way." Molly looks grave, almost heartbroken. "Don't worry, I'm not going to write about it. I couldn't. My journalistic detachment is all gone.

The stuff she told me, about losing your grandfather, then your dad. And what happened to her this week, and to Violet. It's not only scary—it's so cruel."

"I know."

Molly looks at me hard. "What are you going to do, Abby?"

"Good question. I'm working on it."

"I know you are. I want to help, but I don't know how."

I touch her shoulder. "You being my friend helps a lot."

Molly stiffens. "That's not enough. There must be something I can do, Abby. Please!"

I look off into the trees. I only wish she could help. But I've seen enough to know this battle will happen in the spirit world. Molly being with me won't help—and she might end up getting hurt.

I promised Ray-Ray I would try to protect her. I peer into her eyes. "Molly, you need to trust me on this. You need to pay me that respect, okay?"

Her chin drops, her face forlorn.

I hug her. "If there's anything you can do, I'll call. I promise."

Molly sniffles. "Day or night, okay?"

When I go inside, Grandma is sitting up on the couch. She looks at me, a bit worried. "I probably told Molly more than I should have."

"It's okay, Grandma. We can trust her."

〜〜<br>〜〜

That night I go to the fourth Spring.

I've gotten to the point where I just have to read the advancement ceremony through once. Then I immediately go into a vision and things happen.

The Fountain of Amity is all of gold, the pure water falling down through seven basins.

Annie says, "Behold you the Spring of Amity, the fourth waymarker on the path of true magic. At the previous Spring, you learned that power comes through balancing forces. But lest you do evil with your magic, you must learn the lesson of Amity—that is, the law of love for all beings in all worlds. Desire tainted by greed or lust may produce effective magic, but desire sprung from selfless love will always be the stronger. Only by surrendering selfish motives to the higher good does the magician advance farther on the path."

She hands me a gold cup to drink. When I lower the cup, Annie is gone, and I'm standing alone before the fountain.

I'm wondering what to do next, when I hear a voice like faraway thunder, coming from inside the water.

"What do you seek?"

I have to collect my wits to answer. "I am Fighting Eagle, initiate of the Circle of Harmony. I seek to advance on the path of true magic. What is your name, spirit?"

"I am Lebab. I welcome you, Fighting Eagle."

*Whoa.* His power feels enormous. And different from the Great Goddess'. She seemed huge and distant, like the night sky full of stars. He is *here,* now, all around me. Like the earth.

"I-I need your help."

"Yes. And I need your help," Lebab answers. "My power has been bound by magic. One of my five Springs has been closed. Now humans are raising that same force again. Look into the waters."

I obey, and see a vision within the vision. The attic at the Alden house. Fiona stands in a circle with three others, all in hooded robes. They are chanting, striking the air with wands, raising a dark shadow in their midst.

"This is the ritual by which they will raise power, vast power, to augment the evil force. They will draw you there, Fighting Eagle. They will ask you to join them because of your talent. If you refuse, they will take your life and use the terror released by your death to empower them. If they succeed, the Springs will die. But if you can raise *my* power, release it into your world, I can save you and the Springs of Harmony."

"How can I raise your power? What must I do?"

"The knowledge you need is in the book that I gave to your founders."

## 22. The Book of Lebab

*Friday. The day of the full moon.*

Right after breakfast, I tell Grandma I'm going to town early—there's some stuff I need to do on the internet. She's groggy from sleep and the pain meds, and she doesn't ask any questions.

When I get to the shop, I phone Kevin. He answers from his car. He's on his way to the shop now. Violet is still in a coma, no change. I know this is bad. From what I've read online, the longer a patient is in a coma from head trauma, the less likely they are to recover. Then a thought comes: Whatever happens tonight will sway Violet's fate—one way or the other.

Kevin arrives a few minutes later. He didn't realize I was calling from the shop, and he's puzzled. He reminds me that he offered to cover Grandma's shop today.

"I know. I need to talk to you about something else. I need to see The Book of Lebab."

He scowls at that. He goes and puts his bag behind the counter, then sits down and stares at me. "Why?"

"I know. It's only for adepts. But before her accident, Violet told me I should go ahead with the advancement rites as soon as possible, and that I might meet guides along the way. Last night, I spoke with Lebab."

He lets out a breath, rubs his forehead. I know he's exhausted, and I'm sorry to trouble him with this. He looks at me across the glass counter, considering, appraising me.

"Abby, I don't think you should do this. I know you're very talented. I get that. But the stuff in that book—it can blow up in your face. And if Violet couldn't handle banishing this thing, I don't see how any of us can."

I'm already scared enough that this doesn't faze me. "I understand. But Kevin, I can't hide from it. It's going to come for me. The book is my only hope."

He stares at me a few more seconds, then shrugs. "Come with me."

I follow him to the back of the bookstore, where there's a locked room with a glass panel in the door. It's a climate-controlled room for rare and collectible volumes. Kevin opens the door with a key and flips up the light switch.

An air filter gives the room a pure, clean smell. The walls are lined with shelves, some with books set out for display, others with locked glass cases. Kevin uses another key to open one of these. It's packed with oversized books with old, worn covers. He pulls one out and sets it on the reading table.

"Lock the door from the inside," he says. "I'll be up front if you have questions. I don't know that I can answer them, but I'll do what I can."

When he leaves, I turn the lock in the doorknob. I sit down in the oak chair and stare at the book. It's like the one Violet used the day she expelled Raspis—brown leather, brass bindings, gold lettering on the front. The Book of Lebab.

I slide it toward me and lift the cover. On the first page, below the title, I read:

Welcome, good friend on the Path of True Magic.
Herein you will find the Formulae of Magic revealed by
LEBAB.
Use it only in accord with the Five Principles, lest your mind
be baffled and your soul lost in Great Confusion.

As I turn the pages, I see the whole book is handwritten—penned in fine lines of black ink. Some of the writing is cursive, some blocky printed characters. Mixed in with the writing are diagrams, drawings, and glyphs.

I turn back to the first page—and feel a slicing pain. A paper cut, which is strange, because the paper is so old and soft. Worse, drops of my blood have fallen onto the page.

As I suck my fingertip and stare at the red drops, I pass into a vision.

I'm standing again in the clearing, at the start of the spiral maze. Annie is there, this time not wearing her hood.

"Greetings, Fighting Eagle. Before you read the book, it is best that you drink from the fifth Spring."

I take her hand, and we walk along the curving path. This time no guardian interrupts us. When we reach the center, we stop before the fifth Fountain. It appears as a circular curtain of water with no basin, no boundaries. The water seems to be falling, but at the same time motionless. It makes no sound.

Annie says, "Behold, Fighting Eagle, the Spring of Bliss, the ultimate goal of our quest. It is union with your own higher self, that which is a fragment of the One Eternal Mind, the Spirit of the Universe. In mortal life, even great mystics and magicians know this union only in fleeting moments. It can only be reached by surrender, by abandoning all personal hope and desire. But remember this: surrender does not mean abandoning the struggle against evil. To oppose evil and bring good into the world is always our duty. What surrender *does* mean is making peace with the outcome of your struggle, whatever it be, peace with the knowledge that you may fail. That is the final key to Bliss."

She hands me a cup of cut glass or crystal, like a wine glass. I drink. The water tastes like...nothing.

When I lower the glass, Annie is gone. In her place is a slim man of medium height. He has long hippie hair and a beard. He's wearing jeans and boots and some kind of cowboy hat. I've seen him before, but I can't remember where.

He's grinning at me. "Abby Renshaw...it's so cool to meet you at last."

"What is your name, spirit?"

His eyes light up. "In the Circle, I was called Star Hopper."

Then I know him. "But your other name was George Renshaw. My granddad." He died long before I was born. I've only seen a few faded pictures.

"I want to thank you for being so good to Kat," he says. "And I want you to tell her something for me: that I'm still watching out for her, and I'll meet her up the road. Will you remember that?"

"Sure."

"Thanks." He waves a hand at the Spring behind him. "Pretty nice, isn't it?"

I gaze at the silent, silvery water. All the terror I'm living with seems a billion miles away. "Yeah. Bliss is great. But I know I'll have to leave soon. To go back and...uh, *oppose evil*, as Annie said."

"Yeah. Sorry about that. You know, you've done really well to get this far. All of us Renshaws are rooting for you. You're the last of the line, at the moment."

"Right. That has occurred to me."

I must have sounded sarcastic, because he laughs. "Girl, you are a hoot." He tilts his head back at the Spring. "The thing about this is, you have to *let go*. I learned that when I had leukemia. You can only do what you can do, and then the Universe is going to do its thing. All the worrying in the world won't matter. You just have to make peace and move on. See what I mean?"

"Yes. I think so."

"Good. Well, that's it." He shrugs. "Before I go, can I get a hug from my granddaughter?"

"I'd like that."

I open my arms, and we embrace. He feels kind and strong, and really *present*. His fingers press the muscles on my back.

"Dang," he says. "You are a tough little thing!"

~~~

Back in the rare books room, I smile at the memory of meeting my grandfather. Then I drop my eyes to the page below, now stained with my blood.

> General Formula for Raising Power
> This practice can be used for any occasion when you need to summon magic energy. Simply visualize the waters of the Springs flowing into you, and repeat this chant until the power is strong:
>
> By the Sun who daylight sings,
> By the Moon beneath Her Wings,
> By the One Who Shapes All Things,
> I raise the Power of the Springs.

I turn the page and keep reading. The book seems easier to follow now. Maybe that's because I've gone through the last advancement rite. Each section describes a magical operation or *formula*. They all follow a similar pattern: call upon the aid of spirits, declare your intentions, raise energy—usually with a chant—and then point and release the power.

Time passes. I slip in and out of trance, becoming alert suddenly to find myself staring at an unfamiliar page, my lips moving with the words. There are formulas for every kind of magical purpose— "Raising Protective Energy," "Achieving Invisibility," "Traveling Outside the Body," "Bending Events in Time" (whatever that means). I find the banishing ritual Grandma taught me, and the Profound Expulsion Violet used. But both of these have already been used against Raspis. I need to find something better, something that will free Lebab.

Maybe it's as simple as that chant on the opening page: "I raise the power of the Springs."

But how can I be sure? There's plenty I don't understand. And I know I'll never remember everything I'm reading. My hope is that my subconscious mind will take it all in and call up what I need at the moment I need it.

*My only hope.*

〰〰

I hear a loud, persistent tapping.

I raise my head from where it rests, heavy on the pages of the book. I was far away, in trance or asleep. I realize I'm terribly thirsty. And that I really need to pee.

I turn in the chair and see Kevin pushing open the door. "I thought I'd better check on you. It's almost seven."

I'm dazed. "Seven...at night?"

"Yeah."

"Oh my god!" I've been in the rare books room almost ten hours. I reach for my backpack, take out a water bottle, gulp some down. It makes me cough.

"Are you okay, Abby?"

"I think so. Bathroom." I brush past him and go to the little closet restroom across the hall.

When I come out, I'm still trying to clear my head. Kevin's waiting for me in the rare books room. I gaze down at *The Book of Lebab* on the table. I feel supercharged with energy, like I could float away, like I need to run, like I might burst into flames any second.

"Do you need more time?" Kevin asks. "I was going home, but I can stay..."

I'm gaping stupidly at the book. Do I need more time to read it? No—it feels like I've *swallowed* all the knowledge of the book. It's all inside me now.

"No. No thanks, Kevin."

I shut the book and grab my backpack, clutching Kevin's wrist as I step past him. "Thank you very much!"

"Are you *sure* you're okay?"

"Sure?... I have to run!" I hurry toward the front door. I open the door, then pause. I don't know why, but I call back to Kevin, "Listen. If things go well tonight, Violet will be okay."

Outside it's still daylight. Sunset won't be for over an hour. A short time after that, the moon will rise. I unlock Grandma's minivan and get behind the wheel. After cranking the engine, I sit there panting, trying to think.

*Focus, Abby.*

Tonight Fiona and her crew will do some badass magic at the Alden house, aimed at giving Raspis all the power of this special full moon. According to Lebab, they will try to draw me there and either convince me to join them or else murder me and suck up the energy of my death agonies.

I have to try to stop them... but how?

*The knowledge I need is in* The Book of Lebab. *The knowledge of the book is inside me now.*

As I'm struggling to grasp that, I'm startled by my phone buzzing. I fish it out of my pack. Three missed calls—Grandma! She must be frantic, wondering where I am. I start to call back, then decide I'd better not. She'll want to know where I've been and when I'm coming home. Whatever I say will freak her out.

I tap the phone to call Molly.

"Hey, Abby."

"You said I could call when I needed you."

"You know you can."

"Good. I need you to call my Grandma at the house. I haven't been home all day, so she'll be worried bad. Tell her I called you, and that I'm fine, and that I'll be home later tonight."

"Abby, this does not sound like you're fine."

"Then I need you to ride over and stay with her till I get there. Fix her something to eat and keep her company. Okay?"

"But where are you? She'll want to know."

"I can't go into that. Molly, I need you to do as I ask. Please!"

I hear a grim sigh. "Okay. But Abby, be careful."

"I love you, Molly."

But *careful* has nothing to do with it.

≈

I back out of the parking space, put the car in drive, and point it toward Bliss Road. But after less than a block, my inner sense is screaming that it's too early. Nothing will happen before moonrise. I need to arrive at twilight—that seems terribly important.

Somehow, tonight darkness is my friend.

I drive over to Founders Park and stop beside the river. I sit in the Odyssey and watch the blue waters flow below me, flowing down from Harmony Springs as they have for who knows how long.

Tonight, I need to free the power of those waters, use the power to sweep Raspis away. What are my chances, realistically? Probably approaching zero.

I'm only a beginner, after all. A few weeks of study, a crash course in the advancement rites. No wand. No dagger. Just a kid from New Jersey.

My life in New Jersey feels like a hundred years ago. But then I wonder if that isn't my real life, if everything that's happened in Harmony Springs hasn't been some huge delusion. It could be a delusion huge enough to have convinced Grandma and Violet and Kevin...Maybe I could just forget it all and go home.

"You do have a choice to make, Abigail."

My heart jumps. Annie Renshaw is sitting in the passenger seat. Annie Renshaw—who was seen in the coffee shop by Molly, and even Lewis.

"Okay," I admit. "You made your point. You're real. All of it is real."

"True," Annie says. "But you still have a choice. You can go back to your grandmother's house tonight. Avoid the confrontation."

"But then Raspis would still haunt me, right?"

"Probably. He will certainly flourish in Harmony Springs, and the world will grow that much darker. And you *are* still a Renshaw, and there *is* still the curse."

Thinking it over, I realize that I have three options. I can join with Raspis and be possessed, like Margaret was. I can try to run, and be tormented, probably driven insane, as Otis was. Or I can try to stop them, as Annie did. And if I fail, as seems way too likely...

"What's it like to drown, Annie?"

"Painful. For a time. But I don't regret my choice. I did what I knew I must."

What my dad said: "To be dead and have so much regret." Annie, at least, has no regrets.

"But remember, my friend, you might also succeed. There are many on this side of the veil who will try to support you."

*All the Renshaws are rooting for me.*

Then I remember what else my grandfather explained: all you can do is what you can do. Then you let the Universe do its thing.

*Make peace with the knowledge that you might fail—the final key to Bliss.*

Annie is gone. I'm alone in the Odyssey, looking down at the swift, shining water.

〰〰

At dusk I walk down the road toward the Alden house. I've left Grandma's minivan parked up the trail, near the head of Bliss Bayou.

My flip-flops make a little slapping noise on the packed sand as I walk. I probably should have worn running shoes today.

Ahead of me I see a guy in a cap, leaning on a tree. When he spots me, he straightens and picks up a rifle. As I get close, I recognize him as one of Casper Wainwright's sons.

"What you doin' out here, little girl?"

He is *not* someone I was expecting. "I'm, uh, here to see someone. The people who are going to be here tonight."

"Well, you know, this is a *private* party."

Behind him I can see a truck and two cars parked in the front yard. One is Fiona's Lexus.

"Oh, I think they'll want to see me. Tell Fiona it's Abby Renshaw."

He frowns, not sure how to deal with me. Then he yells out, "Hey, Daddy. Come here a minute, will ya?"

In a moment, another man appears from behind the house. Long white hair, and a pistol in his belt: Casper Wainwright.

"This one says she's Abby Renshaw, and that Fiona will want to see her."

Casper looks me up and down with a sneer. "I remember her. Listen, girly. This ain't no Save Harmony Springs meeting tonight."

I suspect I know more about what's going to happen tonight than he does. "If you'll let Fiona know I'm here, I'm sure she'll want to see me."

His face wrinkles. "Guess I better. You just wait here."

He strolls across the yard, climbs the steps to the front porch, and goes inside. A minute later Fiona appears, Casper trailing behind her. She's wearing one of her light-colored business suits and high heels. She steps quickly over to us.

"Abby, what a pleasant surprise. Come in." She glances at Casper. "Thank you, Mr. Wainwright. You gentlemen, please carry on."

I fall into step beside her. As we cross the front yard, she says, "I'm glad you came on your own. He said you would."

"*He* being Raspis."

Fiona sucks in her breath. "Please, Abby. Be more discreet. We don't use that name outside of the circle."

I let that pass. I'm trying to judge if Fiona is completely possessed by Raspis, the way Margaret was.

Inside the house, the chandelier glitters in the hall. We walk into the large parlor. Since the last time I was here, it's been furnished: brand-new Victorian-style furniture and soft Persian rugs. Three men are seated around a coffee table over a decanter and crystal glasses.

One of the men is Adam, Fiona's husband. I also know the other two.

"Everyone, this is Abigail Renshaw, a young lady who has worked with me on Save Harmony Springs. Abby, you know Adam, of course. But I don't know if you've met Mr. Philip Deering and Mr. Elston Tyler."

"Who have worked *against you* and Save Harmony Springs." I say that with a bite of sarcasm.

Fiona laughs like I made a little joke. The three men glower at me. They are not at all comfortable.

"We can't offer you brandy, of course," Fiona says. "But perhaps some tea. Adam, dear, do you think you could fix us tea? Abby and I have important things to talk over."

Fiona leads me to the doorway of the next room. Adam stands and walks over to us. He whispers at Fiona, "Are you sure you know what you're doing?"

She gives him a serene smile. "Everything's going according to plan. Tea, please."

Adam stalks off, looking worried. Fiona leads me into the drawing room. It has pocket doors, the kind that slide into the wall. She closes them to give us privacy.

The room is dim, lit only by the twilight coming in the big bay windows. I feel a little surge of magic. When Fiona switches on a table lamp, I see Margaret Alden standing in the corner, watching us. Raspis is a lurking black figure at her shoulder.

Fiona notices where I'm staring. "They are here, aren't they?"

"Yes."

She takes a deep breath, like someone enjoying pure mountain air. "It must be wonderful to be gifted like you. I've had to work so hard to build up my occult senses. I can hear them clearly now, but seldom actually *see* them—except, of course, in the circle." She waves me to a chair. "Sit down, Abby. Tea will be ready soon. You'll be the first guest for tea in my new house. Isn't that nice?"

I choose a chair as far from the corner as possible, where I can keep an eye on everyone. Margaret and Raspis watch me silently. Fiona settles on the couch like a regal hostess.

"So Mr. Deering and Mr. Tyler are part of your circle?" I ask.

"That's right."

"So the whole development fight was a fake. You've been in it together from the start?"

"Well," Fiona says, "we've had to use a little deception. But all in a good cause."

"What exactly is your cause?"

She spreads her hands. "To save Harmony Springs, of course. That is what Margaret and our patron spirit wish—the springs left undisturbed, as they were a hundred years ago."

"Then why are you working with the developers? It doesn't make sense."

"Well, we also need money. There's lots of money to be made through this magic. We will preserve the land around the springs and make money developing the land farther out. Everyone wins."

I'm struggling to make sense of it. "But why did you need to invent a fake plan by this Texas company?"

"Oh, the plan is real. Elston works as a consultant for Texas-Brighton. He drew up a proposal. You see, people needed to feel that the springs were threatened, so they'd have incentive to rally to our cause and approve the easements."

"But all the vandalism and fighting..."

She presses her lips together. "Things did get a little out of control. I just think our patron needed a certain amount of...energy to grow stronger, so he could help us."

"Yeah. I've heard that he feeds on fear and rage."

In the corner, Raspis hisses like a snake.

Fiona looks shocked. "Oh, I wouldn't put it that way at all."

"What about the Wainwrights?"

"Hired help. Phil employed them for us. They've been useful at different points. Tonight they're just here to make sure we're not disturbed."

*Tonight.* "What happens tonight?"

More stirring in the corner. Margaret speaks: "She knows already."

Fiona seems to hear her. "You're a very smart girl, Abby. I think you know the answer."

There's a knock on the door. Adam opens it and comes in, carrying a silver tea service.

"Lovely," Fiona says. "Thank you, dear."

He sets the tray down on the table. "We need to start getting ready soon," he tells Fiona.

"I know. We won't be much longer."

Without looking at me, Adam goes out and slides the pocket doors shut.

Fiona pours two cups of tea. "Oh, dear. He neglected to bring lemon. But we do have milk and sugar."

"Nothing for me, thanks." I'm afraid it might be drugged.

"Oh." Fiona looks disappointed. "Are you sure?"

I'm playing for time, trying to figure out what to do next—hoping Annie or Lebab or *somebody* will speak to me, give me a hint.

"So what about tonight?" I ask. "Where do I fit in?"

Fiona takes a sip of tea, then sets down the cup. "That's really why we needed to have this talk. You have a choice to make, Abby. Margaret and I recognize your gifts. We'd like to invite you to join our circle."

Well, I expected that. Over in the corner, Margaret and Raspis are watching me. In the silence, I hear the antique clock on the mantel ticking.

"No, I don't think so."

Fiona looks sad. She reaches for her cup again.

My eyes flick back to the corner, drawn by a sudden motion. Raspis has flung out his hand sharply. A jolt of force lurches through the room.

Now everything feels quiet—incredibly still. Fiona is frozen, the teacup suspended near her lips. Margaret stands by the wall like a statue. The clock is no longer ticking.

"Do not be afraid," Raspis says, gliding toward me. "I have simply stopped time so we can speak together *in private*."

His shadow form is huge now: bulky shoulders, long, sleek arms, small and narrow head. For the first time, I see eyes glinting in the blankness of his face. I glance at the door, terrified, wanting to run.

"I know." He lifts his hands reassuringly. "You are afraid of me. But it is a fear you can easily overcome. You have so much to gain as my ally—wealth, power, pleasure. With your gifts, there is nothing we could not accomplish."

He steps closer, his long hands stretched toward me.

"No! Stay away. You hurt my Grandma!"

"Your grandmother was hurt because you opposed me. But it's not too late. You can heal her. You can save Violet."

I stare at his fingertips, inches away. I feel energy rippling across the space between us, caressing my skin, seeping into my body. It's soothing, like a numbing drug, deadening my fears, my will to resist.

"No! Get out!" I leap from the chair, feeling sick and filthy. "Stay away from me. I will never join you. Never!"

His shoulders slump. "Very well. Your choice is made." He waves a hand and floats back to the corner.

The clock on the mantel starts ticking again.

Fiona looks up, confused to find me standing. "Oh, well...you've decided not to join us?" She sets down the teacup. "Unfortunately, Abby, your other choice is...not a happy one."

*Yeah. Tell me about it.* I feel weak, confused. I had some sort of plan when I came here, but I can't remember...

From the parlor outside, I hear men's voices, loud and agitated. An anxious look crosses Fiona's face. She gets up and heads for the doors.

As I follow her, I hear Casper Wainwright: "He threatened to come back with a search warrant. What was I supposed to do?"

Fiona pulls open the doors. Standing in the parlor, facing Casper and the other men, is Ray-Ray Quick.

## 23. Exactly the thing I planned not to do

Ray-Ray locks eyes with me, then faces Casper. "Well, look. There she is. I thought you told me she wasn't here."

Casper shuffles a foot. "I just meant, it's none of your business. This here's a private party, and I was told to keep people out."

"Young man," Phil Deering says. "I know you work with the Harmony Springs police. Are you here in an official capacity?"

Ray-Ray is not wearing his uniform. "Not exactly, sir. I'm just looking for Ms. Renshaw. Her grandmother was worried about her, and I found the car she was driving abandoned up the road. Abby, are you okay?"

*Not really.*

"Abby paid us a visit," Fiona explains. "To discuss some Save Harmony Springs business. Of course, if your grandmother is worried, Abby, perhaps you should phone her. And tell her you're all right."

My brain's in a fog, the lingering effect of Raspis' caress. But piercing the fog is a stab of fear—for Ray-Ray. He needs to leave and not get sucked into this. "That's okay," I say. "Just tell Grandma I'm fine. I'll be home in a little while."

Ray-Ray's not buying it. Even if he wasn't training to be a detective, I don't think he'd buy it. The tension in the room now practically reeks.

"I think you'd better come with me now, Abby," he says.

"Um, okay." I have to get him out of here.

But as I start toward him, I hear Raspis' voice behind me. "No! He has strength that could protect her. They must *both* stay."

That makes me freeze.

"Just a moment," Fiona says to Ray-Ray. "Abby is a guest in my house. I don't think I like your insinuations."

Ray-Ray tenses. "I'm not making any insinuations, ma'am. Although it *is* strange to find the leaders of the two sides of the development fight sharing drinks in your house...while the house itself is being guarded by men with guns, who also happen to be under indictment for criminal mischief."

Now everyone starts talking at once.

"Hold on right there," Adam says.

"Mind your own business, police boy," Casper growls.

"You have no legal grounds..." Phil Deering begins.

As the shouting match continues, Fiona walks calmly over to a desk. The shadow that is Raspis trails behind her. She opens a drawer and pulls out a wand.

"In any case, this girl is a minor," Ray-Ray is saying.

"Ray-Ray," I scream, "you need to leave now!"

But it's too late. Fiona and Raspis have moved behind him. She touches the wand to the back of his head. He turns, startled, like he's been stung. He starts to say something to Fiona.

"Sleep," she says.

His knees buckle, and he sinks to the floor.

Fiona leans over him. The rest of us look on in shock.

Raspis murmurs in Fiona's ear, and she repeats the words to Ray-Ray: "It is good to sleep. You are resting well. You will sleep until your name is called three times. Then you will remember nothing of this."

Fiona stands up, an eerie, triumphant light in her eyes.

"Oh, this is great," Adam says. "Now we're holding the son of the police chief hostage."

"Shut up!" Fiona snaps. "I have to think."

≋

"Ray-Ray Quick...Ray-Ray Quick...Ray-Ray Quick." I call his name softly.

His eyelids flutter, then open. He looks at me, bewildered. "Where are we?"

They left him lying on the floor, and I'm kneeling beside him. He struggles up on his elbows.

"They locked us in a storage room, behind the kitchen," I tell him.

He grips the top of his skull. "Who are *they*?"

"How much do you remember?"

He climbs to his feet, leans on the wall to steady himself, looks around. The storage room is the size of a large walk-in closet. No windows, just an overhead light that I've switched on. The room's empty except for stuff left over from the renovations—drop cloths, cans of paint, a broom and brushes.

"What do you remember, Ray-Ray?"

"I'm not sure...Molly called me from your grandmother's house. They were worried and asked me to look for you. I found your car up by the mouth of Bliss Bayou. Then I drove down the road and saw...Cletis Wainwright, holding a rifle? Abby, what's going on?"

"Sit down. It's a long story."

He slumps with his back to the wall.

I explain that we're at the Alden house, and that Fiona Alden-Gathers and her husband are in an occult circle with Phil Deering and the Texas guy, Elston Tyler. That the whole development fight has been a fraud. That tonight they're doing a ceremony to raise power for an evil spirit.

Ray-Ray looks more and more incredulous. "That's crazy."

"I know." I'm not surprised he doesn't believe it. As both Violet and Kevin have told me, most people, when confronted with supernatural events, will choose any rational explanation—no matter how unlikely.

"So what's your theory, Ray-Ray?"

He rubs the back of his neck. "I don't know. Maybe they bashed me on the head. A concussion can cause memory loss..."

"Okay. Have it your way. They bashed you on the head and locked us in a storage room. Either way, we're in a lot of trouble."

"You're right about that. We've got to get out of here."

He stands up and examines the door. He grabs the knob and shakes hard. It doesn't even rattle. "Steel frame and a deadbolt." He looks around at the walls and ceiling. "This is one of those safe rooms built for hurricanes. The whole house could blow down, and we'd still be locked in here."

"Well, I don't think we need to worry about that."

He sits down beside me again. "They can't keep us prisoner for long. Molly will have the police out looking—how long was I unconscious?"

"Only about ten minutes. I was able to wake you by saying your name three times. That was the magic charm."

He looks startled, then searches my eyes. "You're really serious about this, aren't you?"

"Yeah. It's serious, Ray-Ray."

I think he's starting to believe me.

"So what's your part, then?" he asks. "Why are you here?"

"That's another long story. But to give you the short version, I'm sort of the maiden sacrifice." Despite my trying to sound cool, my voice cracks, with a little pitch of hysteria too.

Ray-Ray's jaw drops. For the first time, he looks frightened. He puts his arm around my shoulder and pulls me close. "Don't worry, Abby. We'll get out of this. I won't let them hurt you."

I've been holding in my feelings all day. Now they break loose, and I shudder. Ray-Ray hugs me—I cling to him. I'm really scared.

As much for Ray-Ray as myself. He's gotten into this mess because of me. And now he could end up dead.

But the main thing he's worried about is protecting *me*.

I've never been in love. I don't really know what it feels like. But I'm sure of one thing: what I feel for him right now is closer to love than anything I've known before.

*Or ever will know. If I die tonight...*

In the back of my mind I hear Violet's words: *"Love is good for you. Take chances."*

I raise my head and look into his eyes. "Listen, Ray-Ray. Just in case things *don't* work out tonight, there's something I want to do. That I don't want to miss doing."

"What's that?"

Sometimes I'm impulsive, and this is one of those times. I throw my arms around his neck and kiss him, hard.

When I lean back, my heart's pounding.

He looks at me, totally amazed. Then he grins, like I'm the freakiest girl he's ever met. "Well. In that case, there's something I want to do too."

"What's that?"

He pulls me close and kisses me again. This time our mouths open and our tongues slide together. The kiss goes on and on.

When it finally ends, I snuggle against him. He feels wonderful— so big and solid. And he's a great kisser.

I start thinking how crazy this is—sitting here making out when we're probably about to be murdered.

But then I hear Violet again: *"Love recklessly. It's good for your magic."*

~~~

I'm resting my head on Ray-Ray's chest, listening to his heartbeat, when the lock turns. We jump up as the door creaks open.

A glimpse shows me that they're all in the kitchen, dressed now in robes. Ray-Ray and I step to the doorway.

"Just Abby is coming with us," Fiona tells him. "You stay here, please."

Ray-Ray grips the door frame. "I don't think so."

Adam, Deering, and Tyler are standing behind Fiona. Their robes are gray and their hoods pulled up.

Ray-Ray takes a step forward.

Elston Tyler raises a pistol. "I wouldn't do that, son."

I scan their faces. Fiona and Deering look calm and determined. Adam looks frightened. Tyler is cold and rock-steady.

Ray-Ray has stopped, but he's not giving up. "Whatever this is, I don't believe you're all willing to commit murder for it. You know you're bound to get caught."

I see Adam's mouth drop open. But Tyler just points the gun higher, aiming at Ray-Ray's heart.

"Son, I'm a gambler. Right now all my chips are on the table. I wouldn't like to shoot you, but I will if I must, then take my chances."

I put my hand on Ray-Ray's chest. "Don't. He means it."

Ray-Ray's shoulders slump. "Yeah, I can see he does."

He takes a step back. Deering closes the door and locks the deadbolt with a key, which I notice he leaves in the lock.

"Come, Abby." Fiona grabs hold of my wrist. "We have lots to do."

She pulls me away, and the men follow. We go out to the hallway and up the grand staircase. The door leading to the attic is open, and we climb the steps.

Since last time I was here, the attic has been wired. Electric lamps hang on the walls of the nine-sided magical chamber. Candles are laid out on the floor, forming a circle, waiting to be lit. Inside stands the ghost of Margaret Alden in her black dress and pearls. Raspis waits beside her, looking solid and oily black.

My throat tightens with fear. "What are you going to do with Ray-Ray?"

Fiona leads me into the circle. "That's actually worked out very well. Our patron explained it to me. You see, Abby, tonight we'll repeat the pattern from a century ago. There's great power in that, because the pattern is already laid down. I will play Margaret's part. You, of course, will be Annie. And your friend downstairs will stand in for Otis. He will watch, paralyzed, as you throw yourself off the dock. Later he will testify that he saw you drown yourself, and was unable to save you. Do you see how perfectly it all fits together?"

Her cheerful, matter-of-fact voice makes it all the more horrifying. I realize that she, like Margaret, is completely under Raspis' control. I look into the faces of the men, who wait at the edge of the circle. Their expressions differ—nervous, cool, grim. But none shows any mercy.

*I'm dead. This is real, and they're going to kill me.*

The fear inside me slips into rage. They're going to murder me, hurt Ray-Ray, probably kill Grandma and Violet and Kevin. All because Raspis promised them money and power. I have a terrible urge to grab Fiona's neck and strangle her.

Beside me, Raspis seems to quiver with pleasure.

Fear and rage both feed him. This is exactly what he wants. I need to get hold of myself.

Fiona walks to a corner outside the boundary of the circle. She opens a large book that sits on a lectern, then consults in whispers with Adam and the others. They are preparing to begin the ritual.

I close my eyes and take deep breaths. In my mind, I drift back to the fifth Spring. I step beneath the silent waterfall, feel it flowing over me, bathing me in Bliss.

I start to feel calm. And an icy determination.

One thing I know for sure: unlike Annie, I'm not walking helplessly off that dock. They'll have to shoot me. Or tie me up and throw me in.

But *that* won't look like suicide. That won't fit with their plans.

"No good. No good!" I hear Margaret beside me. "Her will is unbroken, defiant!"

I open my eyes. Across the room, Fiona stares at me, her mouth hanging open.

"She is warm with love for that boy," Raspis says. "But there is also something else."

I feel his mind probing me. "Agh! She has drunk from the fifth Spring—this very day! The waters of Bliss flow in her spirit. They protect her from despair."

Fiona steps back into the circle. "What shall we do?" she asks them. "What *can* we do?"

"Find a way to break her," Margaret says.

Raspis seems to fade out of the room for a split second, then reappears. "Yes. There is a way. Besides the boy, there is another whose love gives her strength. One who is far more important. The grandmother. She must die first."

My knees go weak.

"Yes," Margaret says. "Then this one will despair!"

Blank terror takes hold of me, blotting out the calm resolve.

"How?" Fiona asks.

"We cannot strike from afar," Raspis says. "Too much protection around the house. You must go there, get close to her."

Fiona sucks in her breath. "No. I couldn't do that."

"You must! You must!" Margaret cries.

Raspis lays a hand on Fiona's shoulder. "It is not hard. You only need to touch her skin. A handshake, a finger on the wrist. Then she will die in the night. We will guide you..."

Fiona is frightened. "It's too risky."

Raspis' hand is still touching her. "There is no other way."

"You can't do it, Fiona." I hope my words will add weight to her doubts.

But they seem to have the opposite effect. She turns on me, frosty cold. "Yes, I can. I can do whatever I have to."

"Fiona! What is happening?" Adam calls.

She looks at the three men, who are watching in confusion from outside the circle. She sets her shoulders and walks toward them.

"There is more preparation I have to do. I'll be gone awhile, maybe an hour." She points at me. "Keep *her* inside the circle. And wait for me."

Fiona hurries down the stairs. Adam shakes his head, obviously annoyed and scared. Deering and Tyler look at each other and shrug.

Margaret and Raspis have disappeared. I realize they have gone with Fiona, to guide her, *to compel her*.

I have to stop them. But how?

First, I need to calm myself again, to squeeze down the fear. I sit on the floor, close my eyes, and breathe.

In a few moments I hear noise outside the circle. I look to see that Adam and Deering have gotten out folding chairs and sat down. Elston Tyler leans against the wall, watching me.

I shut my eyes again. In my mind, I go back to the Spring of Bliss.

I try to think. Fiona will need to change her clothes, then get in her car and drive over to Grandma's. All that will take maybe twenty minutes. Then she'll need to find a way to touch Grandma's skin. It might not be easy. Grandma may be on her guard. And Molly's there, too.

So I might have time. But I've *got* to get out of this attic.

The three men guarding me are frustrated, confused by Fiona's absence. The night is not going as they expected. They're nervous. Is there a way I can distract them just long enough to get past them and down the stairs? Is there some magic to put them to sleep or into a trance?

I think about how Raspis stopped time earlier this evening. That would be perfect. Was there a formula for that in *The Book of Lebab*? I wish I had the book with me now.

*But the book is inside me.* I hear a voice confirming that thought—Lebab's voice. "You gave your blood to the book, Fighting Eagle. It is yours now, whenever you need it."

In my mind, I'm back in the rare books room. *The Book* lies open on the table. As I watch, the pages turn on their own, fluttering as if blown by the wind. When they stop, I lean over and read:

A Formula for Stopping Time

The power to stop time might seem unattainable. But recall that all magic takes place in the mind and nervous system. To halt time, the adept must simply arrest the <u>sense</u> of time in the minds of those present. You may then proceed to act in the normal time stream, while those around you wait in suspension. This effect will last for as long as you can hold the mental construct. In practice, a minute or two is the longest span achievable, before the strain becomes unsupportable.

It sounds fantastic, and I'm no adept. But what choice do I have but to try?

I read the instructions carefully, then open my eyes and stare into the room. I'll only need a few seconds to get out of the attic and down the stairs.

First I call upon the Elementals of water, whispering to myself: "Good friends of water, you sprites that flow beneath the moon, wild ones of sea and stream, I, Fighting Eagle of the Circle of Harmony, pay you my reverent respects and ask that you aid in my working."

In answer, their power seeps into me, lifting me like I'm floating.

I focus the power, use it to form a mental sphere—outside my body, but surrounding the bodies of the three men.

When I feel the sphere is firm and real, I whisper the chant:

Wild ones of sea and stream,
Make time stop as in a dream.

I repeat the chant over and over, feeling more and more power rise. When the power's so strong I can no longer hold it, I cast it into the sphere.

A current of energy ripples across the space between me and the three men.

I stare at them.

They're very still.

Cautiously I stand up. They don't react at all. They look exactly like figures in a paused video.

Oh my god. If Molly could see this!

*Focus, Abby. Keep the sphere intact.*

I lean down and take off my flip-flops. I don't want any noise to break the charm.

Then I tiptoe across the floor, slipping between Phil Deering's chair and the place where Elston Tyler leans on the wall. They stay in suspended animation.

I reach the stairs and go quickly down. The door at the bottom is open. There's a key in the lock, on the inside. I slip out the key, shut the door, and lock it.

I throw the key away and run.

$$\approx$$

Downstairs, I rush to the kitchen and unlock the storeroom door. As I'm yanking it open, Ray-Ray's already on his feet.

"Come on," I tell him. "We're getting out of here."

We run to the entry hall.

"Wait. Do you have a phone? One that works here?"

Ray-Ray checks his pockets. "They must have taken my phone."

*Figures.* I left mine in Grandma's minivan. It probably wouldn't work here anyway. And I don't remember seeing any landline phones in the house...

I hear pounding on the attic door upstairs.

"Listen, we've got to get to my Grandma's house. Fiona's gone there to kill her."

"Molly's there too."

"I know. If you get there, don't let Fiona *touch* anyone. Understand? She can't touch their skin."

Ray-Ray nods. "Okay."

We rush to the front door. I open it quietly, and we creep outside. The full moon is shining through the trees. The road curves in front of the house. At the edges of the curve, I can see the two Wainwright boys guarding each side of the property. Ray-Ray's truck is parked behind one of them.

"We'll have to go out the back," Ray-Ray says. "Cut through the woods."

But I know that's no good. "Casper will be back there."

From upstairs I hear a crashing noise. They're kicking down the door.

"The dock," Ray-Ray says. "Swim across to your grandma's. You can swim, right?"

"Yes, but—"

"Come on!" He grabs my wrist.

We jump down the porch steps and run, bent low.

I see that he's right. Our only chance is to get to the water. Of course, throwing myself into Bliss Bayou is exactly the thing I planned *not* to do tonight.

We dart across the road and splash through puddles. We run over the boardwalk and onto the dock.

Someone yells from the front porch, "They're on the dock. Stop them!"

Ray-Ray grabs my shoulders and points me upstream. "You go that way, I'll go the other. Swim underwater, quiet as you can. Okay?"

"Yes."

He propels me to the edge. I jump off and hit the water.

〜〜<br>〜〜

I'm back in my nightmare, sinking into freezing black depths.

For a second I wonder if it's all been one crazy nightmare—Harmony Springs, studying magic, Raspis. Will I wake up, gasping, in my bed in New Jersey?

Or will I really drown this time?

*No.* This time is different. This time I'm not paralyzed.

I move my arms and kick against the sluggish current. I swim underwater as far as I can, then fight my way to the surface.

As I suck in air, I see the dock thirty yards downstream. The two Wainwright boys are there, joined by the guys in robes. They're all staring in the other direction.

I hear splashing down there. Two of the men raise rifles and shoot.

*Ray-Ray is making noise on purpose, drawing their attention away from me.*

I pray to the Goddess Who Shapes All Things: *Please protect him.*

Then I dive and swim underwater, making for the opposite shore, the fastest way to Grandma's property. But when I surface, I'm disoriented. The moon's passed behind a cloud. It takes me a moment to spot the Aldens' dock. I've gotten farther upstream, but no closer to the other shore.

Worse, I'm starting to tire. I've gone all day on adrenaline, and my body's reserves are draining fast. Already my legs ache from the cold water.

I have to get to shore, or I'll drown for real.

I stay on the surface, breaststroking for the nearest bank.

In about a minute, I'm able to touch bottom. It's cold and mucky under my bare feet. I grab at the tall reeds, then pull my hand back, hissing. I put the hand to my mouth and taste blood.

*That's why they call it sawgrass.*

The shore here is swampy and covered with the stuff. Getting to dry land won't be easy. Of course, there might also be snakes or a gator.

I just want to lie down and cry.

But I think about Grandma and Molly and Ray-Ray. I have to hurry. I cast a sphere of protection around myself, then slog upstream till I find a little gap.

I push toward the bank, shielding my face and parting the sawgrass with my arms. Finally I reach a sandy patch and drag myself onto it. The moon's out again, and I can see shrubs and pines in front of me. Somewhere ahead is the road and Grandma's minivan. I move as fast as I can, shoving aside the ferns and low branches.

Up ahead I see a clearing, bright in the moonlight. As I get closer, I realize it's the old circle at the mouth of Bliss Bayou—the place where I saw the vision the day I went kayaking with Molly.

I reach the edge and stop. Strands of white mist drift across the clearing. In the center, I spot the gray stones set up like an altar.

Standing in front of them are Margaret and Raspis.

"Come in, Renshaw," Raspis says in his slimy voice. "We're waiting for you."

*They were drawn here.* They sensed my escape and had to leave Fiona—to come here and stop me. Then, with a flash of insight, I perceive that we were *all* drawn here to this circle, at this hour, under this full moon.

By the Goddess Who Shapes All Things.

Thomas Renshaw's ring hangs over my heart. I touch it and feel it pulsing with magic.

I know what I have to do. I square my shoulders and walk with confidence, as I've trained myself to do on the track when I march up to the starting line.

I've made it through the preliminaries. Time for the last race.

I'm a muddy mess, soaking wet, bleeding, exhausted. But as I get closer, I sense they're the ones who are afraid. I've given them a lot more trouble than they expected. They certainly hadn't planned on confronting me *here*.

I stop a few yards in front of them. The mist is thickening, forming into a circle that hovers around us, white fog with sparks of gold.

"Your time has come," Margaret snaps. "You've escaped us for the last time."

"No. I think *your* time has come."

Margaret snarls. "You stupid girl! You are nothing compared with us. You have no wand, no circle."

"But I'm alive, and you're not. I belong in this world, and you don't."

"Strike her!" Raspis shrieks. "Strike her now!"

Margaret thrusts her wand at me. The jolt knocks me back a step. I feel terror and despair. An image of drowning myself in the bayou comes to mind. It feels comforting, an end to all the struggle and pain.

But I know it's only an illusion.

"No," I say firmly. "It won't work anymore."

"Who do you think you are?" Margaret screams.

"Me? I am Fighting Eagle, True Magician. And I am Abigail, the last of the Renshaws. *And I am here to end the curse.*"

Margaret lowers her wand. She looks staggered, unsure.

I point two fingers at the shadow. "I banish you, Raspis, by your own true name, from this place and from this world, forever and ever."

He stiffens and falls back a step. But then he sneers. "You cannot defeat me. You're just a frail little girl."

"No, I'm not."

"Your father died and left you. Your mother has abandoned you. Your friends are all going to die. You'll be alone. Just as you are in this moment."

His words strike a new terror in me. I feel my confidence slipping.

"Alone," Raspis says. "All alone!"

"She is not alone." A voice comes from behind me. I turn my head. Annie is there in her white robe, holding a wand.

"She is not alone." Otis steps from the ring of fog beside her.

"Not alone, you bastard!" George Renshaw, my grandfather appears.

I look around. More people are stepping out of the mist, from all directions. Men and women in magic robes or Victorian dress—members of the Circle of Harmony going all the way back to the founders. And then still others, Native Americans wearing ornaments of feathers and shells.

All the people who have lived and practiced their magic by the Springs.

Margaret looks appalled. She collapses to her knees. Raspis stands frozen with shock.

The spirits form a circle around us. I hear Annie and the others start to chant. I recognize their words from the first page of *The Book of Lebab*.

> By the Sun who daylight sings,
> By the Moon beneath Her Wings,
> By the One Who Shapes All Things,
> I raise the Power of the Springs.

The native shamans use different words, but the power is the same. I join the chant, and it grows louder and stronger.

"No," Margaret moans. "No!"

Raspis stands with his arms thrown out, like the limbs of a dead black tree. Then his arms start to shake, like branches creaking in the wind.

The chant goes on and on. I feel the power of all these magicians focused in me, flowing up through my feet. I point my hands, not at Raspis, but at the earth, envisioning the source of the Springs deep underground, the crystal-blue water rising, higher and higher.

I fling up my hands and shout one last time, "Raise the power of the springs!"

The power bursts out of the ground, an explosion of blue light. Raspis shatters into fragments, blown away into the sky.

Blue light falls back into the clearing like a gentle rain.

*No, like a fountain.*

The chanting has stopped. Everything is still. I peer around at the ghosts. They look...satisfied.

Then I hear a rumbling coming from deep below. It grows closer, and the ground trembles. The rumble turns into a deafening roar.

The ground heaves, and I'm thrown off my feet. I black out for a second or two.

Then I'm rolling over, getting to my hands and knees.

The clearing is quiet again. I stand up and look around. The ring of mist is still there, but the spirits have departed.

All except three.

The ghost of Margaret Alden lies on the ground, weeping softly. She's no longer the fierce mature woman. She's the young Margaret again—Maisie—in a white blouse and long skirt.

From beside me, Annie and Otis walk over to her. They help her stand.

"It's all right, Maisie," Annie says. "It's over now."

She looks at them, teary-eyed, baffled. "Annie, Otis...I thought I'd lost you."

"No," Annie says. "It was all just a dream."

"We've come to take you with us," Otis says.

"But I remember...I was alone for so long. I did bad things— terrible things."

"Don't think about it anymore," Annie says.

Maisie looks from one to the other. "Where are we going?"

"Someplace beautiful," Otis says. "We'll all be together."

The ring of mist has been shrinking, contracting around us. Now the three ghosts step into it and begin to disappear.

Annie turns back to me and raises her hand. "Farewell, dear Abigail. And thank you. We owe you much."

"Well...I owe you a lot too. Will I see you again?"

She smiles, looking happier than I've ever seen her. "You only have to call."

Next moment, they're gone.

I'm standing alone in the silent clearing, under the silent moon.

*I'm alive. And I belong in this world.*

I run for the road and Grandma's car.

~~~

When I pull the minivan up in front of Grandma's house, a Harmony Springs police car is parked there. I jump out and run inside.

In the living room I see Grandma sitting up on the couch. Molly is in a chair, talking to an officer, who is taking notes. Another officer is kneeling in the corner, beside Fiona. She's sitting on the floor, clutching her stomach, staring straight ahead like she's in shock.

"Abby!" Grandma calls.

I rush over and hug her.

"Are you okay?" she asks.

"Are *you* okay? Fiona didn't touch you, did she?"

"No. No, I'm fine. But you're all wet. And your arms are cut."

"I'm okay."

Molly's standing beside me. "Yeah? You look like you've been through a blender." She examines my arms, then calls to the officer. "Jim, we need first aid for this girl."

Jim gets up and heads for the door. Molly shouts after him, "And get on the radio and tell them Abby Renshaw's here, and she's okay." She turns back to me. "Ray-Ray's got the whole shift out looking for you."

"He does? Is he okay?"

"Yeah. A little wet, from what I hear." Molly tilts her head toward the corner. "I think the only one who's not okay is Fiona."

I sit down and take hold of Grandma's hands. "What happened with Fiona?"

"She showed up about an hour—no, more like forty minutes ago," Molly answers.

"She said she needed to talk with me," Grandma says. "But she sounded strange, incoherent, almost like she was..." She hesitates.

"Possessed." Molly supplies the word. "All of a sudden, she jumped up and started screaming. Something about you and Margaret and her *patron*. She stumbled around and fell. Then she crawled over to the corner and hasn't moved since."

I look at Fiona, who is staring at nothing. I'm thinking that when Raspis was blown out of this world, he took her mind with him. I shiver.

Jim comes with the first aid kit and starts wiping the muck and blood off my arms.

"So," Molly says. "And how was *your* evening?"

〰

Later, after I'm patched up, after the ambulance comes and takes Fiona away, after Chief Quick and Ray-Ray arrive to check on us and take Molly home, after I finally get a shower and something to eat, I say goodnight to Grandma and crawl up to bed.

But tired as I am, I don't fall asleep.

I'm bruised and sore from the cuts, but that's not keeping me awake. Something else...I'm still charged from the power of *The Book of Lebab* and of that circle, of all the shamans and magicians of the Springs.

I stand up and go to the window. The full moon is high, and I can see Bliss Bayou clearly. I stare for a long time, not sure if what I'm seeing is real.

I put on my shoes and walk quietly down the stairs. I go out through the kitchen and cross the backyard in the moonlight. A little path leads down to a spot where I have a good view of the water.

No question about it: under the bright moon, the water is flowing fast and clear.

Bliss Bayou has changed back to Bliss Spring.

## 24. So, is Guardian of the Springs a viable career choice?

I sleep till early afternoon.

When I finally get up, I feel like a disaster area. The cuts on my arms and legs aren't too bad, but I ache in every muscle. I trudge down to the living room and find Grandma beaming.

"How are you feeling, Abby?"

"Okay. I'm sorry I slept in, Grandma. I didn't get you breakfast."

"Oh, don't worry about that. I got my own. Listen, Kevin called this morning. Violet's awake. They think she's going to be all right."

I slump into a chair and let out my breath. I'm so happy, so grateful.

Grandma continues: "Kevin told me the first thing Violet said when she woke up was 'Abby did it.' So, Abby, what exactly did you do?"

When Molly questioned me last night, I said very little. I was just too tired to sift through what to say and not say. Now I give Grandma the whole story, everything that's happened to me all week, culminating with last night. She listens with a calm, thoughtful expression, like it's all wonderful and makes perfect sense. And like she's really proud of me.

When I tell her about meeting George Renshaw, and give her his message, her eyes glisten with tears. "Oh, my. I've felt so close to him lately, ever since I started spiritual work again. I talk to him now sometimes. But it's so nice to hear that message—and to know you got to meet him."

~~~
~~~

Later, Molly calls to check on me and to fill me in on the news.

As I learned last night, Ray-Ray swam to a safe distance downstream, then got to a phone at a neighbor's house. Within fifteen minutes, three police cars converged on the Alden house. They drove up with lights flashing, but no sirens.

The Wainwrights saw them coming and tried to run, but they didn't get very far. Inside the house, the police found Adam Gathers, Phil Deering, and Elston Tyler. They were sitting in the living room, drinking brandy. Based on Ray-Ray's evidence, all six men were arrested on charges of unlawful imprisonment and attempted murder.

At first Deering and Tyler tried to explain it all as a misunderstanding. But when Adam found out that Fiona was in custody and unresponsive, he cracked. He confessed to the whole Save Harmony Springs conspiracy and the occult circle. He said that Fiona believed she was in communication with the ghost of her great-aunt and with her great-aunt's patron spirit. Adam claimed he only found out last night that they intended to bewitch the Renshaw girl into drowning herself.

Hearing all this, Deering and Tyler also rolled on Fiona. They're angling for a plea bargain. Meanwhile, Fiona's in no position to tell her story. She's under observation in the county psychiatric ward. The diagnosis is catalepsy, brought on by an acute psychotic break.

"The others are all at the county detention center," Molly tells me, "being held without bail. Oh, and my dad says you'll need to come down and give a statement as soon as you're feeling up to it."

*Well, that should be interesting.* "Is Ray-Ray all right?"

"I think so. Last night he was all charged up, with the arrests and everything. Today he seems kind of moody, like he's got a lot on his mind."

"Right." Busting an evil cult, getting shot at, finding out that the supernatural is real. Not to mention kissing a new girl—a girl he thinks is pretty strange. I guess he has a lot to sort out.

*Maybe I should call and help him.*

No. I decide I better give him space.

〜〜〜

Monday morning, I go down to police headquarters and give my statement. I haven't seen Ray-Ray since Friday night, and I'm hoping he'll be there. But he's not. Instead I meet with Chief Quick, a stenographer, and Ms. Ramirez, a county prosecutor.

I've thought hard about what to say, and I rehearsed it with Grandma. Of course, I have to tell the truth. But I also have to consider my oath not to reveal any secrets of the Circle of Harmony.

So I can tell the truth, and nothing but the truth. But the *whole* truth? That's where it gets dicey.

I start by explaining how Molly and I found the magical chamber in the attic of the Alden house. Since then, I say, I've suspected that people were doing evil magic there, and that it was related to the fights and vandalism in the town. Then I had a premonition that something terrible was going to happen the night of the full moon, and that I needed to go there and try to stop it.

So that explains how I ended up at the Alden house. For the rest, I can pretty much repeat what Ray-Ray must have said. We were locked in the storage room together, and then they took me upstairs to the attic. I managed to get away and lock the attic door. Then I let Ray-Ray out, and we made a run for it.

I'm relieved that they don't press me for details about *how* I escaped the attic. And I don't even need to mention what happened in the clearing at the top of Bliss Bayou. In fact, Ms. Ramirez and

Chief Quick don't probe at all into the occult stuff. They only want facts that will help make the charges stick, and the simpler, the better. They seem satisfied that my story matches Ray-Ray's on the key points—that we were locked in the storage room against our will and that at least two of the men shot at Ray-Ray from the dock.

When I've signed the statement, Ms. Ramirez thanks me and says that it's possible I'll have to testify in court, but not likely. I gather she figures that my talking about premonitions on the stand would not be terribly convincing. She says that with all the plea bargaining and Fiona's incapacity, it's looking like the case might never go to trial at all.

I'm actually surprised there's so little interest in the occult aspects of the story. I've had paranoid fantasies of cable news trucks and TV interviewers storming the town. And my mom seeing headlines like "Harmony Springs Preservation Group Linked to Devil Worship" or, worse, "New Jersey Teen Intended Victim of Cult Murder."

Even Molly's blog posts are restrained. She's focusing only on the facts of the arrests and on what she's hearing about investigations into the Alden-Gathers' finances. It's possible there will be further charges of criminal conspiracy or fraud. When I ask Molly about the paranormal angle, she admits that her dad warned her about writing anything that might be construed as libelous, Phil Deering being a lawyer and all.

"Besides," Molly says, "no one wants to talk about that stuff. I think they just don't want to believe it."

"I know what you mean."

"Seriously, Abby. I'm having to rethink my whole paranormal investigations blog. I mean, by following this story, I've proven to myself that the spirit world is real. But just writing the truth won't convince other people. And I'm not even sure I should try."

"These things are secret," I quote, "and should not be taken lightly."

"Exactly. I think I understand that now. I think, at this point in my career, it's better to stick with hard news."

People in town seem much more interested in the fact that Bliss Spring is flowing again. When a hydrologist from the Florida Geological Survey comes out with instruments and diving gear the next day, Molly is on the spot to interview him. He reports that it's a first magnitude spring, with roughly half the flow of the four other springs combined. When asked why the spring is suddenly open again, he says it must be due to a pressure shift in the aquifer—rare, but not unheard of.

Absolutely no mention of Lebab.

People always look for the rational explanation.

~~~

That night, still pondering this, I sit down to do the Daily Ablution. When I approach the fifth Spring, Annie Renshaw is waiting for me.

"Greetings, dear friend. I wondered how you were doing."

I smile to see her. "I'm good. Everything is good."

She peers at me a moment, reading me. "You are surprised that no one is demanding more explanations about the magic you experienced. This is partly due to Lebab's influence. He works to keep these things hidden from those who are not ready to understand. It is best for all involved, and best for the springs."

I can see how that makes sense. "I'm still trying to understand exactly what happened that night. I had a strong sense that I was drawn to the circle at the top of the bayou, that we all were."

"Yes, I definitely believe that."

"Did the Great Goddess do that?"

Annie seems amused. "You mean, was it Her will working through you, or your will working through Her? That's a question a magician can never answer. It is a mystery of our art. The important thing is, you and Raspis were drawn there, to the place where he was formed. He did not perceive it was also the place where he would end, the place where you—where all of us—could most easily raise the power to *unmake* him."

"So Raspis is definitely gone for good."

"Exactly. For *good*."

"And Lebab's power is free again, and that is why Bliss Spring is flowing?"

"Yes, Abigail." She looks deep into my eyes. "But your help is still needed."

"How? What do you mean?"

"As long as humans have lived in this place, there have been magicians who guarded the springs and channeled their power. You saw many of them in the circle that night. Now that the power flows freely again, a new guardian will be needed."

"Me? But I'm only a kid."

Annie laughs gently. "Not anymore. You are a young woman now. More than that, a woman of power."

*Okay. That's nice to hear.* "What would I have to do?"

"You will learn in time if you choose this path. If you do not, another will be found. Lebab is patient. He does not dwell in human time."

"Well, that certainly gives me something to think about."

"Indeed."

"I have another question for you, Annie. That night in the clearing, after Raspis was blown away, you and Otis went to Margaret, and you treated her as though you were still friends, as though nothing had happened."

"She *is* our friend."

"But after what she did to the two of you. She helped *murder* you. How could you be so forgiving?"

"You will understand in time, Abigail. From where we exist now, what happened in that lifetime seems so long ago. It's no more important to us than a quarrel among three-year-olds. But the love we have for our friends, the love of the soul, *that* lasts forever."

〜〜〜

I'm in the shop on Wednesday morning when my phone chirps.

"Abigail Adams. How R U doing?"

I look at the text and smile. It's been several weeks since I've heard from Franklin. "Benjamin Franklin! Fine. How R U?"

"BORE-DUH. Please entertain me with tales of your exciting summer."

*Hmm. How much is it wise to tell him?* "Well, I kissed a guy on Friday night. Not sure where the relationship is going though."

"Nice. If it doesn't work out, can I have him on the rebound?"

Picturing that makes me laugh. "Sorry. He is totally not your type."

"Figures. What else?"

*Well...how can I put this?* "I've done a lot of work for Save Harmony Springs."

"And did U save the springs?"

"Actually, I believe I did."

〜〜〜

I was supposed to fly back to New Jersey this Sunday, but I've decided to stay a little longer. I call Mom to explain.

"Grandma went back to the doctor yesterday. Her ankle is coming along fine. In another week she'll be able to drive, so I want to stay one more week to make sure she's okay. I've gone ahead and changed my flight. I'll be flying home a week from Sunday instead. I hope you don't mind too much, Mom."

"Well, I don't know. I understand your wanting to take care of her. But that will give us only three weeks to look at colleges."

"Actually, Mom, I've been researching that. There's a good college only forty minutes from here, Clermont State. I'd really like to apply there. I could live here with Grandma and commute."

-271-

"Oh, Abby, no! With your grades, there are so many good schools you could go to."

"It *is* a good school. Their graduates seem to do very well. If it doesn't work out, I could transfer to UF in year or two. Then I could still stay with Grandma part of the week. Anyway, I'm thinking of a dual major—English and either business or political science. A degree like that would be really strong for getting me into law school."

"Law school?"

"Yeah, I'm definitely considering it."

*Environmental law*, to be precise. If I do decide that Guardian of the Springs is my path, I figure a law degree will come in handy. Then I could also work on protecting other historic and wilderness places in Florida. That feels like a really good way to spend my life.

"Wow," Mom says. "I *am* glad you're giving this serious thought. But we'll talk about it more when you get home, okay?"

"Sure, Mom."

"I guess I'll have to get used to the idea that my little girl is growing up."

∿

*Thursday, almost a week after the full moon.*

I meet Molly at the antique shop, and we head over to the Presbyterian church. The Save Harmony Springs committee is reorganizing under Reverend Johnson and Jonas Carter. Even though the development plan by the Texas-Brighton Land Company turned out to be bogus, they feel that the organization is still needed. It's only a matter of time before new development interests show up. The committee wants to keep the idea of preserving the springs alive.

Molly and I walk down Main Street, over the broken sidewalks, under the huge oak branches and Spanish moss. If it's possible, I think I love this place more than ever.

I ask Molly about Ray-Ray. I still haven't seen him since the night of the full moon.

"You and Ray-Ray." Molly laughs. "When did I become your go-between?"

"What do you mean?"

"You keeping asking me about him. He keeps asking me about you. Hey, I just had a thought: why don't you talk to each other?"

"I know. But—"

"Tell me: did something happen between you two that night? I mean, other than dodging ghosts and bullets?"

"Such as?"

"Something romantic?"

"Well...kissing happened."

"I knew it! And how did you feel about that?"

"I felt great. I'd like it to happen some more."

"So why haven't you called him?"

"I know. I've thought about it a bunch of times. But I don't want to pressure him. I figure if he wants to see me, he'll call."

"Right," Molly says. "I'm sure normally he would. But in this case, there may be a problem."

"He doesn't really like me that much. It was just something crazy that happened, in a crazy situation—"

"No, that's not it."

"Then what's the problem?"

"Abby, think about it. He's already had his heart broken once this summer. If he has feelings for you, he's going to keep them in."

"But why?"

"Duh! Because you're leaving in a few days and might never come back."

"Oh!" Damn, I hadn't even thought of that. I guess I still have a lot to learn about men.

"Actually, Molly, as far as me leaving and not coming back? There's been a slight change in plans."

~~~

On the second Saturday in August, Harmony Springs celebrates Founders Day. Just like on the Fourth of July, most businesses close early and everyone heads down to the park for a picnic.

Because of her foot, Grandma's not up for going to the picnic. But she won't be alone for the afternoon. Kevin and Violet drive out to visit, and we all have lunch together. Violet's walking a little slowly, but it's great to see that same sparkle in her eyes. The three of them talk about doing more Circle of Harmony rituals together, maybe even initiating new people.

I leave them to their magical schemes and borrow Grandma's car. I've been invited to join the Quick family at the picnic. I find Molly and her parents in one of the groves overlooking the river. They've got a table spread with food, and Chief Quick is resting on a hammock, sipping a beer. Ray-Ray's nowhere in sight.

Molly grins at me. "He's down at the swimming hole. Wanna go swimming?"

"Sure."

We walk down the path to the inlet. It's crowded with people splashing around, swimming out to the raft, or just relaxing in the shallows. Kids are running off the dock and jumping in.

I'm looking around for Ray-Ray, when suddenly he's right in front of me, wearing a swimsuit and dripping wet.

"So, Abby," he says. "I hear you're staying another week."

"That's right."

"And that you're planning to come back next year and live here."

"Yeah. Things might change, but that's definitely my plan."

"Nice." He looks me over. "So, you going swimming? I *do* know you can swim."

I pull the band out of my ponytail and shake my hair loose. "You know, Ray-Ray, sometimes a person wants to jump into things herself. But other times, she needs a little encouragement."

Ray-Ray takes the hint. He swoops in and lifts me off my feet, then carries me, marching out onto the dock.

"Finally!" Molly shouts. "That's what I'm talking about!"

Because I'm a normal girl, I laugh and shriek. "No! Don't throw me in!"

But because I'm also a woman of power, I say softly in his ear, "Jump in with me."

And he does.

## Author's Note

Harmony Springs is fictional. You won't find it on any Florida map in what we've more or less agreed to call the real world. But you *can* locate and even visit a town called Micanopy, which looks suspiciously like downtown Harmony Springs. If you'd like to see what the springs themselves might look like, try the glass-bottom boat rides at nearby Silver Springs State Park—another remnant of what we around here like to call "the real Florida."

The Circle of Harmony is, of course, also fictional. But the nineteenth-century occult revival and utopian communities in Florida were real things. Those interested in this peculiar corner of the past might enjoy looking up the histories of the Florida towns of Ruskin, Estero, and especially Cassadaga.

I'm extremely grateful to my beta readers: Nancy Berkowitz, Peggy McKnight, Dakota M. Lu, and particularly John W. Kelly (who pulls no punches). An author cannot succeed without thoughtful and serious feedback.

My copy editor, Christina M. Frey of Page Two Editing, worked with me line by line to make this book the best it could be. Her dedication, acuity, and thoroughness surpassed all my expectations. Sincere thanks also to author Jana Oliver and her husband, Harold Buehl, for generously sharing their knowledge of the publishing business, as well as authors Tyra Burton and Kathryn Hinds, for years of friendship and support.

Last and most, to my beloved M, who reads every word and does magic every day: this book's for you.

## And thank you!

Thank you for reading *Ghosts of Bliss Bayou*. Please consider posting an honest rating and review on Amazon, Goodreads, or other sites. The algorithms of the publishing business make these reviews extremely valuable to authors.

Abby's adventures continue in:

- *Ghosts of Tamgrove Hall* (novella)
- *Ghosts of Lock Tower*
- *Ghosts of Prosper Key* (novella)
- *Ghosts of the Mermaid Spring* (novella)
- *A Demon on the Lion Bridge*

I love hearing from readers. You can connect with me at

Web: triskelionbooks.com or jackmassa.com
Facebook: Facebook.com/AuthorJackMassa/
Twitter: @JackMassa2

www.ingramcontent.com/pod-product-compliance
Lightning Source LLC
Chambersburg PA
CBHW050013180626
46810CB00002B/402